# Resurgence

Rebecca Deel

Copyright © 2017 Rebecca Deel

All rights reserved.

ISBN: 1979822263
ISBN-13: 978-1979822268

# DEDICATION

To my amazing husband.

# ACKNOWLEDGMENTS

Cover design by Melody Simmons.

# CHAPTER ONE

Veronica Miles drew in a ragged, painful breath. She twisted her hands, feeling for play in the ropes holding her suspended from the ceiling of the dank stone cell she'd occupied for an unknown length of time. Might be one day or a year. No windows in this hole to help her distinguish night from day.

One thing she did know. She had been here too long. Had someone missed her? She must have missed her check-in by now. Was anyone looking for her? Veronica shoved the panic welling inside behind a mental brick wall. Of course someone was looking for her. At the very least, her handler knew she was MIA. He would spread the word of her disappearance.

Warm liquid trickled down her arms. While the ropes binding her hadn't loosened despite repeated attempts to free herself, she was losing more blood. What she wouldn't give for a sharp knife.

Water, too. Her lips were split from repeated slaps to the face and lack of water. She desperately needed fluids. Yeah, she'd get right on that as soon as she freed herself.

Raising her head to take in the dim surroundings took a shocking amount of effort. If she managed to free herself, how would she escape the room? She didn't have a weapon or lock picks handy, and she was weak.

She made it a practice never to lie to herself despite the fact she was a consummate liar for her job. Veronica knew to the marrow of her bones if she didn't free herself in the next 24 hours, she would die in this cold room at the hands of ruthless men who wanted information she wouldn't provide. To break would cost another man his life, one who had suffered horrendous wounds at the hands of creeps like these. He deserved better. She wouldn't be the weak link in a chain leading to his death.

The question she wanted answered was how these thugs tracked her down. She'd been careful to keep her role in the previous mission a secret and her current assignment was in a different part of the world. How did they find her?

Later. She would figure that part out later, after she was free and safe. Veronica scanned the room again, searching the shadows for anything to use as a weapon once she freed her hands.

Her heart sank when she realized there was nothing. No furniture to take apart. No eating utensils since her captors didn't feed her. Fine. She'd dredge up enough strength to fight hand-to-hand. Wouldn't be the first time she saved herself. But she had never been so broken and bruised. In her current weakened state, this fight might be her last.

Regret swelled at the realization she wouldn't meet the Fortress operative whose life she'd saved months before. His strength and courage in the face of the injuries he suffered called to her as nothing else had in her life. From the reports, he had returned to full operational status. She wanted to see his face, assess his recovery herself, and know that she had made a difference in someone's life.

Footsteps echoed in the hallway outside her cell. Veronica froze, hardly daring to breathe. She bit back a moan when she realized the footsteps headed her direction.

She had a reputation in the DEA of being an ice queen, a woman with no feelings. Her fellow agents didn't know the real Veronica Miles. If they did, they would have never believed the falsehood. Veronica felt too much. Showing weakness made you a target. She wasn't a victim anymore despite her dreams each night.

She wanted to laugh, considering her circumstances. She hadn't been a victim for years until she was captured by these goons and turned into a punching bag for them to vent their rage and frustration.

Focus. She had to focus if she wanted to survive the next encounter with Interrogator. As the key unlocked the door, Veronica willed herself to stand tall with her head raised to face her captor. She would never spill the information the creep wanted so badly. To do so would hasten her death and turn a good man over to this pack of wolves.

The cell door opened and a shaft of bright light temporarily blinded her. She refused to look away from the large shadowed figure now entering the room.

"Still with me, I see."

That gentle, silky voice would haunt Veronica's nightmares for the rest of her life. If she survived, that is. The contrast between someone with a smooth, cultured voice doling out vicious beatings was stark. Made Interrogator all the more horrifying.

"You are a strong woman, Ms. Miles." A pause. "I like a good challenge."

That was her, all right. A challenge. Her own father viewed her the same way. He had never beaten her into submission. This thug sure wouldn't. The price of failure was too high.

"Are you ready to cooperate now?"

His crooning voice sent cold chills racing over her aching body. How could pure evil sound so gentle? Veronica stared at Interrogator, mute in her defiance.

"I suppose not." Interrogator shook his head with a sigh. "You're making this more difficult on yourself. Tell me what I want to know and all your pain will stop."

Right. He'd end Veronica's misery by killing her.

"I brought something special to encourage you to change your mind." Interrogator showed her the velvet bag in his hand before he turned to close the door. "I'm told by our other guests that I'm particularly skilled with this tool."

She refused to take her gaze from his. What was the point? She would find out soon enough what he had in mind for her. She prayed she was strong enough to endure. If she broke, the operative she was protecting with her silence would die.

He laid the bag on the ground and reached inside to pull out a whip. Although an instrument of pain and torture, the whip was beautiful. The supple leather sang as Interrogator snapped the leather on the ground in front of her.

Veronica kept her face blank although dread pooled in her stomach. Oh, man. The next few minutes would be excruciating. She'd been on the receiving end of her father's belt too many times to count growing up and still had the scars to prove it. How much more damage would an actual whip do?

"Ah, I see you recognize this." His chuckle echoed in the stone chamber. "One last chance, Ms. Miles." He moved a step closer. "I'd rather spend my time with you in much more pleasurable ways."

Veronica remained mute.

A broad smile stretched his mouth. "As you wish. Before I'm finished, you'll be begging to give me the information I want."

She tried to keep Interrogator in her sight, but he casually strolled behind her. Veronica twisted her bound wrists, desperate to free herself and face her tormentor. Useless effort, like the other times she tried. The ropes attached to the rings in the ceiling were spaced far enough apart that she couldn't turn. All she could do was wait for Interrogator to begin his work.

She didn't have to wait long. The whip cracked. Pain exploded across Veronica's back as her scream echoed in the stone chamber.

## CHAPTER TWO

A tropical breeze blew across Adam Walker's face, the humidity bad even in this early morning hour. The wind did nothing to cool his overheated body in his black uniform.

He activated his mic. "Report," he whispered to the black ops team moving into position to breach the compound looming in the darkness. His gut tightened as he awaited the responses from the Shadow unit. The group of four men and one woman were aptly named. They melted into the shadows.

"In position," Nico Rivera, the unit leader, murmured. Rivera hadn't been happy to cede leadership of this mission to Adam. Tough. Adam owed a debt to Veronica Miles. Her information had saved Adam's life when he'd been captured by a drug lord. She also saved the lives of the Fortress CEO's family. Fortress owed her big.

One by one, Trace Young, Joe Gray, Samantha Coleman, and Ben Martin checked in. Relief filtered through Adam. His gut screamed at him to move, that Veronica Miles was in serious trouble.

He forced himself to hold position until the timing was right. Moving too soon would get them all killed and leave

Veronica in the hands of men who would torture her for long days before killing her. "On my mark."

Adam waited in stillness until the guard rounded the corner. "In five," he whispered in the comm system. They had watched the guard's rotation long enough to time the rounds and check for blind spots, the window of opportunity short, but workable.

When he judged the timing to be accurate, he said, "Go."

The Shadow unit left no sign of their passage through the danger zone. When the guard rounded the next corner, Adam slipped from the darkness of the forest and, with swift and soundless steps, crossed the open expanse to the darkened corner of the compound wall.

He dropped flat on the ground behind a thick bush. Their informant's intel had been spot on. The window to the storage area in the basement was big enough for Adam to slip through. Barely.

Grabbing his glass cutter, Adam attached the suction cup and made a hole large enough to reach inside and unlock the window.

He'd almost completed the circular opening when a door five feet away opened. Adam froze. Light spilled into the courtyard, dispelling the shadows he and the Shadow unit needed to work in safety.

A man's laughter rang out as he stepped outside into the early morning. "She won't give you trouble tonight, Fritz. I made sure of it. I'll be back later today to continue my interrogation. A good day's work on my part. The woman will give me the information I want during my next visit. She's close to breaking. Now, however, I have a date. My woman has been waiting for me for hours and she is not patient."

"Yes, sir. What do we do with your guest while you're away?"

"Every thirty minutes, dump a bucket of cold water over her."

"Sir?"

"Just do it," the boss snapped. "You don't have to understand my methods. If my orders are not carried out to the letter, I'll know and you will take her place. In case you've forgotten, I do enjoy my work."

"Yes, sir." A mixture of anger and fear filled the underling's voice.

With another laugh, the other man climbed into a luxury car parked in the driveway and cranked the engine.

As the vehicle purred to life and left the compound, the remaining man uttered vicious oaths in the direction of the retreating taillights. Winding down, the thug spun on his heel, stomped into the house and slammed the door.

Fury filled Adam's gut. What had these men done to Veronica? From the words uttered by the boss, at least she was alive. If the woman they talked about was the missing DEA agent.

He returned his attention to the window. "Thirty minutes between visits to the target," he whispered to the unit assisting him in the rescue.

"Copy that."

Made their timing even tighter. Adam and Nico had to find, free, and remove Veronica from the compound before the next visit by the thug.

As the clock ticked in Adam's head, he wondered how soon the thug would make his first visit to Veronica to carry out his orders. This clown might not know why he was supposed to dump water on the agent's head twice an hour, but Adam did. Sleep deprivation, keeping her on edge. Yeah, he was very familiar with the routine. Special Forces soldiers were trained to resist interrogation. He figured Veronica had been trained, too, though not as well as Adam.

He removed the circle of glass, slid his arm inside, and unlocked the window. A moment later, he dropped lightly to the concrete floor in a storage room full of boxes. He eased the door open a crack.

The lights in the hallway were dimmed, which suited Adam's purpose well. No one was on guard duty in the hall. "Moving into the hall," he whispered into the comm mic.

"On your six," was Nico's reply.

Adam had twenty minutes to free Veronica and leave the compound before the thug was scheduled to visit her. He scowled as he moved into the open with soundless steps. If the creep stayed on schedule. Something in his voice as he talked to his boss told Adam he wouldn't stick to the time line.

Didn't matter. Adam would handle any obstacle thrown at him. Veronica Miles wasn't dying on his watch.

If the intel Maddox received was correct, the DEA agent was being held prisoner in the third room on Adam's right. His jaw clenched. This was no ordinary basement. The place reminded him of the subterranean chambers where he'd been held and tortured by drug lord Peter Collins. A cold stone pit where he thought he would die. His sister and his friends from Fortress had rescued him with help from Veronica. He intended to return the favor.

Adam twisted the knob, wasn't surprised to find it locked. He pulled out his lock picks and went to work. Seconds later, he opened the door wide enough to slip inside a room lit by one dim bulb in the ceiling.

His heart clenched at the sight of the woman suspended from the ceiling by ropes tied around her wrists. Her head lolled against one upraised arm, dark hair covering part of her face, her breathing shallow and labored.

Despite the bruises, Adam recognized Veronica from the picture Zane sent him. "Target in sight," he whispered to the team.

"She alive?" asked Sam, Shadow unit's medic.

"Barely."

"Nico?"

"Stay with the plan."

"Copy."

Adam crossed the expanse of the room. "Veronica, can you hear me?" he murmured. He saw the instant she became aware she wasn't alone in the room and began gathering her strength to resist further torture.

And the boss thought this woman was nearly broken? The guy was an idiot. The DEA agent was nowhere near the breaking point. "I'm with Fortress Security."

Her eyelids lifted a fraction, assessing him. A second later, she gave a slight nod of acknowledgment.

Excellent. He moved a step closer, Ka-Bar in hand. "I'll cut you down. Hopefully, we'll be gone before someone comes to check on you." Adam reached up to make the first slice when Nico's voice stopped him.

"Tango approaching."

His eyes locked with Veronica's. "Company," he whispered.

"Go. Run." Panic flared in her eyes.

He cupped her cheek, barely making contact, afraid of causing her more pain. "I won't leave you here alone." By the time the key was shoved into the lock, Adam's back was pressed against the wall beside the door, knife still in his hand. This clown couldn't raise an alarm if Adam and the team at his back were to complete this mission with minimal bloodshed.

When the door swung open, Adam shifted enough to keep Veronica in his sight as well as the slim man now entering the room carrying a large plastic bucket. His lip curled in disgust. The creep was fifteen minutes early.

He set the bucket down. "You're awake." He reached behind him without turning and closed the door. "Good. You ready to talk yet?"

"What do you think?" Veronica kept her gaze on her captor.

A low chuckle. "That's what I figured. The boss thinks you're ready to tell all. I know better. You need more persuasion."

Persuasion? Adam's eyes narrowed. What kind of persuasion? From what he'd seen in the lousy lighting, the boss had beaten Veronica repeatedly in an effort to obtain the information he was after. What did this guy think he could do to convince her to talk?

Slim twisted to the left and reached for a switch on the wall. The ropes holding Veronica slowly lowered until she was kneeling on the floor, arms still stretched above her head.

"Not so smug now, are you?" Another chuckle. "I have a few minutes before I'm supposed to dump water over you, long enough for what I've wanted to do since I laid eyes on you the first time."

He swaggered closer and reached for his belt.

## CHAPTER THREE

Adam's jaw clenched, raw fury exploding in his gut. No way was he allowing this creep to touch Veronica. Slim had just signed his own death warrant.

"After I'm finished, my friends will want a turn." Another laugh. "Should keep you busy and awake until the boss comes. By that time, you should be good and ready to tell him everything he wants to know." The man began unzipping his trousers.

Enough. In four steps, Adam came up behind the man and clamped his hard hand across his mouth. He thrust the Ka-Bar into the Slim's kidney and twisted. Adam dropped the body to the floor, wiped the blade on the dead man's shirt, and turned to look at the woman watching him. Would she label him a murderer now?

He knelt in front of her. "I'm going to cut the ropes now. The pain in your shoulders will be excruciating, but you can't make a sound." When she nodded, Adam sliced the ropes with one swipe of the razor-sharp blade.

Veronica gasped, then clamped her mouth shut. Although she didn't utter another sound, the tears tracking down her face told the story of the pain she was in.

"I'm sorry," he murmured.

"Adam," Nico said. "Clock's ticking."

"I have to get you out of here," he said to the woman now leaning on him for strength. "Can you move under your own steam?"

A nod.

Though Adam wasn't convinced, he said, "Good. Let's go. Nico?"

"You're clear."

He grasped Veronica's upper arms and, keeping them aligned with her body to minimize the pain, lifted her to her feet. She sagged a second, then straightened, indicating for him to lead the way.

Adam clasped her hand, figuring that was the only place not likely to have injuries. "Coming out now."

"Go," Nico murmured.

Sig in his hand, Adam pulled Veronica into the hall and sped to the storage closet where he'd entered the house. Footsteps echoed on the stairs leading to the basement hallway. "Another tango, Nico."

"I'll take care of him. Get your girl to safety."

He blinked at the comment, discomfited by the term. Brushing that aside, he hustled the agent into the dark room and locked the door. "Window," he whispered to her. "There's a bush less than a foot from the wall. Get as close as you can to the roots without attracting attention. I'll be right behind you. Go."

She turned, hesitated. "Do you have a backup weapon?" she whispered.

A smile curved his lips. Instead of replying, he grasped the second Sig strapped to his calf and handed the weapon and extra magazine to Veronica without a word.

When Adam shifted closer to lift her to the window, he noticed her shirt was ripped to shreds across her back, the material wet. Water? He drew in a breath and caught the scent of copper. Blood. The light was too dim to make out how bad she was injured. Damage assessment would have to wait until they were on the plane.

Hands at her hips, he boosted her to the window. Once she was through and flat on the ground, Adam hoisted himself up and scrambled through the opening.

Veronica shifted her weight. When she would have risen to run, Adam placed a hand on her shoulder to hold her in place. Right on schedule, the guard came around the corner and walked his path at the front of the house. He talked on his phone, not paying attention to his surroundings.

Through Adam's ear piece, Ben whispered, "Fifteen seconds."

Adam counted the seconds in his head, willing the guard to move faster. He had to have Veronica in the forest before Ben's explosives went off. They needed the chaos for cover.

Finally, the security guard turned the corner of the house. "Go, Veronica," he whispered. "As fast as you can to that grove of trees to the right. I'm on your six."

The agent leapt to her feet and raced for cover with Adam on her heels. Three seconds before the clock ran out, he slung an arm around her waist and hustled her behind a cluster of trees at the edge of the forest.

He nudged her back against the largest tree trunk and covered her with his body. A second later, the ground shook as a massive explosion ripped through the night. A fireball from the detached garage turned the sky orange. If they'd been near the house, the fire would have backlit them, making them a prime target.

"Go," Adam ordered the rest of his team as he gripped Veronica's hand, tugging her into a run. Shouts and screams behind them spurred him to move faster. He worried she couldn't keep up the grueling pace for long. He prayed she lasted long enough for them to get her to safety. If not, they'd have a firefight on their hands. From what he and the others had observed, Fortress was outnumbered 3 to 1. Not terrible odds. They had faced worse.

Gunfire peppered the ground on either side of them.

"Under fire," he said, dragging Veronica into denser cover.

"Copy," Nico said. "Converging on your location."

A bullet whacked into the tree by Adam's head, sending splinters of bark into his cheek. He growled. The shot came too close to his principal.

"There." Veronica yanked at his hand and pointed to a mound of large rocks. "We can pick them off and protect your team."

Amazing. Most principals would either be hunkered down or trying to flee in a blind panic. Not the woman at his side. She not only wasn't running, she was thinking clear enough to consider the safety of his teammates.

"Do you have enough ammunition?" she asked.

"More than enough for the seven of us to take care of business."

"Fantastic. Let's go to work."

As the tangos flooded the forest in search of them, Adam, Veronica, and the Shadow unit targeted the enemy bent on killing them all. Ten minutes later, Nico's voice came over the comm. "Hold your fire."

Immediately his unit stopped firing. Adam signaled Veronica to hold her fire. An eerie silence settled over the forest. "Trace, Joe?" Adam scanned the area, waiting for the sniper and spotter's replies.

"We're clear." This from Trace.

"Clear," Joe agreed.

"Move out." Adam lifted Veronica to her feet. "We're on a short clock." The massive explosion and gunfire would draw unwanted attention to their location within minutes. This part of Mexico was filled with federales and cartels who hated Fortress. If Adam and the others were captured, the province officials would make sure they disappeared. He didn't want to even think about what would happen to Veronica.

He circled Veronica's waist with his arm and urged her to move faster. "How are you holding up?"

"Fine."

Not so fine. She was trembling and, whether she knew it or not, leaning more heavily on him the further they ran. He didn't think she would make it to the SUV under her own power. He could handle her weight alone, but she would slow him down.

"Nico," he murmured. "I'll need cover soon." He didn't dare say the word help for fear the DEA agent would run herself into the ground, possibly causing herself more harm.

"Copy. I'm fifty feet to your right." A moment later, Shadow unit's leader moved to Veronica's other side. He nodded at her. "I'm Nico."

"Veronica. Thank you for getting me out of that torture chamber."

"Our pleasure, ma'am."

She turned her head to eye Adam. "Who are you?"

"Adam."

"I'll never be able to repay you for saving my life."

"You already did, Veronica."

She frowned.

He knew she didn't understand. Once they were in the air flying toward U.S. airspace, Adam would tell her what he meant. Everything else would have to wait until she was safe.

At that moment, she stumbled and would have gone down if not for his hold on her. Adam righted her. "Veronica, we need to move faster and you're weak from blood loss and dehydration. Will you let me carry you?"

When she swayed, he took the decision out of her hands and lifted her into his arms. Veronica hissed, arching her back away from the arm supporting her.

"Wrap your arms around my neck and rest your upper body against my chest." Adam kept his voice calm and matter-of-fact despite the firestorm raging inside him. What had those creeps done to her? "That position will take the pressure off your back."

With the adjustment in her position, the agent relaxed her weight against him. "Better. Thanks."

Her weak voice alarmed him. He needed to get her checked out, pronto. "What happened to your back?" She was silent long enough Adam figured she wouldn't answer.

Finally, she responded. "The interrogator used a whip." Her head rested against Adam's shoulder. "He was angry that I wouldn't cooperate."

Nico growled and activated his mic. "Sam, did you catch that?"

"Copy. I'll be ready."

"Who is Sam?" Veronica whispered in Adam's ear.

Goosebumps rose along his skin. He frowned at his reaction. What was wrong with him? She wasn't trying to attract his attention. He knew from past experience that she was so weak now she couldn't hold her head up. "A medic. She'll look at your wounds once we're in the air, Veronica."

She sighed. "Call me Vonnie," she murmured.

"Your friends call you that?"

"Family."

But he wasn't family. Was she delirious? "Your co-workers have a nickname for you?"

"Roni or Nica. Hate them both."

All right, then. Guess he'd call her Vonnie. He and Nico picked up the pace. Adam tried to minimize the jarring, but with the uneven terrain and fast jog, he couldn't help but hurt her. "You still with me, Vonnie?"

"May I have water?"

"As soon as we reach the SUVs. You'll have to take it slow, though. No guzzling or you won't be able to keep down the liquid."

"Thanks," she whispered, then went totally limp.

"Vonnie?" No response. Oh, man. Had she fallen asleep or lost consciousness? He couldn't stop to check her. Emergency sirens split the night's peace as vehicles sped toward the compound now a quarter mile behind him. They made so much noise, Adam couldn't hear if anyone was on their trail, a situation which made his skin crawl.

By unspoken common consent, Adam and Nico broke into a run. Ten minutes later, the team assembled at the two SUVs. "Sam, ride with us."

"I'll drive." Nico motioned for Trace and Joe to take the second vehicle. "Ben, you ride shotgun with me."

While the others tossed their gear into the appropriate vehicle, Adam climbed into the backseat with Vonnie in his arms. Sam got in on the other side. Once Nico drove toward the airfield, the medic asked, "Did Ms. Miles say what kind of injuries she had?"

"No. When I got into the room, her breathing was shallow and labored. Her face is bruised and the back of her shirt is soaked with blood."

"Cracked or broken ribs. Sounds like her captors beat her with their hands as well as the whip." Sam touched Vonnie's forehead. "She doesn't seem to have a fever. I'll administer antibiotics in her IV anyway. In this tropical climate, she could develop an infection. When we're airborne, I'll clean her wounds." She hesitated. "The easiest way to clean and disinfect her back is in the shower. I'll need help if she's still unconscious."

The thought of another teammate assisting with Vonnie's care made Adam's gut tighten into a knot. "I'll do it."

"Good. I was going to ask you to help anyway. She seems comfortable with your touch."

He frowned. "Why would that...." Adam froze, unable to continue. No. He tightened his hold on the woman in his arms.

"We don't know what happened to her before we arrived, Adam. It's not uncommon for women prisoners to be sexually assaulted."

The operative swallowed hard. He didn't want that for any woman, but especially this one. She'd risked everything to save his life. He pressed a soft kiss to her temple, praying he'd arrived in time to spare Vonnie from rape.

# CHAPTER FOUR

Veronica surfaced from the deep pool of darkness, opened her eyes, and saw nothing but blackness. She stiffened. Had she lost her sight? How would she escape her captors if she couldn't see?
"You're safe, Vonnie."
Vonnie. That voice. She recognized this man's voice. Black velvet that stroked her, soothed her. "Adam?" she asked, voice raspy.
A slight squeeze from his muscular arms. "We're two minutes from the plane. Once we're on board, Sam will treat your wounds."
She desperately wanted to lift her head and look for this Sam person. Couldn't. Had she ever been this weak before? She couldn't remember a time when she had no way to defend herself. She trained ruthlessly, pushing herself so she would never be helpless again. Yet she still had no strength. If Adam weren't holding her up, she would have slumped into a spineless mound on the vehicle's seat.
"Hello, Ms. Miles, I'm Sam," a woman's voice said from nearby.
Sam was a woman. Thank God. Veronica shuddered in relief. She huddled closer to Adam. She just needed a few

minutes to gather her strength, then she'd shift away from the operative and fend for herself. Hopefully.

Adam dipped his head until his lips hovered over her ear. "I've got you," he whispered. "I'll help you through this, however long it takes."

Not knowing how to answer him, she remained silent.

The vehicle slowed to a stop. There were no lights. For a second, panic flooded her. Why weren't there any lights at the airfield? Had she trusted the wrong people? Maybe Adam and his friends weren't from Fortress.

"This is a private airstrip," Adam said as though he knew the source of her distress. "Lights would have invited questions we didn't want to answer. The owner was paid a lot of money to look the other way tonight. He doesn't know who we are or why we need the airstrip, and frankly doesn't care. Money speaks louder than words in this part of Mexico. For his sake and that of his family, it's safer not to know anything."

She prayed she hadn't made the biggest mistake of her life. If she didn't hurt so much, Veronica would have laughed at herself. The biggest mistake she'd ever made was signing on for the latest mission with the DEA. She'd trusted the wrong person and her misplaced trust had cost her big. Would her lapse in judgment cost her life? Only time would tell.

"You're safe with me," Adam whispered against her ear.

Was she? She thought so, but her current situation reminded her that she wasn't as observant as she had assumed. If she was wrong about Adam, she would be dead soon enough.

Adam opened the door and climbed out with her still in his arms.

"I can walk," she protested although she wasn't totally sure of that statement. She'd give it a shot, though.

Appearing weak went against everything she projected to others.

"Indulge me."

Sensing he wouldn't give her the opportunity to try, she lapsed into silence again. Adam carried her straight up the stairs into the cabin of the plane. She glanced around at her dimly lit surroundings. Nice. Really nice. The black ops business must net a good profit.

A moment later, Adam's teammates streamed into the cabin, loaded down with black bags. All of them were large men with the exception of Sam, the pretty medic.

As soon as the door was secured, Adam sat, still holding her in his arms. He activated the intercom system. "Get this bird off the ground, Craig." Within seconds, the engine roared to life. They taxied down the runway and lifted into the air just as a swarm of vehicles with flashing lights poured onto the airfield.

Once the plane was level, Adam stood. "Sam." He carried Veronica toward the back of the plane.

"Where are we going?" she asked.

"Sam needs to check you over."

She shook her head. "I'll be fine."

"Your back is a bloody mess. If she doesn't treat you, you'll develop an infection. We're six hours from medical care we trust. You've been through enough trauma without adding an infection to the mix. Let her treat your injuries."

From the stubborn set of his jaw, he wouldn't take no for an answer anyway. When she nodded, Adam carried her into a luxuriant bedroom with an attached bathroom.

"Ms. Miles, I need to look at your back." Sam set a large black bag on the bed. "I have to know what we're dealing with before I can treat you."

The operative holding her slowly set Veronica on her feet. Her legs buckled. Adam grasped her arms, keeping her from sinking to the floor of the plane.

"I'll be quick." Sam circled behind Veronica, tried to lift the back of her shirt, and couldn't. "Ms. Miles, the blood has dried, causing the shirt to stick. I'll hurt you if I don't wet the material before trying to loosen it."

"Sit for a minute," Adam said. He shifted her to the edge of the bed, then sat beside her and bent over.

Veronica's eyes widened. He was taking off his boots and socks.

"Someone has to hold you up while Sam cleans your back, Vonnie. The easiest place to do that is in the shower." He glanced at her, his eyes dark with understanding. "I'm leaving my pants and shirt on. You have my word I won't look." He straightened after setting aside his footwear and looked at her, waiting for her to either accept his help or reject it.

Veronica weighed her options and realized she didn't have any. She was too weak to help herself and Sam needed another pair of hands. The idea of one of the other men touching her made her swallow in revulsion.

"What is it going to be, Vonnie?" he asked softly. "Me or someone else?"

"I trust you, no one else."

Satisfaction glowed in his eyes. He nodded, glanced at the medic. "Let's get this done, Sam." He stood and began removing his vest and weapons.

The woman walked to the bathroom. Seconds later, the shower came on. Sam returned and opened her bag. She pulled out sweat pants and a black t-shirt. "You can wear this when you're cleaned up. Should be loose enough to be comfortable."

"Thanks."

Rather than drawing things out, Adam lifted Veronica again and carried her into the bathroom. He stepped into the shower with her and set her on her feet. "Face me, Vonnie. Let the warm water work on your back for a minute, then Sam will take a look at you."

"Ms. Miles, your shirt is basically in tatters in the back," Sam said. "Will you let me cut the rest of it off?"

"Sure. Please, call me Veronica. Ms. Miles is too formal for the group who saved my life less than an hour ago."

"Okay, Veronica. Adam, hook your arms underneath hers and around her shoulders. That will give Veronica support but leave most of her back exposed for me."

"Are you okay with me doing that?" he asked.

She nodded. How could she refuse? She moved her arms away from her body just enough for him to slip his arms around her.

"Let me take your weight."

Good suggestion since she was about to collapse against him any minute. Setting her jaw, Veronica leaned against his massive chest. Good grief, Adam was seriously ripped and as strong as an elephant. He didn't appear to be suffering any fatigue from carrying her such a great distance over rough terrain. What she wouldn't give to be that strong. She would be again, she reminded herself. As soon as she rested, fueled up and hydrated, Veronica would be back to her normal self.

"I'm ready, Adam," Sam said.

"Go ahead."

Veronica glanced at him through her lashes. He was as good as his word. The operative's eyes were closed. "Adam?"

He shifted his face closer to hers. "What is it, Vonnie?"

"Are you allowed to tell me your last name?"

The man holding her stilled a moment, then said, "Walker."

Shock held her immobile. "The one captured in Belize?"

A faint smile curved his mouth. "The same. You saved my life."

"You saved mine tonight. We're even now."

"Not even close. Fortress still owes you. You saved the lives of my boss's family. He has a sweet little girl named Alexa who's alive and well because of you. She stole all our hearts. We'll never be able to repay you."

Veronica ignored Sam's poking and prodding, choosing instead to focus on the fascinating man in front of her instead of the worsening pain from her back. "Did my handler ask Fortress for a rescue?"

He didn't say anything.

Dread curled in her stomach. "Adam?"

"Fortress has a lot of contacts."

"That doesn't answer my question."

"One of the contacts asked for our help."

How could that be? She had missed several check-ins. Why didn't Dane send in the DEA?

"Veronica, a couple of these lash marks need stitches." Sam's fingers pressed lightly on Veronica's rib cage.

She gasped.

"Breathe," Adam said.

"Sorry," the medic murmured. "I don't feel any breaks. Are you hurt anywhere else?"

"Bruises, which you've seen."

"Vonnie," Adam said, his voice soft. "Don't hold back information. Sam wants to help you. The sooner you recover, the faster you can defend yourself if someone else comes after you."

She scowled, glancing up at his rugged face again to be sure he wasn't peeking. He wasn't. Veronica rested her forehead against his chest. "My legs."

The operative holding her upright stiffened.

"I'll need to check," Sam said.

Veronica's cheeks burned as she stood still, waiting for the inevitable questions. Man, she didn't want to talk about the scars with anyone, but especially not with Adam Walker within hearing range.

Sam unfastened her jeans and eased them down and off. "Looks like the jeans protected your legs. Just a few cuts, none that need stitches." A pause. "You want to tell me about the scars?"

And there it was. Veronica shook her head.

Adam growled.

She felt an irrational need to comfort him. Ridiculous. This man was obviously a warrior, used to hardship. Adam didn't need her to coddle him. "It was a long time ago," she whispered.

"Shouldn't have happened."

Veronica wished her mother had believed the same thing.

"Any other injuries I should know about, injuries I can't see?"

She shook her head.

"We're flying you to see a doctor contracted with Fortress. You need to tell him everything that happened to you. If there's any possibility of sexually transmitted diseases or pregnancy, you have to tell him. Don't hide the truth because you don't want to face it. You're too strong for that and your health depends on your honesty, Veronica."

"I understand." She didn't know what had been done to her. She'd been unconscious for a number of hours before she woke up in that torture chamber, hanging by her wrists from the ceiling.

The water shut off. Sam grabbed a clean towel and gently dried Veronica's back. "You need fifteen stitches. Do you want me to do them, or should I use butterfly bandages and let the doctor stitch you? If I do them, you're likely to have scars back here."

Adam snorted. "Sorensen isn't a plastic surgeon. He'll leave scars as well."

"You do them, Sam." Veronica would rather get the ordeal over with. The sooner the wounds were closed, the better.

"It will be easier with you stretched out on your stomach." She wrapped the large towel around Veronica's body and secured it. "Can you make it to the bed on your own? If not, Adam can carry you."

"I'll make it. It's safe for you to open your eyes now, Adam."

"I'll walk with you," he said. "I have to grab my Go bag to change into dry clothes anyway."

Between Adam and Sam, Veronica made her way to the bed and laid on top of the mattress, face down.

"Let me know when you're finished, Sam." Adam grabbed his bag, returned to the bathroom, and shut the door.

"I'll numb your back," the medic said as she unwrapped the towel. A moment later, Sam injected the numbing agent beneath her skin. As she waited for the medicine to kick in, she prepared her suture kit. "So how do you and Adam know each other?"

"We don't. I was on another mission when I heard rumors of Fortress hunting for a missing operative in my area. One of my contacts passed on his location to me." She glanced around to be sure Adam was still in the bathroom. "I've been keeping tabs on him ever since."

"Why?"

"To check on his progress." She'd been sickened at the trauma Adam had suffered. If only she had learned his location faster, he wouldn't have suffered so much at the hands of that drug lord.

"Tell me if you feel this." Sam leaned over her back.

"Pressure. No pain."

"Perfect. That's what I want. You'll feel a few tugs. I won't take long. This will be easy since I normally have to work under fire."

She let the medic work in silence for a few minutes. "Is Adam good at what he does?"

"The best," came the prompt reply. "Maddox hires the best in the military and law enforcement."

Veronica understood that. The DEA hired only the best and until this mission, she'd considered herself on the top echelon of her agency. Now, she wasn't sure she trusted herself or the people she worked with.

## CHAPTER FIVE

While Adam waited for a signal from Sam, he took a quick shower, soaping off the sweat, stench of carbonite, and Vonnie's blood. After drying off, he dressed in another black t-shirt and black fatigues. Another swipe with the towel over his military-short hair, and he called it good. Pretty, he wasn't. Not after the drug lord finished working on him.

He reached into his bag and pulled out his satellite phone.

"Maddox."

"It's Adam. We have her."

A sigh of relief drifted over the speaker. "She okay?"

"They worked her over before we located her and got her out. We're flying straight into Bayside."

"Exccllent. I'll alert Sorensen so he's prepared. Who took her?"

"Don't know. Whoever it was didn't stick around for the party. Also, the creep interrogating her left before we rescued her. The ones left behind on guard duty were low-rent talent."

"Any good?"

"Nope. Outnumbered 3 to 1, we didn't sustain any injuries. Boss, we need to know who's behind her abduction. Got a feeling they'll keep coming after her. The creep who interrogated Veronica beat the crap out of her, including using a whip, in order to obtain information. If he meant to kill her, he wouldn't have kept her alive as long as he did." A fact which still made his stomach twist into a knot.

"Agreed. What do you want to do, Adam?"

"Protect her until we unearth the people after her and take them out. We still owe her. Always will." And he was fascinated with the woman, although he didn't plan to tell his boss that bit of information. He wasn't taking a chance on Maddox replacing him on her security detail.

"You want a safe house?"

He considered that a moment, rejected the idea. "Not yet. I'm taking her home with me. She needs time to heal before she's ready to face the truth." Hard days were ahead for Veronica Miles. The betrayal was going to hit her, hard.

"Whatever you need, it's yours. When will you arrive at Sorensen's clinic?"

"Five hours."

"I'll meet you there. The Shadow unit is needed in another country by tomorrow night."

Adam frowned. "There isn't anyone else you can send? We haven't even put our boots on U.S. soil yet."

"Not this time. See you in a few hours."

He shook his head. Fortress was understaffed. Even superstars like the Shadow unit needed downtime. A quick rap on the door signaled it was safe for him to leave the bathroom.

Adam shoved the phone into his pocket and opened the door. Vonnie was dressed, stretched out on her side, gaze locked on his the moment he stepped from the bathroom. The wariness in the depths of her eyes disappeared at his entrance to the bedroom. "How are you?"

"Better."

Not about to take the tough agent's word at face value, he turned to Sam. "You agree?"

"She's feeling good right now." Sam indicated the IV. "Fluids to rehydrate her system. I gave her a mild pain killer, nothing that would hide a serious problem should it arise while we're in the air. She needs to rest, Adam. Stay with her while I change into dry clothes."

When Veronica held out her hand, Adam couldn't refuse the silent request. He set his bag aside, carefully climbed onto the bed to sit beside her, and threaded his fingers through hers.

In less than a minute, she was sound asleep. Though he longed to touch her soft hair, Adam contented himself with studying her face. Why would anyone want to beat her with fists and whips? His jaw clenched. When he tracked down the creep who caused Veronica's injuries, Adam would be dishing out his own form of punishment.

Sam emerged from the bathroom a minute later, bag in hand. When Adam swung his legs over the side of the bed, preparing to cede his place to the medic, Sam indicated for him to stay.

He settled back as the other woman left the bedroom. The bathroom light was on, giving the room some illumination so Veronica wouldn't wake up in the dark.

Rage filled him anew at the horrible conditions she'd been kept in, the trauma and pain she'd suffered. Someone was going to pay for that.

An hour later, Veronica stirred, gasped, moaned.

He checked, saw she was still asleep. No doubt she dreamed of her ordeal in captivity, an experience Adam was all too familiar with. "You're safe, Vonnie. I have you."

She shifted closer, drifted into a deeper sleep after whispering his name. Veronica woke an hour later. "Adam?"

He squeezed her hand. "Right here. Go back to sleep. You're safe."

"Sorry I wasn't faster," she whispered. "They hurt you."

"I'm fine now, thanks to you. Rest, sweetheart." He couldn't stop the endearment from spilling from his lips. What was up with that? He had never been one to call the women he dated sweet names and this one was a virtual stranger. Except she didn't feel like one. "I'll watch over you."

"Stay with me."

No way. She couldn't really mean that. Could she? "I'll be here. Sleep, Vonnie."

She edged closer until her face was pressed against his ribs and her body went boneless against him.

For the remainder of the flight, he kept one hand intertwined with hers. The other cupped the back of her head. He worried she wouldn't like the hold, but when he removed his hand, she grew restless.

When the landing gear came down four hours later, Veronica woke with a start.

"You're safe, Vonnie. We're getting ready to land."

"Okay. Adam, I have to get up."

Based on the amount of fluids the medic had been pushing through the IV, he wasn't surprised. "Sam needs to remove the IV first." He let go of her hand and swung his legs over the side of the bed, his hand feeling oddly empty without her smaller one nestled in his.

Adam opened the door. "Sam, Veronica's awake."

The medic followed him into the bedroom. "How do you feel, Veronica?" she asked as she removed the IV.

"Better. Thanks for your help, Sam."

"No problem." She smiled. "I hope I see you under different circumstances next time. How about a cookout at your place, Adam?"

He blinked, leaning one shoulder against the wall. As far as he knew, the Shadow unit didn't socialize much except with each other. "Sure. Call me when you're in town next time. We'll grill hamburgers."

"Perfect. I'll bring the baked beans. It's my grandmother's famous recipe. You should invite Veronica to join us. It'll be fun."

Interesting. "Deal." After Sam left the room, he helped Veronica to her feet. "Okay?"

She nodded.

"I'll wait here for you. Call out if you need anything."

Her face flooded with color.

While he waited for her to emerge from the bathroom, Adam cleaned up the room and made sure everything was in the correct place in his Go bag. By the time she left the bathroom, his gear was ready for the trip to Sorensen's clinic. What would she say about recovering in an animal clinic?

As soon as the plane depressurized and the stairs were lowered, Nico hefted Adam's bag over his shoulder while Adam escorted Veronica from the plane. After settling his principal in the backseat, he turned to the Shadow unit's leader. "I owe you. Anytime, anyplace."

The other operative was silent a moment. "She's more than a job to you?"

He lifted one shoulder, not ready to explain his connection with the agent. It didn't make sense to him and sure wouldn't make sense to Rivera.

With a nod, Nico handed over his Go bag and returned to the plane. As the SUV drove away from the airfield, the refueling truck arrived at the plane. Minutes later, Adam walked Veronica into the back door of Sorensen's animal hospital.

"Are you kidding me?" she muttered. "You brought me to a vet for treatment?"

"Sorensen is one of the best trauma surgeons in the country. When he burned out, he retired from active missions with Fortress. Now, he's one of our company doctors." He hesitated, wanting her to trust Sorensen, but not wanting to distress her even more than she already was. "He's the one who treated me when my teammates brought me back from Belize."

She stopped in the doorway, glanced at him. "But you're okay now?"

His hand automatically touched his scarred cheek. "A little beat up, but fully recovered, thanks to you."

"About time you got here." An irritated voice came from his right. Typical Sorensen. "I've got a full house today. Don't have time to waste. Thought I'd seen the last of you, Walker. What are you doing back here?" The grouchy trauma surgeon scowled. "You better not have messed up my handiwork. I spent a long time putting you back together last year."

Adam held up his free hand to forestall more of the doctor's tirade. "Not me this time, Doc. This is DEA Agent Veronica Miles. She's been an unwilling guest in a compound in Mexico."

"Treatment so far?"

"Sam Coleman stitched up her back, gave her fluids and a mild pain killer plus a standard antibiotic. She was afraid to do much more without your consent."

Sorensen grunted, his hand coming up to tilt Veronica's head to the side to get a better look at her injuries. Veronica shifted closer to Adam.

He slid his hand down to hers and squeezed. He wouldn't leave her until Sorensen kicked him out to examine his patient.

"The clown who did this to her is dead?" the doctor growled.

"Not yet." He would be soon if Adam had anything to say about it.

"This way, Ms. Miles."

"It's Veronica."

"Veronica, then. Come with me." When they reached an exam room reserved for Sorensen's human patients, the doctor glared over his shoulder at Adam. "Go wait in my office."

Rather than follow Sorensen inside the room, Veronica turned to Adam. "Hey," he murmured, his arms wrapping around her, tugging her against his chest. "You okay?"

"You're sure he's one of the good guys?"

"Positive. His bark is worse than his bite."

"I heard that," the doctor called. "Not funny."

"Vonnie, his office is right across the hall. If you need me, I'll be inside the room in seconds." He tilted her face up to his with one finger under her chin. "Promise me you'll tell him everything that those scumbags did to you."

Her gaze searched his for a moment before she nodded.

The knot in his stomach eased. Without thinking about what his actions might say to Veronica, he leaned down and brushed a soft kiss across her mouth, then turned her toward the exam room and nudged her inside.

Once the door closed behind Veronica, Adam sagged against the wall. What was wrong with him? He'd never kissed a principal and this one was so wounded he had no right putting his hands on her aside from keeping her upright. Would she be angry with him?

He closed his eyes a moment. He should ask Maddox to replace him. Obviously he wasn't objective about her. He'd never forgive himself if her safety was compromised because he was distracted.

## CHAPTER SIX

Veronica climbed on the exam table, almost numb with shock. Adam Walker had kissed her. Did it mean anything beyond a gesture of comfort? Man, she hoped so. The black ops warrior attracted her as no other man had in a long time.

And, no, it didn't make any sense. She didn't know him, not really. She'd built the fantasy of him in her mind when she found out where he was held captive in Belize.

So what was her excuse for keeping watch over him for the past year? She told herself her interest was pure, that she had a vested interest in his recovery. Maybe she had an unhealthy obsession. She was definitely exhibiting behavior far outside her norm. After all, once she returned to her normal life, she wouldn't see him again. What a depressing thought.

Sorensen examined her face, his expression dark and forbidding. "Sleaze bags," he muttered. "Any other injuries I should know about?"

Veronica told him about the beatings with fists and whip, and endured the teeth-grinding examination by the doctor. She knew he was only doing his job. Didn't mean she had to like it. She'd always hated dealing with doctors.

"Sexual assault?" he asked bluntly. "And don't lie to me. I need to know for the sake of your health."

She shook her head. "I don't think so, but I was unconscious for an unknown length of time. When I was awake, they threatened me with rape. If Adam hadn't arrived when he did, I would have been assaulted." The thought of Adam finding her after that kind of assault made her stomach revolt. Would he have looked at her differently? Somehow she didn't think so. The Adam Walker she'd learned about over the past year had more character than that. If anything, he'd be inclined to hunt down the man who assaulted her. She couldn't let him do that.

"I'm going to give you another round of fluids and a stronger antibiotic just to be safe. I imagine the interrogator practiced using his whip on more than one person. Go to the room on your right and make yourself comfortable on the bed. You'll be here for at least a couple days." He stood, turned toward the door, paused with his hand on the knob. The doctor spoke to her over his shoulder. "Walker's a good man to have at your back." With that, he left the room.

What did he mean by that? She already knew Adam was a good protector. Veronica tugged her shirt back into place with a grimace. He'd seen the operative kiss her. Did his statement mean Sorensen approved?

She slid from the exam table and had to grab the edge to hold herself up. Man, she was still weak. Hopefully in a couple days, she'd be back to normal. Veronica slowly walked to the door.

Adam straightened from the wall and slipped his arm around her waist to lend his support. "Where to?"

"Bed. He's keeping me for two days." Unless she could convince him to release her early.

"Not surprised." He bent down and lifted her into his arms.

"I can walk a few feet." Maybe. It galled her to be this weak.

"Save your strength for what's important. Healing." He placed her on the bed, then tugged the sheet over her. Adam dragged a chair to her bedside and sat. "What did he say?"

"I'll recover, but I should see a plastic surgeon to minimize the scarring on my back."

"If you need a recommendation, he has several doctors he trusts."

Honestly, she didn't want to see another doctor anytime soon. Besides, what were a few more scars on her back and legs? She never went to the beach without a cover-up anyway and she didn't care what other people thought of her scars. Well, not much, she amended.

Another thought occurred to her. Would Adam find the scars distasteful? "I don't know if I want another doctor working on me. When do you have to leave, Adam?"

"I'm staying."

"But your boss must have another assignment for you." Veronica's handler always had another mission lined up for her. She couldn't remember when she last took time off for herself.

Veronica didn't have close family contacts anymore so she was the perfect choice for many undercover assignments. Most of the time she didn't mind taking on the more dangerous tasks. She'd been to too many funerals of fellow agents and witnessed the devastation of their families.

"You're not getting rid of me that easily, Vonnie."

Her lips curved. The last thing she wanted to do was get rid of Adam. She liked having him around.

The doctor came into the room and set up the IV. "Keep her still, Walker. No walking the halls until after hours. My waiting room is full of cats, dogs, a parrot with an attitude, and curious pet parents with a direct connection to the Internet. Anything unusual shows up on their social media pages."

"I know the drill, Doc. We'll stay in here until the coast is clear."

With a nod, Sorensen left, closing the door behind himself.

"Interesting man." Veronica turned her head. "Do you still have an extra weapon? I feel vulnerable without a way to defend myself."

The operative reached down to his calf and grabbed the sweet Sig he'd loaned her earlier. "Sorensen has weapons stashed all over his clinic. We're careful to protect his identity, but leaks happen. He has enemies, the same as we have, and the doctor has a family to protect."

Veronica blinked. "He's married?"

Adam shifted in his seat as he chuckled. "He also has twin boys at home. Sorensen takes any threats to him or his family seriously."

A short while later, her eyes grew heavy. She couldn't find a comfortable position on her back so she turned on her side to face Adam, trusting him to watch the door.

"Rest, Vonnie. I'll keep watch."

"Who will spell you?" she murmured. "You have to be exhausted." She knew he hadn't slept on the plane. Every time she woke, Adam reassured her she was safe with him.

"My backup will be here soon."

Who was his backup? She should be on edge, worried since a stranger would be at her back while she was vulnerable. Instead, she let go and slid into sleep.

Sometime later, she woke with a start at a quick knock. She and Adam pointed their weapons at the door.

"Coming in soft," a male voice said from the hallway.

Adam must have recognized the voice because he lowered his weapon. "Come."

Not so trusting, Veronica kept her weapon trained on the doorway and the man with buzz-cut blond hair walking into the room. His eyebrow soared when he noted the Sig in her hand.

"Ms. Miles, glad to see you on U.S. soil." He extended his hand. "Brent Maddox."

Keeping her gaze locked on the potential threat, she asked Adam for confirmation. Receiving it, she set aside the Sig and shook the Fortress CEO's hand. "Thank you for sending Adam and the others. I'm indebted to you."

"Not in my book, Ms. Miles. I still owe you for saving the lives of my wife and daughter. Tell me the size clothes and shoes you wear."

Bemused at his insistence, she gave him the information. Veronica's agency wouldn't go to this much trouble for her. Was this how Maddox treated all his employees?

Maddox turned his attention to Adam. "I'll be in the hall. Both of you get some rest."

For the next two days, Veronica slept more than when she'd been injured previously, including the time she'd been down with a nasty case of the flu. Finally, Sorensen agreed she was fit enough to travel.

"If you have a setback, call me or one of the Fortress medics. If you see your own physician, make sure he can be trusted not to report your injuries. A record in the medical system will tip off your kidnappers that you not only survived, but you're back on your home turf. We don't want you in their hands again."

"Thank you, Dr. Sorensen." Veronica leaned up and kissed his cheek. The gruff physician turned beet red as he patted her shoulder.

"Just see that you take care of yourself." He glared at Adam. "Watch out for her, Walker. I don't want her back here anytime soon."

Adam saluted the man, then he and Maddox escorted Veronica out the back door of the clinic and into the black SUV waiting to take them to the airfield.

Within minutes, they boarded the Fortress jet. This time, Veronica insisted on sitting in the seats like a normal passenger. "I slept for two days. I'm much stronger than when you brought me here."

Once airborne, Adam retrieved three bottles of water from the galley. "Staying hydrated helps with the soreness."

Veronica eyed him as she drank deeply. "Where are we going?"

"Nashville."

"Why?"

"Fortress headquarters is there. Plus, that's where I live."

Something in his expression told her there was more to what he was saying than the simple words conveyed. "I need to report to my handler after we land."

Adam and his boss exchanged grim glances.

"Adam?" She reached over and gripped his hand. "Tell me."

"Vonnie, Dane Carver is dead."

## CHAPTER SEVEN

Cold seeped into Veronica's bones, setting off convulsive shivers. She fought to keep her teeth from chattering with marginal success. Dane was dead. She had talked to him an hour before she was captured by the thugs who tortured her in that death chamber. He didn't say anything about a medical problem, and he would have told her. They had been friends since she joined the DEA.

Adam didn't mention a medical issue. Her heart skipped a beat. Was his cause of death medical or something more sinister? "How did he die?" she asked, voice hoarse. His wife, Cissy, must be devastated.

Adam laced his fingers with hers. "The police report indicates he committed suicide."

"No." She shook her head, rejecting that possibility. "Dane would never do that."

"Are you sure?" Maddox leaned forward, gaze intent. "People hide things from others, even those they love the most. Maybe he was more troubled than he let on, Veronica."

"Dane adored his wife. Her father committed suicide soon after she and Dane married. Cissy made him swear he would never put her through that, no matter what. I'm telling you he wouldn't kill himself. Especially now. Cissy is pregnant with their first child. They've been trying to have a baby for years. I've never seen him so excited about anything more than this baby." She swiped tears from her face. "How is Cissy? Is the baby all right?"

"You'll have an answer by the time we land in Nashville." Maddox stood. "I'll let you know what I learn." He walked to the front of the plane, sat at the table, and pulled on a headset.

"Come here," Adam murmured. He took the bottle from her unresistant fingers and wrapped strong arms around her.

Veronica's head rested against his chest. She couldn't stem the tears flowing down her cheeks. She couldn't believe her friend and mentor was gone. Flashes of the dinners she had shared with Dane and Cissy, the weekends spent with them between missions, the birthday and anniversary celebrations all ran through her mind.

How could this happen? She had a hard time believing Dane was so distracted by anything that he would compromise his safety. He'd drilled into her the need to be vigilant.

"I'm sorry, baby." Adam's large hand cradled the back of her head.

She drew in a deep breath, two, a third before she could speak. "Me, too. Adam, I need to see Cissy. I have to go to her."

"It's not safe. That's one of the first places your captors will look for you."

"She's my friend. I have to do this."

"Even if the visit might cost your life?"

"It won't. I'll be careful. I'm not stupid, Adam. I know these creeps won't give up." She also knew they would look for the people who ripped her from their clutches, especially the operative holding her in his arms.

Adam was silent a moment, then eased away to look her in the eyes. "Are you positive Dane wouldn't kill himself? Not for any reason?"

"There is no question in my mind that someone murdered my handler."

"Where did Carver live?"

Her lips curved. "Nashville. I'm based there as well." Their proximity to each other made it easier to keep up with Adam's recovery. Of course, she didn't dare follow him. He was too good an operative to miss someone trailing him. No, she made discreet inquiries through a contact in black ops who was friends with the medic on Fortress's Durango unit.

"Veronica." Maddox covered the microphone on his headset with his hand. "Cissy has been admitted to St. Thomas-Midtown as a precaution. She took her husband's death hard."

"And the baby?"

"Seems fine, but the doctors are keeping a close watch on her."

"Can she have visitors?"

"I'll arrange for you to see her." He moved his hand, turned back to his open laptop, resuming his conversation over the headset.

She frowned. "How can Maddox guarantee I'll see Cissy?"

"The boss knows a lot of people. If he says he'll get you in, bank on that happening."

Veronica knew she should pull away from Adam, but was too comfortable to move. He didn't seem inclined to release her, either. She reminded herself not to assume anything, especially not to credit the Fortress operative with feelings he couldn't possibly have for her. As upset as she was, she still caught the sweet name Adam called her. Perhaps he called all the women in his life by sweet names.

She hoped not. She wanted to be special to someone, but figured that dream would never come true for her. Perhaps Adam wouldn't mind if she stayed in his arms a few more minutes. Adam holding her made Veronica feel safe and secure though experience taught her safety didn't come from another person. She'd always had to protect herself, even during her childhood.

She must have drifted off because sometime later, Adam rubbed her arm, murmuring her name to wake her.

"We'll be landing in a few minutes, Vonnie."

Veronica disentangled herself from the man who had held her for hours. "I'm sorry. I didn't mean to fall asleep on you. You should have nudged me to my own seat."

He cupped her cheek, his gentle touch a stark contrast to his hard hand. "You needed to be held."

She couldn't deny it although she was embarrassed to admit such a weakness. To give herself time to collect her thoughts, Veronica glanced out the window and saw that it was dark. "What time is it?"

"After midnight, too late to see Cissy."

She blew out a breath. "Can you drop me at my place? I left my car in the garage." She always took a taxi to the airport when she left on a mission. Otherwise, the parking fee would be astronomical. Sometimes she was out of the country for weeks.

"You can't go home right now."

Veronica stiffened. "I know how to protect myself."

"You're still recovering from a horrific ordeal and your reflexes aren't up to par yet. If you stay in your own place by yourself, you'll be on alert instead of resting."

"Take me to a hotel."

"I have something better in mind."

This ought to be good. "Do tell."

"Stay at my place."

She twisted in her seat to face him. "I can't stay with you."

"You don't trust me?"

"Of course I do." Seriously? This alpha warrior had risked his own life to free her and hustle her out of Mexico. How could he think she didn't trust him? "I can't put you out that way. You need rest as much as I do and you won't if you're watching over me."

"Vonnie, I'll be watching over you, whether you're in my house or not."

"Be reasonable." He couldn't be serious. "You can't stay awake 24/7. You have to sleep sometime."

"I arranged for friends to provide backup."

"Who?"

"Remy and Lily Doucet. They're with Fortress as well and I've worked several missions with them. I'd trust them at my back anytime, anywhere."

"A brother-sister team?"

"Husband and wife. Lily's a spitfire and Remy adores her. Both of them are as fierce as they come."

She blinked, surprised. "Maddox allows married couples to work together?"

"He says they fight harder to protect each other. So far, he's been proved right."

"What are their backgrounds?"

"Lily was an Army sharpshooter before signing on with Fortress. Remy was an NYPD homicide detective."

A fellow cop. Some of her tension faded. "They don't mind helping?"

He shook his head. "They just returned from a mission overseas and are happy to remain on US soil for a while. Maddox authorized them to be on your protection detail."

"That's just wrong," she muttered. "I know how to use a gun and I'm well trained in defense tactics."

Adam gave her a lopsided grin. "Might as well give in, Vonnie. We have your back for the foreseeable future."

Truthfully, she didn't mind all that much. The thought of facing her empty house made her skin crawl. Who could she trust aside from Adam and his friends? Her cover had been blown. No one but Dane knew she'd been assigned a deep-cover mission in the Chihuahua province in Mexico and he would never tell. Who found out and gave her identity away to the creeps who abducted her? "All right. You win." She slid him a pointed glance. "For now."

Satisfaction filled his gaze. "Lily and Remy will be waiting at my place."

Once the plane landed, Maddox signaled Veronica to wait. She hated being on this side of a protection detail. It wouldn't be for long, she reminded herself. She and Adam would figure out who was behind her kidnapping, then everything would return to normal. Except things would never be normal again without Dane.

Five minutes later, the Fortress CEO returned to the plane. "Everything is clear, including your SUV, Adam. Report to my office tomorrow morning before you go to the hospital to see Mrs. Carver."

"Yes, sir." Adam helped Veronica to her feet, grabbed his Go bag, and preceded her to the stairs. Stubborn man didn't trust his boss's word that it was safe for her to leave the plane, although she appreciated his diligence and protectiveness. The DEA could use a man of his caliber.

Veronica lifted her duffel bag of clothes and followed. Once she settled in the passenger seat of a black SUV, Adam circled the hood to climb behind the steering wheel.

She liked driving this time of morning. Not much traffic, the only time that was true in this booming metropolis. Plus, Nashville was pretty at night. Veronica was surprised to discover that Adam lived a few miles from her house. Nice. Maybe they could swing by her place tomorrow or the next day to replenish her clothes supply. She didn't expect Fortress to supply her with a new wardrobe.

Provided it was safe enough. If her place was under surveillance, she didn't want the watchers to see Adam.

Maybe a nighttime visit would be better. Easier to blend into the surroundings at night. Adam couldn't blend in during the daytime. His rugged good looks and obvious physical fitness made fading into the background impossible.

Veronica sighed. Now she sounded like a grade school kid experiencing her first crush.

Adam drove to the back of his ranch-style house. The back door opened and a muscular man walked outside.

She gripped the Sig, never taking her gaze from the man approaching Adam's side of the SUV. If he made so much as one suspicious move toward Adam, he was a dead man.

"Relax, Vonnie. That's Remy." Adam squeezed her hand and opened the door to greet his friend. "Sorry for interrupting your night, Remy."

Veronica opened her door so she could hear the conversation and be ready to defend Adam should he need backup. Didn't look like he did, though.

"No problem. We're glad to help."

After glancing around to be sure no surprises lurked in the darkness, Veronica exited the vehicle.

Adam held out his hand to her. "Veronica, this is Remy Doucet. Remy, Veronica Miles."

"Nice to finally meet you, sugar."

Remy's Cajun accent was pleasant to Veronica's ears. "Finally?"

"You gave us Adam's location in Belize."

"You were part of the rescue team?"

He nodded. "Thank you, Veronica. Adam is a good friend. Lily and I owe you a debt."

"You don't owe me anything, Remy." Her gaze shifted to Adam. "I'm glad you got him out in time."

"Let's go inside," Adam said, voice gruff. "Remy, my Go bag and Vonnie's duffel bag are in the cargo area."

"I'll take care of it. Lily's waiting."

As soon as they entered the kitchen, a small blond woman turned, smiled at them. "No new injuries, Adam?"

"Not this time. Lily, this is Veronica Miles. Lily Doucet, Vonnie."

"Glad you're safe, Veronica." Lily motioned to the kitchen table. "I have water heating for tea or I can make you coffee if you'd prefer."

Her eyebrow rose. "You have tea, Adam? I pegged you as a coffee-only man."

"I am. The tea is for Claire."

Claire? Veronica's breath froze in her lungs. Adam had a girlfriend? Pain stabbed her heart. Why wouldn't he? The operative was an amazing man. Of course he had a woman he cared for. But if so, why did he kiss her? Maybe the kiss meant nothing but a gesture of comfort after all.

"Speaking of Claire," Remy said, depositing their bags to the side of the door. "She insisted you call as soon as you got in."

"It's two in the morning." Adam scowled. "She should be sleeping."

"Yeah, she said you'd fuss, but for you to call anyway." Remy clapped his shoulder. "She won't sleep until she hears from you. Might as well give in so she'll rest."

"I'll call her after I get Veronica settled."

Lily handed Adam a mug of coffee, then stood with her arms crossed and a scowl on her face. "Call her now. I'll take care of Veronica. Put your sister out of her misery."

Sister. Claire was his sister. Veronica dropped into the nearest chair, relief rolling through her in a tidal wave. What was wrong with her? Must be weaker than she thought from the interrogation sessions because her emotional equilibrium was way off.

Adam took a sip of coffee, tapped Lily on the nose, then left the room, cell phone in his hand.

"Do you want tea, coffee, or something else, Veronica?"

Mindful of her need to keep hydrated, she opted for water. Within five minutes, Adam returned and held out his hand to her. "Come on. I'll show you where you will be sleeping." He looked at Remy.

"We're on duty until you wake. Get some rest."

Grabbing her duffel bag, Adam led her from the kitchen to a guest room. "This okay?"

Compared to where she'd been living the last few weeks, this was like being in a luxury hotel. "It's great. Thank you, Adam. For everything."

"Bathroom is through the door to your left. There are towels and washcloths under the sink along with soap, my sister's favorite body washes, and new toothbrushes and toothpaste. Use whatever you want."

He set her bag on the bed. "I'll be across the hall. If you need anything during the night, come get me." Adam kissed her cheek.

A smart woman would have let him go on to bed. She didn't do the smart thing. Veronica cupped his face between her palms, searched his startled gaze a moment, then slowly moved closer and kissed him.

The kiss started out light, a first date kind of kiss. For a few seconds, Adam let her explore. Then his arms came around Veronica and drew her against him. She heard a door close and the earth moved. She found herself caged between the door and Adam.

His tongue brushed her bottom lip, asking silent permission to deepen the kiss. With a soft moan, Veronica opened her mouth and was swept away on a tide of heat. Man, Adam Walker's kissing talent was off the charts. She wrapped her arms around his neck and held on for dear life as fireworks exploded in her head.

For long minutes, she indulged in exploring the taste and texture of Adam's mouth. When he broke the kiss and shifted his attention to her neck, Veronica realized he was slowing them down, allowing them both to catch their breath and cool the ardor burning them up.

"Vonnie," he whispered against her skin. "That kiss got out of hand. Should I apologize?"

"Please don't." Her hand clenched on his nape.

Adam held her close for a few more minutes, then sighed. "I have to leave now. While I still have enough control to walk out of here." He stepped back so she could move away from the door. "See you in a few hours." Without turning around, he left the room.

Veronica sank onto the bed, more buzzed than if she had consumed a whole pot of coffee, and realized the truth. She was in so much trouble.

## CHAPTER EIGHT

Adam woke from a restless sleep, needing to burn off the charged emotion still revving his system. After changing into jogging clothes, he walked to the darkened kitchen, saw Remy staring out the back door with a mug of coffee in his hand. "Problem?"

"Not unless you count the coyote prowling the neighborhood."

He shrugged into a light jacket and checked that his Sig was accessible. "He doesn't bother me so I leave him alone. Everything quiet?"

"Nothing unusual. Going for a run?"

"Can't sleep."

Remy turned. "You okay?"

"Things on my mind." More like someone. Veronica Miles captured his interest without trying, and that was before the sizzling kiss. Every time he woke during the night, he ached to hold her close and exchange more dynamite kisses.

Remy's intent gaze said his friend wasn't buying the explanation. "I'll make a new pot of coffee while you try to outrun your problems. Not going to work, though. Women are complicated."

"Who said anything about a woman?"

"Please. You're talking to a man who adores his wife, mother, sisters-in-law, and nieces. I know that look because I've seen it in the mirror more times than I want to admit. Veronica?"

No point hiding the truth from one of his best friends. "Yeah."

"Things will work out, Adam. Take your time. You've been hurt and I think she has, too."

He flinched at the direct hit. Yeah, he had been hurt, but he moved on with his life. Adam clapped Remy on the shoulder and went out into the early morning. He ran the first half mile at a slower pace, giving his body time to warm up and loosen stiff muscles and joints. He still felt remnants of the drug lord's handiwork first thing in the mornings.

He completed the next four and a half miles at a faster pace. As he pounded the pavement, he considered Remy's words. Despite his friend's worry, Adam didn't pine for Jessica. He'd been engaged to the kindergarten teacher before the deep cover mission that landed him in the enemy's hands. Adam had warned Jess he might be gone for months and unable to call. She assured him she would be fine, and she'd see him in a week or two.

That was his first clue she didn't understand the danger he faced every time he deployed. Should have known then their relationship wouldn't work out. Instead, he took Jess at her word, assuming she would understand if he was absent longer than a couple weeks.

He managed to call once a week until he was captured. Adam's stomach lurched, remembering agony at the hands of a sadistic killer bent on expanding into weaponized viruses, afraid at the time he wouldn't make it home to her or his sister. He had escaped, thanks to Claire, her husband Zane, Remy, Lily, two SEALs, and the Durango unit. If the team had arrived one day later, he wouldn't have survived.

Adam understood what Vonnie survived. He'd been there himself. At least her interrogator hadn't used chains, knives, and fire on her.

Once Adam was stateside, Jess came to see him. His lip curled. The woman he planned to spend the rest of his life with had taken one look at his injuries, handed him the engagement ring, and walked away without a backward glance. He hadn't heard from her in more than a year.

Comparing how he felt about Jessica to the firestorm Vonnie stirred in him, Adam was grateful the teacher walked away rather than try to stay the course with him, then ultimately leave when she realized she wasn't strong enough to be an operative's wife. She would have been miserable, their home a war zone instead of a place of safety, comfort, and love for them both.

Adam didn't know where this thing with Vonnie might go, but he wanted to find out. For the first time since Jessica walked out on him, he looked forward to spending time with a woman away from work. The question was, did she feel the same interest in him?

He huffed out a laugh as he turned the corner and ran toward his house. Why would Vonnie be interested in him? He had his share of dates before Jessica and Belize. After the drug lord finished with him, no woman showed any interest. His time in the torture chamber scarred him inside and out.

But Vonnie kissed him. That had to mean she was attracted. Right? Adam frowned. He'd drive himself crazy with this line of thinking. He didn't have the answers to any of the questions. Only Vonnie had them.

He slowed to a walk in his driveway. When he opened the back door, Remy turned and tossed him a bottle of water. "Your girl is awake. I don't think she slept any better than you."

Adam guzzled half the water before asking, "How do you know?"

"She stumbled in here after you left and begged for coffee. Once she drank a cup and poured a refill, she admitted she slept an hour or two."

Adam glanced toward the hall, concerned. Did she feel worse? "Maybe I should ask Jake Davenport or one of the other medics to check Vonnie when we go to Fortress headquarters."

The other operative rolled his eyes. "Won't make her happy. Veronica told Lily she's tired of being in bed and dealing with doctors. Sending her to Jake will spread the aggravation to you."

He grunted. Couldn't blame her. He felt the same after escaping the basement in Belize. Adam cared about Vonnie, enough to make her angry with him by calling in Jake.

After showering, he dressed, strapped on his weapons, and grabbed another light jacket. No point in making medical personnel uncomfortable when he entered the hospital fully armed.

In the hall, he noticed her bedroom door was cracked. Adam tapped on the door and eased it open. Veronica straightened from tying her running shoes, a smile curving her mouth when she saw him.

"How far did you run?"

"Five miles."

"Give me another few days and I'll run with you."

"Deal." He moved closer. "How do you feel, Vonnie?"

"Like I've gone ten rounds in the ring with an MMA champion." She placed her palm against his chest. "Adam, I'm fine. Please, don't worry so much. Dr. Sorensen might be a grouch, but he's good at what he does."

"You didn't sleep well."

She frowned. "Remy is a tattletale? Good to know. I'll be sure to keep deep, dark secrets to myself."

"He's concerned about you, Vonnie." So was Adam.

"I can look after myself. It's nobody's fault I had nightmares starring the creep who interrogated me for three days." Her cheeks flushed. "I also had a hard time going to sleep in the first place."

He analyzed her tone of voice, noted the way she wouldn't meet his eyes. "Why?"

"Your serious kissing skills, Walker."

Grinning, Adam wrapped his arms around Veronica. "I didn't sleep well myself. I was distracted by a beautiful woman sleeping across the hall from me."

She leaned her cheek against his chest. "What are we doing, Adam?"

"Exploring an attraction."

Veronica was silent a moment. "I don't know how to play relationship games."

"I don't play games." Not anymore. Life was too short to waste time with high school antics, especially given his high-stakes career. "I want to see where this goes."

"What if it doesn't go anywhere?"

Based on their kiss, he didn't think there was a chance of that happening. "We'll part ways as friends. I'll always be here if you need me, no matter what happens between us."

She seemed to melt against him. "Same goes for me. I will always have your back."

Adam captured her mouth in a gentle kiss, and released her. "Come on. We need to eat before meeting Maddox."

"What could he find out in five hours?"

"You'd be surprised. Fortress has people working 24/7. One of them is my brother-in-law, Zane Murphy. Zane is our resident tech guru. He's magic with computers and electronics."

"Handy. You like him?"

He clasped her hand. "Yeah, but don't tell him I said that. He thinks I put up with him because of Claire. Keeps him in line."

Remy and Lily went home to sleep when Adam left with Veronica. At Fortress headquarters, he escorted her to Maddox's office. Helen, the boss's assistant, hadn't arrived yet so Adam knocked on the door. A moment later, he and Veronica were seated in chairs in front of Maddox's desk.

"How are Rowan and Alexa?" Adam asked.

Maddox's face lit up. "Good. Lex started taking karate."

"Good for her. What sparked her interest?"

"Jon Smith and Eli Wolfe have been working with her and Rowan on self-defense tactics. They convinced my girls that training in martial arts is a great equalizer."

Adam wasn't surprised. The two Navy SEALs spent a lot of time with Maddox and his family and they loved Alexa as much as the rest of the Fortress operatives. Situational awareness and martial arts training would help the boss's wife and daughter protect themselves until help arrived should they be attacked by enemies of Fortress again. He couldn't think of anyone better to give the women pointers on self defense than the two fierce SEALs.

"Veronica, I made some calls and cleared you to see Cissy Carver." Maddox looked troubled. "I'm afraid your reception might not be what you're expecting."

"Why not?"

"She's not seeing visitors. Her blood pressure is too high and she's refusing to speak to anyone except her physician."

"We're good friends. I don't think she'll mind."

Maddox didn't look convinced.

A knock on the door brought Adam to his feet. He placed himself between Veronica and the visitor, although he wasn't too worried about a gunman storming into Fortress without being stopped in his tracks long before he reached the boss's office.

Zane rolled into the room, file on his lap. His eyes narrowed when he saw Adam. "You look like you haven't slept in a month. Take a nap or something before Claire sees you."

He scowled at his brother-in-law. "Yes, Mother. Z, this is Veronica Miles. Vonnie, Zane Murphy, my pain-in-the-neck brother-in-law."

Zane shook her hand. "Nice to meet you, Veronica. R.J. Walsh is a friend of mine."

Veronica smiled. "So you're the famous Z spoken of so highly by R.J. He says you create amazing video games."

"In my spare time." He sent a pointed glance at Maddox. "Not that I have much of that these days."

Maddox smiled. "What do you have for me?"

Zane tossed the file on the desk. "I'm still digging. No one reported Veronica missing."

Adam curved his hand over her shoulder, felt the tension vibrating through her.

"How can that be? I've been out of touch for more than five days."

"I don't know, Veronica," Zane said. "I report what I find."

"If the DEA didn't tell anyone I was missing, how did Fortress know to look for me?"

"R.J. contacted me, said Dane touched base with him and asked for help."

Adam frowned. Why didn't he go through his normal DEA channels? Didn't he trust his own people?

"That doesn't make sense," Veronica said. "Why didn't he go through the chain of command? There were other operatives in the area who could have searched for me within hours of the first missed check-in."

Adam clenched his jaw. Veronica wouldn't have suffered at the hands of her captors if her handler had alerted the chain of command. If the man wasn't dead, Adam would have paid Dane a visit. You didn't leave one of your own behind, no matter what. He should have mounted a rescue effort, even if he relied on Fortress for backup.

When Adam missed his first check-in, Fortress had immediately started the process to locate and evacuate him. Thanks to Veronica, his friends arrived in time to save his life. "We'll find out what happened, Vonnie." He laced their fingers together, ignoring the surprise on his boss and brother-in-law's faces.

She nodded. "At least Dane tried to help, although he used Fortress to do it. I want to see Cissy now."

Adam checked his watch. "It's still early. We'll go by your place first, then stop at a coffee shop for caffeine-free tea or coffee for Cissy."

"Perfect." She turned to Adam. "Thank you for everything."

"Veronica, don't report in yet," Maddox said.

"I have to."

"Not until we know what's going on," Zane said. "Do you have family who will worry about you?"

"No." Veronica sighed. "All right. I'll hold off for another day. I can't justify keeping silent after that."

Adam walked with her to the SUV. After fighting through rush hour traffic, he parked in her driveway. "Anything seem off?"

She scanned her house and the surrounding area. "Not so far."

"Will you let me check before you go inside?"

She slid him a narrow-eyed glance.

He laughed. "That's what I thought. Do you have an extra house key or should I show off my lock-picking skills?"

"I can pick my own lock, thank you."

Adam met her at the front of the SUV and walked to the porch. He pulled lock picks from his pocket, glanced at her door, and froze. Fresh scratches. "Wait."

Her gaze zeroed in on the knob. Veronica's lips pressed into a thin line. "Someone broke in."

## CHAPTER NINE

Veronica's chest tightened. That was not what she wanted to see. She slid the borrowed Sig from the small of her back, wondering if her alarm company knew about the breach in her security.

She signaled Adam to take the left while she took the right. They could clear the house faster if they split up. Pleased that he nodded and indicated for her to proceed, she tried the knob, found the door unlocked.

Turning the knob, Veronica eased the door open a crack and listened. No noises to indicate the intruder was still in her place. She slipped into the house, leading with her weapon. She quartered the living room, fury heating her blood. The intruders had trashed her house. She hadn't spent much time here, but she loved this place and had chosen every stick of furniture and decoration in it. Whoever broke in had systematically destroyed every piece of furniture she owned. Now she'd have to start all over again.

Veronica shoved her emotions down deep and continued searching through this part of the house. She didn't relax until Adam returned.

"Clear."

"Same here." She slid the Sig away and gestured around her. "Look what they did to this place. What could they possibly have been looking for?"

"You."

She folded her arms. "I'm not in the cabinets, but they broke every dish I own. This destruction was pointless."

"Depending on when they broke in, the purpose was to find out where you were or punish you for escaping their clutches."

"I guess there's no point in telling myself this was the work of random thieves." Her security system was too good for run-of-the-mill criminals.

"Have you noticed anything missing?"

"Not so far. I'll do a quick walk through before I call the cops."

"Might be best to let your alarm monitoring company make the contact. You're supposed to be out of the country, remember?"

"I'll tell them a neighbor reported suspicious activity here and have them check. They'll file a report with the police." She started in the bedrooms. "Try not to touch anything. Your prints are on file. I don't want your name connected to their investigation."

"I don't need your protection, Vonnie."

"Tough. You're getting it anyway. I don't want you at risk."

Adam chuckled. "My job is all about risk and so is yours."

"That doesn't mean I want to shine a spotlight on you. You're important to me." More important than he realized. She had the stitches, bruises, and cuts to show how much she wanted to protect him. How far were these jerks willing to go to get their hands on Adam?

She slumped against the wall in her bedroom, dismayed at the wholesale destruction. Her clothes were ripped to shreds, her mattress spewing stuffing, sheets in tatters. The contents of her dresser littered the floor, nail polish, perfume, and various body lotions poured over the intimate apparel. Shoes were scattered around the room. "I need to shop for clothes. Looks like they destroyed every outfit I own."

"I'm sorry, Vonnie. We'll go to Green Hills Mall after we visit Mrs. Carver. Can you tell if anything is missing?"

The only thing of value she kept in this room was the safe with her weapons and real ID. Veronica never carried her real documents on a mission. She never knew when her belongings might be searched.

She picked her way across the room to the large ornate mirror hanging on one wall. Behind the mirror was a large wall safe. Veronica checked the contents of the safe and breathed a sigh of relief. All her documents were still inside along with her weapons, shield, and a few hundred dollars in cash. She stuffed the money in her pocket along with her personal cell phone and creds wallet, which she might need since she was stateside. She also removed her laptop and case along with her favorite Sig and backup weapon. These would come in handy.

"Nothing is missing from here." She closed and locked the safe. Once the mirror was back in place, she handed Adam the Sig she'd borrowed. "What kind of thief trashes the house without finding the safe? There aren't any scratches to indicate they tried to get inside it."

"A thief with a message to send," he said, his expression grim. "Let's check the other rooms and get out of here."

Veronica made a sweep of the remaining rooms and found nothing was missing. "I don't understand what they wanted," she said once they were on the way to the hospital. "They didn't take anything to make the break-in look like a robbery."

"Unfortunately, you can't tell the alarm company that or they'll know you were inside the place."

"At least the police can investigate, look for finger prints."

"Would you rather have Fortress take care of it?"

"You have a CSI team?"

"Of course. If we handle the investigation, you won't have to worry about the police figuring out you're in town. We can upgrade your alarm system and replace your locks." He sent her a narrowed glare. "They're crap locks, Vonnie. You need to protect yourself better."

"I haven't had a problem before now," she protested.

"These clowns wanted you to know they could get to you in your safe space."

She tore her gaze from his. He was right. No matter how much the upgrades cost her, she couldn't afford to put off the investment in her safety. "Can you arrange for Fortress to take care of everything?"

Instead of replying, Adam activated his Bluetooth. "Z, it's Adam. Veronica's house was broken into. Everything is trashed. I want a team of crime technicians at her place. She also needs a security upgrade. Top level, top priority."

"I'll take care of it. Who is your monitoring company, Veronica?"

She told him the name and said, "Can Fortress monitor my system?"

"We'll add you to our monitoring list by the time your system is online. You'll need to cancel your contract with the current company in the next few hours."

Hours? Wow, Fortress didn't mess around. "I'll call in a few minutes."

"Good."

"Z, Vonnie needs replacements for her belongings."

"We'll take care of it. You need anything else, Adam?"

"Not at the moment."

"I'm still digging through the DEA's system, flagging any reference to Veronica."

"That information is classified," Veronica said.

"Want me to stop?"

Her gut told her he wouldn't back off even if she asked him to. If he was as good with a computer as Adam claimed, Veronica needed to know the information Zane might unearth. "No. Do me a favor?"

"Name it, sugar."

"Flag references to Dane Carver as well."

"You got it. I'll get back to you." Zane ended the call.

"Fortress doesn't have to replace my belongings, Adam."

"Part of the package because you're involved with me."

Figuring she would lose this argument, Veronica opted to call her alarm monitoring company and cancel their service. By the time she finished, Adam turned into the parking lot of the coffee shop. After purchasing a cup of herbal tea, they drove to the hospital.

Adam curled his fingers around hers as they walked. Despite playing the role of a doting boyfriend, the operative was on alert. In the elevator, he wrapped his arm around her waist, positioning his body between her and the other occupants of the car.

"I hate this," she said after they exited the elevator. "I don't want to be your principal."

"My role as your bodyguard is temporary. You're more to me than a job, Vonnie. I hope you know that."

"Sorry. I'm trying not to be crabby."

He stopped her a few feet shy of Cissy's room. "You might be grumpy, but you're still the most beautiful woman I've ever seen." The operative brushed his lips over hers.

How could a soft, simple kiss make her heart rate zoom out of the stratosphere? She was in so much trouble. At least, her heart was. This warrior was fast slipping beneath her guard and she couldn't find a way to keep him out. Truthfully, she wasn't sure she wanted to try. He fascinated her. No man had caught her attention for a long time.

Adam trailed his rough fingers over her cheek with a light touch. Another light kiss before he continued to Cissy's room. He knocked and pushed open the door.

A gasp greeted him. "Who are you? What do you want?"

"I'm Adam, Veronica's boyfriend."

"Boyfriend? She never mentioned a boyfriend. Why haven't I heard of you?

"The relationship is new, Mrs. Carver. We brought you some herbal tea."

"Veronica's here?"

She scooted past her "boyfriend" and walked into the room. Cissy's dark hair was spread over the white pillow, her belly distended, her brown eyes red-rimmed and swollen. "Cissy, I'm so sorry about Dane." She reached for her friend's hand as Adam set the tea on her rolling table.

"Don't touch me!" Cissy's face reddened with fury. "I don't want to see you."

Veronica's hand dropped to her side. Cissy didn't want to see anyone or just her? "Why not?"

"It's your fault my husband is dead."

"I had nothing to do with Dane's death. I was out of the country, Cissy."

"He protected you and you're nothing but a traitor."

## CHAPTER TEN

Shock rolled through Veronica's body. Traitor? What made Cissy say such a thing? Veronica had spilled blood to protect intelligence secrets. "Did Dane say that?"

"He was so upset, said there was a ton of evidence to prove you were passing information on the other agents. How could you turn on the people who protected you? I trusted you and you stabbed my husband in the back. I thought we were friends."

"We are." They had been. Now? She didn't know what was going on, who convinced Dane she was a turncoat, but she would find out. The thought of Dane believing she was guilty gutted Veronica.

"Not anymore, Veronica. Get out or I'll call security." Tears streamed from Cissy's eyes. "Don't come near me. I never want to see you again."

Veronica blinked to keep her own tears from falling. She wanted to protest, proclaim her own innocence, but one look at Cissy's face told her the effort would be futile.

Fine. She'd prove her innocence to Cissy and her DEA co-workers. Maybe she and Cissy would be friends again once she realized Veronica was innocent. As for the people she worked with, she already knew suspicions would linger long after proof of innocence was presented and might mean the end of her career with the DEA. That thought hurt so bad she almost couldn't breathe.

"We need to go," Adam murmured, nodding at the monitor showing Cissy's spiking blood pressure.

"The tea is from Adam," she said and left Cissy's bedside. Her friend might still enjoy the tea.

Adam didn't say anything as they walked to the SUV. He unlocked the vehicle and tucked her inside. He cupped her cheek. "I'm sorry, Vonnie. She will regret her words when you prove her wrong."

"You believe I'm innocent?" How was that possible?

"I know you are." His finger trailed over her still bruised cheek. "I saw what they did to you. I know how you suffered at the hands of your captors. When we finish our investigation, Mrs. Carver will believe you're innocent." He circled the hood and slid behind the wheel.

"Why do you believe me when people who worked with me for years think the worst? You don't know me."

"I know enough." He drove from the lot and headed toward the interstate. "Can you power shop to replenish your wardrobe?"

"Watch me."

"Excellent. While we cut a swath through the mall, think about who has a reason to set you up."

"Not Dane."

"Everyone is under suspicion, Vonnie, including Dane and Cissy. Dane was concerned enough when you missed your check-in to send us after you. I'm grateful he had the foresight to do so despite his suspicions."

"Or he worried I would commit treason." She couldn't stop the swell of bitterness flooding her soul. "He watched my back for years, and though he believed the worst of me at the end, he didn't abandon me." No need to pin a medal on him for nobility. He probably wanted Fortress to find her and haul her back to face justice.

"Maybe he didn't fully buy your guilt."

Possible. She pressed her fingers against her eyes. She still had trouble focusing, and the fuzziness caused her thought processes to be slower than normal. "If you're right, Dane must have left a trail in his investigation. That might be why he's dead."

"Someone killed Dane to stop him from nosing around."

"So they thought I would give up? No. Way. I'm going to clear my name and take down the creep who killed my friend."

"Good girl. Did you have a system with Dane where you received messages from him that he didn't want in the system?"

Her head whipped his direction. "How did you know?"

"We have fail safes at Fortress."

"But something went wrong when you were in Belize, didn't it?"

"We had a couple of traitors." His eyes glittered. "One was my teammate."

"Oh, Adam. I'm sorry." How devastated he must have been.

"It's behind me now."

Was it? Veronica wasn't so sure. At times since Adam rescued her, she noticed shadows in his eyes, as though he remembered painful things in his past. Was he thinking of his captivity or something else?

Maybe he thought of someone else. Her heart squeezed. Was there a woman Adam cared for? No, Adam wasn't that kind of man. He wouldn't kiss her if there was a woman who had a claim on his affections. Perhaps there had been a woman in his past. Later, when there was time, she might ask. Veronica didn't want to hurt him by dredging up the past, but neither did she want to lay herself open for unnecessary hurt. And this dark warrior could hurt her more than any other person in her life.

Adam parked in the garage attached to the mall. Once inside, Veronica led him to the store where she bought most of her wardrobe and had the best chance of finding everything she needed in one stop.

She tried on several changes of clothes and while in the dressing room, counted the money she'd taken from her safe. Enough for her purchases, although there wouldn't be much left over for other expenses. She needed access to her account without alerting anyone. Maybe Zane could help her.

Adam hauled her bounty from the mall and into the garage.

"Do you think anyone knows I'm in the country?" Her gaze scanned the interior of the concrete structure as they approached the SUV. A motor ran somewhere close. Veronica listened for the car to shift into gear and drive from the garage. But there was no change.

Her skin prickled. Someone could be talking on their cell phone if they had good reception in here. She didn't like it.

Adam stopped at the back of his SUV and hit his remote to unlock the vehicle. He deposited her purchases in the backseat, his gaze scouring their surroundings. "Get in the SUV." His attention focused on the right side of the garage, the area where the engine still idled.

She reached for her Sig. A brush of fabric nearby had her spinning toward the right.

A man dressed in black from head to toe darted into the deep shadows, gun in his hand.

"Gun," Veronica said, moving to a more protected position behind a concrete column. Rapid gunfire echoed, obliterating all other sounds. If someone planned to sneak up on them, she and Adam wouldn't hear them coming.

She fired two rounds in the direction of the thug. Her shots pinged off the concrete wall at the height of his head.

She didn't have a good shot from this position. In the lull, she heard muffled curses from her target.

A glance at Adam revealed he was shifting position, trying for a better angle himself. He crouched and ran past four vehicles. Before he reached his final destination, their quarry ran. Seconds later, the car which had been idling shifted into gear. Tires squealed on the pavement. A tan four-door sedan barreled around the corner and raced past them.

Adam and Veronica fired two rounds each. Though the back and side windows of the vehicle shattered, the driver, hunched low, raced from the garage and disappeared.

"You okay?" Adam asked as he jogged toward her.

"Peachy. You?"

"Same. Catch a license plate?"

She scowled. "No. Happened too fast."

He grinned. "And that irks you, doesn't it?"

"You bet. I'm supposed to notice details."

"Let's get out of here. That question you asked me earlier? I'd say the wrong people know you're back in town." Adam drove the SUV from the garage. As soon as they were clear of the structure, he called Zane. "Need a favor."

"Name it."

"Pull the video surveillance in the garage at Green Hills Mall."

"What am I looking for?"

"Cream-colored four-door sedan laying rubber as it barreled out of the structure about two minutes ago. Shooter tried to take out Vonnie."

"Injuries?"

"None on our part. Don't know about the shooter. He was dressed in black, including a ski mask, about six feet tall, two hundred pounds. He was trained, Z. Maybe law enforcement."

Veronica's breath stalled in her lungs. A fellow cop? Her stomach soured.

"A hit?" Zane asked, his voice barely above a growl.

Adam's hand wrapped around hers. "That's my guess."

"That can't be," Veronica protested. "We don't assassinate people."

"Law enforcement doesn't," Zane agreed. "Someone guilty of treason is trying to cover his tracks. He knows you won't let Dane's death slide, that you'll fight to clear your name. The investigation is more likely to stall if you're dead. I guarantee there would be a massive influx of proof of your guilt after you were dead and unable to defend yourself. And with your handler gone, who would take up the fight?"

No one, she realized. No one cared enough to put their career on the line to fight for her. She remained silent, unwilling to admit the truth to men who would fight to the death for each other and their fellow operatives. Though wheelchair bound for three years, Zane had gone to Belize with Claire to free Adam. None of her fellow DEA agents risked themselves to rescue her.

"The car description was generic. Anything to distinguish it from the thousands of others in the area at the time?"

"Yeah," Adam said, his tone wry. "The windows have been shot out and the side panels have bullet holes."

Zane chuckled. "I'll see if I can locate your car. Veronica?"

"Yes?"

"We'll figure this out, sugar. Hang in there."

"Thanks, Zane."

"Adam, I'll tell the boss what's going on. Expect him to contact you."

"Copy that." He glanced at Veronica. "I checked the SUV for tracking devices before we left your place and before we left the garage."

"How? I didn't see you drop to the ground."

Amusement swirled in his gaze as he handed her a small, plastic device that fit in the palm of her hand.

"What's this?"

"Detects activated tracking devices and bugs."

She stared at the gadget with serious envy. "I don't suppose Maddox would part with one of these."

"I'll get one for you."

Veronica grinned. "You give me the best gifts."

"Whatever keeps you safe, Vonnie. Now, where's your drop site?"

"A post office box in Brentwood."

Adam drove onto the interstate and headed toward the post office. "Take your battery out of your phone."

She stared at him a few seconds, sighed. "Someone pinged my signal. I should have thought of that. It's a secure phone, DEA issued."

"It's in the DEA database which Zane is surfing with ease. I'm sorry, Vonnie, but indications are someone in your unit is out to get you."

## CHAPTER ELEVEN

Adam parked in the lot outside the Brentwood post office. "Do you visit this box often?" he asked Veronica.

"I clean it out once a month when I'm in town. I have boxes in five different locations, each under a different name. This is the one Dane and I agreed would be the drop for emergencies."

Smart. Even if someone guessed she and Carver had a drop, they probably wouldn't know about all five of them. "I assume there was no record of the boxes in the database?"

She snorted.

"How good are your IDs?"

"I haven't had any questions."

Maybe, but he'd prefer Zane check the trail and add his magic touch to keep Vonnie safe. "I want the names and addresses. Let's make sure there aren't any mistakes. Do you have the key to your box?"

"I grabbed that along with my cell phone and money." She pulled a small key chain from her pocket and dangled it from her hand. "Let's go."

"Wait." He grabbed a Nashville Sounds baseball cap from his glove box and tugged it on her head. "Not much of a disguise, but it will have to do."

They walked into the mail room together. She unlocked box 487 and pulled out a handful of envelopes. All but one were full of papers. Inside the SUV, she said, "I need a secure place to read these."

"Fortress headquarters is closer than my house."

"That will work."

Adam took his time, turning squares, backtracking, quick turns, some weaving in and out of traffic, looking for a tail. While he maneuvered through the streets of Brentwood and Nashville, Veronica kept watch on the mirrors.

"Nothing." She twisted in her seat. "It's been over an hour. I think we're clear, Adam."

Still watchful, he drove to Fortress. How long, he wondered, would it take for the people after Veronica to realize he was involved with her, not just as her bodyguard? Five minutes of observation would reveal he felt something for the DEA agent seated beside him. He didn't intend to hide it. The more people who knew she was under his protection and that of Fortress, the better. Smart people didn't mess with Adam or his friends.

He escorted her to the elevator and up to the fifth floor. His fingers laced with hers, Adam walked into the communication room. His brother-in-law turned, held up his finger in a signal to wait, then returned his attention to the three screens spread out at his work station.

"Copy that, Nico. I'll send you the information within the hour." Zane spun his chair to face Adam and Veronica. "What do you need?"

"A quiet, secure place to check intel Carver sent to a drop for Veronica." He inclined his head toward the screens. "The Shadow unit?"

"Yeah. They need information on a child trafficking group."

Man, Nico's group was tasked with the worst of the horrible assignments. All the units took on terrible jobs, but this unit seemed to have more than their fair share. Couldn't be easy. "Are they ever assigned anything easier?"

"Not in a while. What do you have, Veronica?"

"I'm not sure. Dane sent several things to one of my drop boxes. I haven't looked at the information yet. Too busy watching the mirrors for a tail."

"Did you check the other boxes?"

She shook her head. "Not yet. The one I checked is for emergency use. There shouldn't be anything in it except junk mail for the past two weeks."

"Anything I can help with?"

"Veronica has five different IDs she's been using for the post office boxes," Adam said. "Run a check on them and see if anyone has been inquiring about her."

"Give me the names and addresses. I'll do the scan while you and Veronica see what Carver sent. The conference room is open, Adam. I installed a scanner in there. It will save time if you scan the documents Carver sent and project them on the wall screens so you both can read them. I'll check with you in a few minutes, bring some water for you."

"Thanks, Z." A minute later, he opened the door to the conference room. Adam had always liked this room, especially at night. The windows showed a great view of the city.

He noted Zane had added several screens on the wall. Nice. Adam flipped a switch and the windows turned opaque.

Veronica shook her head. "We use blinds to block windows."

"Fortress likes gadgets." He extended his hand for the envelopes. "I'll scan these in. Might take a few minutes."

He slit open the envelopes with his Gerber knife and slid out the contents of each one. Adam spent several minutes scanning the pages, taking the earliest post marked date first. By the time he finished and sent the first file to the screens, Zane entered the room.

"Everything work okay?"

"Perfect. The scanner will come in handy when we plan missions."

"That's what I thought." Zane handed Veronica a bottle of water and tossed a second to Adam. "So, what do you have?"

The three of them turned to the screens. The more he read, the colder Adam felt.

Zane turned his head to stare at Veronica. "Do you have an explanation for this?"

Her face pale, she shook her head. "I don't know where Dane obtained this information, but it's not true." She turned to Adam. "I didn't do this, Adam. I would never betray you like that."

"You didn't know him a few days ago," Zane snapped. "He was a stranger to you. Easy enough to sell information on someone you don't know. How do we know for sure this isn't the actual truth? You could have been lying to protect yourself all along. Maybe you just got caught."

"Enough, Zane," Adam interrupted, his voice soft.

"If she's one of those responsible for your time in that death chamber, she has a lot to answer for."

The angry SEAL was correct. Veronica hadn't been part of his life for long. However, she had provided critical intelligence to aid Fortress in the past, including Adam's rescue. What he knew of her to this point led him to believe she was innocent.

Adam faced Veronica. She didn't protest her innocence again, just waited, resignation and sadness in her eyes. The DEA agent expected him to condemn her like her handler and his wife had done.

Without taking his gaze from hers, Adam said to his brother-in-law, "Vonnie is innocent, Z."

Tears sparkled in her eyes as she sent him a tremulous smile.

"Think with your head, not your heart, man."

"I am. Look at the screen again, Z."

The tech guru scowled. "What am I supposed to be seeing?"

"The date of the first packet of information."

"What about it?"

"That's about the time Vonnie went to Mexico."

She straightened in her chair. "He's right, Zane. The date is the day after I arrived in Mexico. I was kidnapped six days later."

"The information looks like it went to Dane's email at work." Adam took his empty water bottle to the trash. "Can you trace it back to the source, Z?"

He dragged a hand down his face. "Yeah." A glance at Veronica. "I'm sorry, sugar. Adam's captivity is a sore spot for all of us."

"I understand. I wouldn't turn over my worst enemy to a terrorist like the one Adam faced in Belize." A wry smile curved her lips. "I have the scars to prove it."

Adam froze for a second, then slowly turned toward Veronica. "What did you say?"

"What scars?" Zane demanded.

She remained mute. Stubborn woman. "Sweetheart, look at me." Adam waited until her gaze locked with his. "Tell me."

"The interrogations weren't only about DEA operations and agents in Mexico. The interrogator also wanted information on you."

## CHAPTER TWELVE

Adam stared at Veronica across the conference room table, unable to believe the words coming from her mouth. "The interrogator asked about me by name?"

She nodded, breaking eye contact with him and focusing on the half-empty bottle in her hands.

He blew out a breath, his gut tightening into a knot. "How much of the interrogation focused on me, Vonnie?"

"Most of it. I refused to tell him anything. That's why the beatings grew more intense and he resorted to using the whip. I don't know how much longer I would have been able to hold out, but I refused to give you up, even if he killed me."

She'd suffered to protect him. Adam's heart hurt at the knowledge. "Zane, give us a minute." He had things he needed to say to her and he didn't want an audience.

"I'll be in the comm center." The SEAL left them alone.

Adam circled the table and knelt in front of her. "Vonnie, why didn't you tell me?"

"What was the point? You rescued me and I'm healing. I endured for you and my fellow agents."

"But you suffered the most to protect me. Why didn't you give me up? I can look out for myself."

Her face flushed. "I kept tabs on you after your rescue from Belize. Over the months, I came to care for you. You started to matter to me. I don't regret what I went through, Adam. You're safe and that's all that's important to me."

He cupped her face between his palms and kissed her, his touch gentle, showing her without words that he appreciated her sacrifice. His own teammates hadn't risked themselves to protect him as she had. That she gave so much for a man she didn't know left Adam almost speechless. He pulled himself together to murmur, "Thank you for protecting me, baby."

He suspected Zane was talking to Maddox about security for Claire. If the person targeting Adam couldn't get to him, he might go after Claire instead. He should ask Remy and Lily to protect his sister.

Adam eased back. "Will you talk to Zane and Maddox about your interrogation?"

She flinched. "I'll handle it."

"Let's read the rest of the files so we know what we're up against."

"Nothing good," she muttered.

They spent the next hour reading the rest of the documents sent to Veronica's handler, each more condemning than the last, including lists of people's names and operations he didn't recognize, but she did. The last envelope contained information on Adam and his assignment in Belize. His jaw clenched. How had the traitor gotten information on him? Zane was obsessive about protecting Fortress operatives. The tech guru had bots set to alert him the moment any operative or the alias in use was mentioned on the Net.

"These are people I worked missions with since the DEA hired me along with the names of the operations. Some of the operatives were killed in missions gone bad. Information leaked and we were ambushed in some cases."

And the only common denominator in all the information was Veronica. So whoever set her up intended to use her as the scapegoat for everything, not just Adam's capture. What concerned him the most was if she returned to the DEA, no one in the agency would trust her or watch her back. The woman who fascinated him wasn't safe working for or with her own agency. Someone had a target on her back. The shooter in the garage could be connected to the interrogator or Veronica's own agency.

He tapped a couple keys and sent a copy of the files to Zane and Maddox, then they returned to the comm room. "Zane, if the boss is free ask one of your underlings to cover for you and come meet with us."

Zane contacted Maddox, turned. "He's free for the next hour and says you owe him. He planned to surprise Rowan at the coffee shop."

"I'll make it up to him." He clasped Veronica's hand and led her the short distance to Maddox's office. Helen waved him through. After a quick knock, he opened the door to the office.

Maddox glanced up from his computer screen, his expression grim. "They did a number on you, Veronica. No wonder your handler thought you were dirty. I'm not surprised someone shot at you."

"I'm not either." Veronica sat.

"How can I help, Adam?"

"I hate to put Vonnie through it," Adam said, "but you need to hear what she went through and why."

Maddox's eyebrows rose as Zane joined them.

"He needs to listen," Adam said. "Claire might be in danger."

"Okay. Shoot."

Adam faced Veronica. "The story is yours to tell." He didn't want to hear what she suffered on his behalf and dreaded her reliving the experience, but the other two men might hear something he missed in the storm of emotion swamping him. Plus, Zane had a right to know everything since Claire was at risk.

Adam scooted his chair close to Veronica's and laced their fingers together to offer silent support. Although she was tough, as evidenced by her injuries and the length of time she endured the various methods of torture, Adam would make her take a break if he felt she needed one.

"Dane assigned me to another undercover op in the Chihuahua province two weeks ago."

"The mission?"

"Locate a warehouse where drugs were being packed and shipped up to the United States. We tracked shipments of fentanyl that were laced back to this particular manufacturer, but he moves his packing locations every few days. He has several dilapidated buildings he uses for one or two days at a time. The equipment and raw materials are packed up each time. Because he packages small quantities, the operation is easy to move. Makes him hard to pin down. He's paranoid and never sleeps in the same place each night, sometimes moves in the middle of the night."

Maddox scowled. "Hate drug lords."

"As you know, this drug is deadly. We couldn't let more hit the streets here."

"How many undercover ops are you sent on each year, Veronica?" Zane asked.

Her gaze darted to Adam for a second, then refocused on Zane. "All my missions are undercover and always outside the US."

Adam's heart clenched. "Vonnie, that isn't healthy or safe for you. No one should work overseas constantly. Why didn't Dane assign you to operations here?"

"I was the most logical choice. I don't have close family ties. That's why the agency hired me, to work undercover missions beyond our borders."

In other words, she was disposable. How could Dane and the others have valued Veronica so little? She had saved countless lives over her career with the DEA. Adam glanced at Maddox and Zane, saw in their expressions the same fury scalding his gut.

"Did you have a partner?" Zane asked.

She shook her head.

"When this matter is resolved, we'll talk," Maddox said. "Continue."

"Six days after I arrived in Mexico, I met with one of my confidential informants. He was to give me the location of Escobar's operation for the next day. My orders were to confirm the location and Dane would send in a team the following day, working in conjunction with the local police."

Maddox grunted. "Law enforcement in Chihuahua is in the pockets of the drug cartels."

"We worked with law enforcement in that area numerous times in the past to put a dent in the drug trade. But this time something went wrong. Carlos must have been followed because someone chloroformed me. I woke up in the room where Adam found me."

"Were you interrogated by a team?"

"One man, someone I called Interrogator. The light was dim in that chamber. I never saw his face. By the time the chloroform wore off, either he or one of his cronies had hit me a few times in the face. My eyes were swelling. From that point on, he focused on other areas of my body."

"How much damage?" Zane asked.

"Mostly soft tissue."

"She has stitches in her back, lacerations from the whip," Adam added, figuring she intended gloss over the worst of what she'd suffered.

"What did Interrogator want to know?" This from Maddox.

"In the beginning, he questioned me extensively about DEA operations and the agents working them."

"He knew you were DEA?"

She nodded. "He called me by name from the beginning."

"I assume you didn't take your ID with you on the mission."

"Never. I entered and would have left the country under a fake ID."

"One of the five IDs you used for your post office boxes?" Zane asked.

"No. This one was DEA sanctioned."

So the agency would have known when she entered the country and in the right place for Escobar and his men to grab her.

"We'll come back to the missions," Maddox said. "What did Interrogator want to know about Adam?"

"Everything. Where he lives, his family, his friends, missions he'd worked, where he was assigned and which team he was working with. He was especially interested in his role in Belize, whether he sabotaged the drug cartel."

"What did you tell him?" Zane asked, his voice soft.

Adam scowled at his brother-in-law.

"Nothing, Zane. I didn't know anything. The only thing I allowed R.J. to tell me was how Adam was doing." She faced Adam. "If I had known more, I still wouldn't have told Interrogator. By the time I was taken, I had developed an attachment to you despite the fact I'd never laid eyes on you." She turned back to Maddox. "I wouldn't know Adam if I passed him on the street before my rescue. The Interrogator knew more about Adam than I did."

"How long did he question you about Adam?"

She was silent a moment. "I don't know. Without windows in the room, I couldn't gauge time based on the sun."

Adam tightened his fingers around hers. "The night we rescued you, Interrogator left to go to his girlfriend. Sounded like she demanded his time in the evenings. How many times was he gone for an extended length of time?"

"Three, I think. I can't guarantee that. I lost consciousness a couple of times. He might have rested from his labors. He was enthusiastic in his work."

Adam's eyes burned.

"Did anyone else question you?" Maddox asked.

"No."

Adam straightened. Something in Veronica's voice raised red flags. Then he remembered the clown who came into the room. "The man I killed in that room came while his boss was gone, didn't he?"

She nodded.

"He touched you?"

"He taunted me, threatened more."

Yeah, he knew what this guy planned to do. If he wasn't already dead, Adam would go back and kill him.

"What about the missions, Veronica?" Maddox leaned forward, arms folded on his desk. "What can you tell us about them?"

"They're classified."

Amusement lit the CEO's eyes. "I have a higher security clearance than you do."

A slow smile curved her mouth. "Somehow that doesn't surprise me. Most of the missions were a bust. I did what I always do, visited the area with my professional camera in hand and took pictures of people, buildings, and landscape."

"That was your cover story?"

"It gave me an excuse to come and go frequently. After a raid, I stayed around for a number of days before claiming to have another gig somewhere on the other side of the globe. The DEA would send me to the place I'd named en route to another mission."

"Most of the missions mentioned in the emails were a bust?"

She nodded. "The information was good. My confidential informants are careful. They never let me down before."

"Sounds like you have a leak." Maddox studied her expression a moment. "What about future missions? Anything you would be working if you hadn't been kidnapped?"

"Dane assigned me to a mission in a different part of Mexico. I was to leave two days ago to find an offshoot of the same drug cartel shipping heroin to the US." She wrinkled her nose. "This cartel is also into human trafficking."

"What group?" Zane asked.

"Los Diablos."

"In Rivas?"

"Yes, why?"

He looked at Maddox. "What do you want me to do?"

"Contact Nico. Pull the Shadow unit out of there."

"It's a government contract, boss."

"I'm not sacrificing my people for a few bucks. Something is very wrong with this picture. First Adam, now Nico's team? Tell him to evacuate immediately. I'll make a couple calls, see what I can find out on my end. You have Claire covered?"

"Smith and Wolfe are with her." Zane grinned. "She put them to work, hauling her equipment to a wedding rehearsal. Her bodyguards are quite a hit with the bridesmaids."

Adam and Maddox chuckled.

"What do you think is going on?" Veronica asked.

The smile slid from Maddox's face. "I don't know, Veronica, but I intend to find out."

## CHAPTER THIRTEEN

Since Maddox had another meeting scheduled, Veronica and Adam followed Zane back to the comm center.

When he sent his co-worker back to the research division, Zane turned to Veronica, his expression sober. "You said you kept up with Adam's progress through R.J. Walsh. Did you ask anyone else about Adam, even in passing?"

And risk Adam's safety? No way. She had a vested interest in his continued recovery. "Only R.J."

"You think R.J. might be talking to someone about me?" Adam asked.

"Maybe. Not likely, though. If it wasn't him, then I want to know who connected Veronica to you." Zane frowned. "And Nico's team. That's even more troubling."

"I didn't know Nico and his team existed until they helped Adam." Veronica sat in a chair next to his work console. "If someone is setting me up for the fall of Nico's team, he overplayed his hand. There is no trail to link me to them until three days ago."

"The Special Forces community is a close one. Hard to believe one of them is responsible. I can't see R.J. running his mouth."

"But it's not unheard of," Adam pointed out. "We've both suffered the consequences of loose lips. We need to check out R.J., see if he's connected to other leaking incidents."

"Agreed." Zane strapped his headset in place, then grabbed his cell phone. "Hold a minute while I text Nico his new orders."

"If he can, you know he'll call and argue."

"Yep. He'll lose."

Sure enough, less than a minute later, a call came into the switchboard. Zane glanced at one of his screens. "Nico." He punched a button. "No, it's not a mistake and you can't stay," he said instead of the standard greeting. He listened a moment, then said, "Look, Maddox ordered you out. The DEA has an operation going down there to deal with Los Diablos and Veronica's captors know about it. They pressed her for information. You can't stay, Nico, or you'll be caught in the crossfire. We'll keep an eye on them through the satellite feed. That's the best we can do right now. I'll contact the pilot, have the plane ready for you to return to the US immediately." He touched a key and disconnected the call, a scowl on his face.

"I take it he wasn't happy," Adam said.

"Not even close. Los Diablos prefers trafficking kids. They claim they're less trouble to keep in line. According to Nico, they have a full stable right now."

Veronica's stomach twisted. There were a lot of sick people in the world. Child predators were the worst of the bunch. She didn't blame Nico for being furious. Even though Fortress would keep tabs on the cartel, those children would still suffer, maybe die.

She clenched her fist, still determined to figure out what was going on and clear her name so all of them could go back to their jobs. If she still had a job when this situation was resolved. If Veronica left the DEA under a cloud, no law enforcement agency in the country would touch her. She'd be black listed.

What would she do for work? She'd worked for the DEA since graduating from college. Now she might not have a choice but to consider other options.

"Veronica, did anyone else know you were helping someone outside the agency with intel?" Zane asked.

"Probably. We pass on tips to other agencies when we pick up chatter. They do the same for us."

"How common is it to aid an outside agency like Fortress?"

"Depends on the case. If we stumble on intel and pass it along, we expect the same in return."

"Fair enough. What organizations have you aided besides Fortress?"

"Only R.J.'s organization, Trident." Veronica frowned. Before her rescue, the only connection she had to the two private security firms was R.J.

"R.J. is already on the top of my list to investigate. Who else would know you aided Fortress in finding Adam?"

"Dane, Carol Rossi, and Graham Norton, all with the DEA."

"I'll dig into their backgrounds as well. In the meantime, what are you and Adam going to do?" His eyes filled with sympathy. "You know you can't go back to work, right?"

She gave a short laugh. "Not unless I want a bullet in the back. But I need to go into the office at some point."

"With the evidence I'm seeing, they'll escort you right into a cell. Hard to uncover the truth from behind bars. You might want to rethink that choice."

"Why don't we talk to R.J., Carol, and Graham individually," Adam suggested. "We'll find out where they are and talk to them."

"Are Carol and Graham in the country?" Zane shifted to the console and keyed information into his computer.

"They were both due for time in house. They should still be in town."

He nodded. "R.J. should be at home unless he goes to rehab in the next hour."

"He's injured?"

"Bullet to the thigh on his last mission. His principal froze. R.J. leaped on top of him to knock him from the line of fire. Bullet hit R.J. instead."

"We'll start with him," Adam said. "What do you need from us to find the other two?"

"Veronica, do you know the phone numbers for Carol and Graham? I can hack into the DEA system, but if you know the numbers it will save time."

"I didn't hear you say that," she said. "I'm still a cop, you know."

Zane flashed a grin at her. "Maybe we can change that."

"Recruiting?"

"Always. Numbers?"

After Veronica gave him the information, Adam said, "Vonnie needs a cell phone."

Zane went to the cabinet on the far side of the room for a phone. After returning to his computers and entering information, he handed her the phone. "It's secure so don't worry about your signal being traced or unwanted ears listening to your conversation. The number programmed into the phone is Fortress." He glanced at Adam. "After you key in your number, make sure you put in mine as well as Maddox's."

"How much do I owe you?" Veronica asked.

He waved off her suggestion of payment. "You're involved with Adam now. We always protect our operatives and the people who matter to them. Maddox figures the cost of the secure phones are worth every penny if our people aren't worried about the safety of their loved ones."

Made sense. The government wasn't so accommodating to their agents.

Adam placed his hand on Veronica's lower back. "Send R.J.'s address to my phone."

"Already done. Let me know when you're ready to see Carol or Graham. I'll ping their phones and give you their location."

Back in the SUV, Adam programmed R.J.'s address into the navigation system. "Let's see what R.J. knows about you and your situation."

## CHAPTER FOURTEEN

Adam parked in the driveway of a two-story brick home. R.J.'s place was situated on a country road outside Nashville, the nearest neighbor at least a couple of acres away. Nice, private, quiet. The kind of place to raise a family.

He turned off the SUV and caught Veronica's hand when she reached for the handle. "Wait." He pulled out his phone and texted Zane to let R.J. know they were in his driveway. Adam had just been given a medical clearance to return to duty. He'd rather not land back in a hospital because of a paranoid, overzealous Special Forces soldier.

"What are we waiting for?" Veronica asked.

"Permission to approach the house. You don't walk up unannounced to the home of someone in black ops, not unless you have a death wish. It's too dangerous."

"Doesn't he have a security system?"

"Of course. Probably includes cameras. He doesn't know who we are, Vonnie." He slid a look her direction. "At least, he doesn't know me except for the name. Have you met him?"

She shook her head. "I've only spoken to him over the phone."

"We'll wait. I have no intention of going to a hospital with injuries I can't explain."

A minute later, Zane sent a text telling him it was safe to approach the door.

"We can go now." They met at the front of the SUV. "You take the lead."

She looked surprised. "Why?"

"He's your contact. He might respond better to your questions."

"Good thing I'd already planned to take the lead."

He chuckled as he rang the doorbell. Adam made sure he faced the camera so R.J. got a good look at him. The operative should run a check on him with Zane and confirm his identity as well as Veronica's.

"Why doesn't he answer the door?" she whispered after a minute passed without a sign of R.J. coming to let them inside the house.

"He's waiting for a visual confirmation from Zane."

Seconds later, the door was unlocked and swung open. A man well over six feet stood in the doorway, leaning on a crutch, weapon clutched in his free hand. His dark eyes scanned them from head to toe, stopping at each place where they had weapons concealed. "Loaded for bear, aren't you?"

"Smarter to be prepared for the worst," Veronica said.

His lips curved. "True. I'm R.J. Walsh."

"Veronica Miles. This is Adam Walker."

"Please, come in." He limped out of the way. "Living room is on the right."

Though the thought of this man at his back with a weapon made Adam's skin prickle, he followed Veronica into the house, making sure his body was between her and Walsh. Pictures of Walsh's family were on the wall and mantle. Cute kids. A boy and a girl, maybe between 7 and 10 years old.

He settled on the sofa with Veronica, keeping Walsh and the door in full view. Was this the man who set up Veronica?

"Thank you for seeing us on short notice," she said. "I'm happy to finally put a face with the voice. How do you know Zane?"

"Served together in the SEALs. He's a good man. Shame about that IED."

"That's what put him in the wheelchair?"

"Yeah. Lost his whole team in that explosion. Don't know if I would have bounced back nearly as well as he has."

"He's a vital part of Fortress," Adam said. "We wouldn't be nearly as effective without his skills. He also saved my hide down in Belize."

"He had help," Walsh said, his words clipped.

"Yes, he did." Veronica leaned forward. "You passed along the information from me so Zane and the others could rescue Adam. You've been a great go-between, R.J. You also were instrumental in saving my life a few days ago. Thank you for contacting Fortress on my behalf. I don't think I'd be alive right now if not for your help."

He shrugged. "We have to help each other in this business. Walker, you look good for a man who spent time as a guest of Peter Collins in his chamber of horrors."

Adam lifted one shoulder. "Takes more than a thug to take down a Marine."

"Did you hear about Dane?" Veronica asked Walsh.

A frown. "No. What happened?"

"He's dead."

The operative stiffened. "And you think I killed him." A statement of fact, not a question.

"You tell me."

"I had no reason to kill him."

"Even if he was responsible for Veronica's capture and torture?" Adam asked. Beside him, Veronica jerked. He shifted so his thigh pressed against hers.

"Why would he arrange her kidnapping, then send in rescuers?"

"He might not have expected Adam and the others to arrive so fast," Veronica said. "If the DEA were in charge, the rescue would have taken much longer to organize."

Walsh snorted. "We don't have that kind of luxury."

"Good thing for me."

"Look, Veronica, nothing personal, but I don't know you. I had no reason to mete out vigilante justice over someone I've spoken to on the phone a handful of times."

"What did Dane say when he called you?"

"What are you looking for?"

"Anything to help us figure out who killed him."

"How did he die?"

"Car accident," Adam said. "The police report said he lost control of the car, maybe due to mechanical failure, and hit a grove of trees, head on." Zane had included that bit of information in the text granting him permission to approach Walsh's house.

"That's not possible," Veronica said. "Dane was obsessive about his vehicles. He worried about Cissy's safety while she was on the road."

"Then we need to look at his car."

"I'd rather not have to break into the police impound lot. Makes a visit behind bars much more likely."

Adam smiled. "We wouldn't get caught, but breaking in won't be necessary. I have a friend who works for Metro police as a homicide detective. He can get us in there legally, although the other way would be a challenge and more fun."

"Your idea of fun leaves something to be desired, Walker." Despite her words, Veronica's eyes sparkled with humor. "What did Dane say when he called, R.J.?"

"You missed your check-in on an op in the Chihuahua province and he was worried. He wanted me to get word to Fortress."

"Did he say why he wanted Fortress to find me as opposed to the DEA?"

"Just said something odd was going on in his unit."

Another finger pointed straight at the DEA. Someone Veronica worked with was out to frame her for treason and possibly the murder of her handler. "How long have you been in contact with Veronica?" Adam asked.

"Two years. Why?"

"Has Dane ever contacted you before?"

"Sure. Like I said, in this business, we help each other. Trident spends a lot of time in areas where the DEA is gathering intelligence or setting up a sting."

So did Fortress, but Maddox wasn't in the habit of contacting other agencies to rescue his operatives. Had Cissy misunderstood Dane? Maybe he wasn't convinced Veronica was guilty. Perhaps he knew someone was setting her up and suspected one of his own as the culprit. "Did he mention anything like this happening before now?"

"Nope."

"How did you know to contact me?" Veronica asked. "I never heard of you before our first phone conversation?"

"Dane owed me a favor. I helped another of his agents out of a jam. I needed information, fast. You had been working in the area where we had a mission scheduled to rescue a five-year-old girl."

"I remember that. I had to leave for another assignment right after we talked so I never found out how the mission went. Will you tell me how it turned out?"

"She's a happy seven-year-old, getting ready to turn eight. She has a few nightmares. Other than that, she doesn't seem to have suffered many repercussions."

"Have you heard rumors about treason in the DEA ranks?"

His eyes narrowed. "Other than you selling out? No."

"And yet you still contacted Fortress on my behalf. Thanks for that."

Walsh inclined his head in acknowledgment. "Your information is spot on every time. I owed you for that at least. If you are guilty, the feds will deal with you on their terms."

"They already tried," Adam said, his voice soft. "Someone shot at her a couple hours ago."

"Huh. Kidnappers trying to reacquire their prize or co-workers targeting her?"

"That's what we're looking into," Veronica said. "Has anyone asked you about me in the last few days?"

Walsh shifted his weight, stretching out his injured leg with a wince. "A couple of people besides Dane. Carol Rossi and Graham Norton both contacted me, looking for information on your whereabouts."

"What did you tell them?" Adam leaned his forearms on his thighs.

"Nothing. What could I tell them?"

"You didn't mention calling Fortress?"

Anger flared in Walsh's eyes. "I'm not a newbie to this game, Walker. After Dane's call, I knew better than to trust anyone with that information. I figured if you and your friends saved Veronica, you'd stash her somewhere safe." His gaze shifted to Veronica.

"Tell me," she said.

"Norton said you and he were very close. You didn't call him as soon as your feet touched U.S. soil."

"He's a friend who wants to be more. I don't." She stood. "Thank you for speaking to us, R.J. How soon will you be back at work?"

"Three or four months. I have a lot of physical therapy ahead of me." He limped to the front door ahead of them.

"I noticed the pictures of your family." She smiled. "They're beautiful. You're a lucky man."

He nodded. "They are my world."

"I'm sorry I didn't get a chance to meet them as well."

"They're not here." He slammed the door behind them.

Adam thought about his words as he walked with Veronica to the SUV. He waited until he was driving from Walsh's home before he said, "What do you think about Walsh and the interview?"

"Something more is going on with him than restlessness from being sidelined."

"He said his family wasn't there, not that they were out running errands or at the doctor or dentist. They aren't living at the house with him at the moment."

"Wonder what happened?"

"Divorce rate is high in our business, Vonnie."

"Same with law enforcement, unfortunately. It's hard when your spouse is gone most of the time."

True enough. He knew many military buddies who divorced because of the multiple deployments and difficult adjustments when the loved one returned home. He glanced at Veronica. "Tell me about Graham Norton."

"There's nothing much to tell."

"Vonnie."

She flashed him a look filled with irritation. "We've been on several missions together. He is also deployed overseas quite a bit."

"I thought you didn't have a partner."

"I don't. Remember, I gather intel, then my handler sends in the rest of the team. Graham has been on those teams."

He was silent, waiting for her to continue.

Finally, she sighed. "He wants more than I can give him, Adam."

"What does that mean?"

"We went on a few dates. He pressed for more."

"You didn't want more?"

"I don't feel the same way he does. The chemistry isn't there for me. He's a friend, nothing more. I didn't think it was fair to go to dinner or a movie when he was hoping for a more serious relationship, so I quit accepting his invitations. And before you ask, yes, I did explain how I felt. I like him, Adam, but only as a friend. I didn't want to hurt him by giving him hope for more when there's no chance more will develop."

He squeezed her hand. "He's not taking no for an answer."

"Not really."

"Maybe I can help with that."

"No."

Her flat tone and narrowed eyes had his lips curving. "You expecting me to call him out for a duel at dawn?"

"I can handle him myself."

"I didn't think otherwise. I merely meant that knowing you're dating someone new might encourage him to focus his attention elsewhere."

Veronica was quiet a moment. "Are you serious about us dating, Adam?"

His head whipped her direction. "Definitely. You game to try?"

"It will be a challenge."

"Everything worthwhile is." Another squeeze of her fingers. "You're worth the effort."

"I hope you still think so as we dig deeper into this mess. The more we learn, the guiltier I look. Whoever is framing me is doing a great job. You would be better off staying as far away from me as you can."

## CHAPTER FIFTEEN

Adam drove to a nearby cafe and parked in the adjacent lot. "Come on. I'm starving and you didn't eat much this morning."

"I'm not hungry."

Her emotions were running high, but her body still needed fuel to function at peak efficiency. "We still need to eat. If you don't find anything here to tempt you, we'll try somewhere else."

When they walked into the cafe, Adam's stomach growled. Veronica nudged him. He winked at her and led her to the order counter. Ten minutes later, a cafe employee brought food and drinks to their table.

After they returned to the SUV, Adam asked Zane for Carol Rossi's location. Seconds later, he received the address. He showed the screen with the information to Veronica. "Recognize this?"

She groaned. "That's the DEA office."

"Maybe we should try Graham next because I'm not taking you to your office. I'd rather not have to bust you out of jail."

"She's a good friend. I'll ask her to meet me somewhere neutral."

"Think she'd do it without telling anyone?"

Veronica nodded.

"It's your decision. However, your meeting place must be somewhere defensible with many exits, too many for your fellow agents to cover if Carol sets a trap for us."

"Us?"

He sent her a pointed look. "You aren't going by yourself. If she's a true friend, she will understand why the man you're dating is watching your back."

"You're right." She pulled out her phone and typed a text. A minute after she hit send, the reply came back. Veronica did a fist pump. "She agreed. We're meeting at Cool Springs Galleria in two hours. She has an appointment in the area anyway."

"Perfect. Lots of exits and a crowd to get lost in if it's necessary." He drove toward the interstate. As he accelerated on the entrance ramp, Zane called.

Adam tapped his Bluetooth. "You're on speaker with Veronica."

"You holding up okay, Veronica?"

"Adam is taking good care of me."

"What did you learn from R.J.?"

"Not much." Adam summarized the few pieces of information they picked up while interviewing Walsh.

He sighed. "I'm not surprised based on what I discovered over the last few hours."

"Talk to me."

"R.J. is in hock up to his eyebrows."

"Why?"

"Gambling. That's why his wife left him and took the kids. Apparently a bookie sent a leg breaker to her work to collect on the debt. This clown threatened to hurt the kids if R.J. didn't pay."

Adam scowled. He'd expected Zane to tell him Walsh was in debt because of the house, land, and the kids' private tuition, not this. Probably shouldn't be surprised, though. Some guys needed the adrenaline rush even while stateside. His addiction to adrenaline might have cost R.J. his family.

He didn't understand why a man would risk losing the people who mattered most in his life. The only person left in Adam's family was Claire. He and Claire lost their grandmother a few months earlier. At least he'd been home to support Claire through the grieving process. Nana lived long enough to ride herd on him through the worst of his recovery from Collins' handiwork.

"Is there a sudden infusion of cash into his bank accounts?" Veronica asked.

"Not that I can find. However, he might have an offshore account. That will take me longer to track down and I need a direction to start the search."

"Not worth your effort at this point. Check his email. See if there's an indication of him being the leak."

"Copy that. Adam, Carol is on the move. Do you want me to send the link so you can track her signal?"

"She agreed to meet us at Cool Springs Galleria in two hours. Keep an eye on her signal. If it look as though she's heading somewhere else at our meeting time, let me know."

"No problem. In the meantime, I'll dig into Carol Rossi's background. Let me know when you're ready for Graham Norton's location."

After Adam ended the call, Veronica twisted in her seat. "What did you think about R.J.?"

"He's skating on a razor-thin ledge and about to plunge over a cliff."

"You thought that before Zane told you about his gambling?"

"He is restless, edgy, and paranoid. If his wife hadn't left him already, she would have walked out soon."

"Why do you think that?"

"If Walsh doesn't get help soon, he'll fall further into paranoia. He could endanger himself and his family."

"How do you know?"

Would she consider him weak? Might as well find out now. It was no secret he'd sought professional help after his time with Collins. "I experienced the same symptoms after I was freed in Belize. Maddox guilted me into talking to a Fortress counselor. He used Claire and my grandmother's safety against me. He was right."

"Talking to the counselor helped you?"

"Didn't stop the nightmares." He still suffered from those, though not as frequently. "She did help me not to reach for the nearest weapon every time Claire or Nana walked into my room. Does the DEA offer counseling services to their agents?"

"Of course."

"You take advantage of it?"

She remained silent.

"I'll take that as a no. Once you're cleared, you should think about talking to someone."

"I've talked to you and Maddox."

"Not the same, and you know it."

Veronica turned away to stare out the window. "I'll think about it," she muttered.

Adam wanted to push her for more of a commitment for the sake of her mental wellbeing, decided to let it alone for now. They drove in silence the rest of the way to Cool Springs.

In the mall, he bought them both a cup of coffee in the food court as they waited for Carol to arrive. "Are you angry with me?" he asked Veronica.

"Of course not. You care. I can't fault you for that." She cupped her hands around her cup. "Do you really think I need counseling?"

"You went through a traumatic experience in Mexico. I'm amazed at how strong you are, but there can be repercussions later. If you start having issues, I want you talk to a DEA or Fortress counselor."

Her shoulders relaxed. "Okay."

"Nica!" a female voice called. A woman with long red hair pulled back into a ponytail hurried toward them. When she reached their table, she hugged Veronica. "I've been worried about you. Where have you been?"

Veronica patted the seat beside her. "Sit so we can talk. Carol Rossi, this is Adam."

Carol dropped into the seat, her gaze locked on Adam. "Adam Walker?"

"That's right."

A slow smile curved her lips. "I was beginning to think you were a figment of Nica's imagination. I'm glad to finally meet you, Mr. Walker."

"Adam, please." He slid the extra coffee he'd purchased to the agent.

"Thanks for the coffee. Call me Carol." She turned to Veronica. "What is going on? Dane was acting like a grumpy old bear for days before...." Carol stopped, horror dawning in her eyes. Her hand clamped on Veronica's. "Nica, have you heard about Dane?"

"I know he's gone."

The other agent sighed. "At least I don't have to deliver the bad news. Where have you been for the past two weeks? You didn't tell me you were leaving."

"Mexico. Dane sent me on another assignment in the Chihuahua province with orders not to tell anyone I was leaving the country."

"No one knew you were going on an assignment. Graham was driving everyone nuts, demanding to know where you were. He's been worried sick about you."

Adam draped his arm around Veronica's shoulders. Seeing his action, Carol's eyes widened, comprehension dawning in her gaze. Exactly the reaction Adam was after. He wanted Carol and any others she talked to after this to know he cared about Veronica. If she went missing, he would never rest until he found her and brought her home, no matter how long it took.

"Dane asked me not to tell anyone in the office where I was going," Veronica said.

Carol's cheeks paled. "Nica, if anything had happened to you after Dane's death, no one would have found you."

When Veronica's gaze shifted to Adam, he gave a slight nod. He wanted to see Carol's reaction to the news of Veronica's captivity.

"I was captured by Los Diablos, Carol."

She gasped. "What? How did you escape?"

Veronica reached for Adam's hand. "Adam and some of his friends found me."

Carol turned widened eyes Adam's direction. "How did you know she needed help?"

"Dane reached out to someone with contacts in Fortress, told him Veronica was missing."

"He must have done that right before he died. Nica, what is going on with you?"

She blinked. "What do you mean?"

"Come on. First you disappear and have to be rescued by an outside group, then we're told you're a person of interest in an investigation."

"A person of interest?" Veronica's mouth gaped. "In what investigation?"

"I don't know. We weren't told."

"Who wants her brought in for questioning?" Adam watched Carol's face and body language for signs she held back information.

"Clay Forrest, Dane's boss."

"Does he know she's back in the country?"

"I don't know. Maybe. He told us to let him know immediately if you contacted anyone in the office."

Adam stilled. "Did you?"

"Not a chance. The guy is a jerk. He's not worried about anyone but himself. Look, Nica, if you're in trouble, I can help."

Veronica was already shaking her head. "It's too dangerous, Carol. I don't want you caught in this mess. Someone took shots at us this morning in Green Hills."

"That was you? The incident is all over the news."

Great. Adam scowled. Not what they needed. Someone would check the security cameras in the area. They wouldn't see anything through the windows of his SUV. Bear, Fortress's car guru, applied a special coating to the windows to prevent cameras from obtaining a clear picture of the occupants of their vehicles.

That left the store cameras. Hopefully, scanning the footage would take a while. Anything to slow the feds down. Unfortunately, if they did ID Veronica, they would also have photos of him. How long would it take Veronica to realize he was now at risk for government harassment?

He should warn Maddox and Zane so they were prepared for scrutiny. The clock was now ticking. They needed to figure out who was trying to frame Veronica before the feds caught up with them. If they arrested her, he might not be able to get to her before she met with a fatal accident.

## CHAPTER SIXTEEN

"I want to help, Nica. Please let me," Carol pleaded.

Veronica clasped her friend's hand. "The best thing you can do is be my eyes and ears in the office. If you hear anything related to me or Dane's death, I need to know. Other than that, I won't risk your safety." Her heart clenched as she shifted her gaze to Adam. "It's bad enough I'm risking Adam's life by involving him."

"I involved myself, Vonnie." Under the table, he laid his hand over hers. "My choice. I would make the same one every time."

What had she done to deserve this man in her life? He'd been through so much, yet he didn't hesitate to put his life on the line to protect her.

"Not good enough." Carol leaned closer to them. "No offense, Adam, but Nica needs more than just you to make it out of this unscathed."

"She didn't leave Mexico unscathed. Los Diablos wanted information from her, and they weren't happy when she refused to talk."

"Is that what happened to your face?"

"The interrogator was unhappy that I wouldn't cooperate." Understatement. No need to tell Carol too many details. She didn't want to give the other woman nightmares. They still had a job to do. At least Carol did. Veronica wasn't so sure about her future with the DEA.

Her friend frowned. "I'm sorry. I don't understand why Dane called in Adam instead of sending us. Wouldn't be the first time we rescued an agent in trouble. I've never known Dane to call in outsiders to help one of our own."

Veronica thought about what to share and realized if Carol framed her, she already knew about the files. On the other hand, if she was innocent, the news might help Carol protect herself. Veronica's friends might be a target, too.

"Someone sent Dane files supposedly proving I'm spilling information on our agents and ongoing operations. Because he called in Adam, I'm hoping Dane didn't believe I was guilty of being a traitor."

"You wouldn't do that. I've worked with you for five years, Nica. You would take a bullet for any of us. I can't see you stabbing us in the back."

Relief spiraled through her. At least one person in her office believed she was innocent. "Thank you."

"I'll keep you updated on what I hear, but I'll look in our files, see if anything pops."

"Be careful, Carol. I don't want anything to happen to you." She didn't know if she could live with the guilt if Carol ended up injured or worse trying to help her identify the real culprit.

"I'll be careful. I promise. How should I contact you?"

"The number I texted you from is secure. No one can trace the number to me."

She nodded. "I'll buy a throwaway phone and text you the number. We'll figure this out, Nica." She stood. "I need to go."

"We'll follow you out," Adam said. He had a bad feeling about allowing Carol to be involved in the investigation. Veronica's friend would be under suspicion as well. Might be wise to ask Maddox for an operative to keep an eye on Carol when she was away from the office.

Veronica finished the last of her coffee, and took the empty cups to the trash. They trailed a distance behind Carol as she walked to the parking lot. When her friend approached the silver SUV she loved, Carol clicked her remote to unlock her car.

In the next instant, her vehicle exploded in a ball of fire. Carol was thrown backward and lay crumpled on the ground. Adam and Veronica were far enough away the blast rocked them and made them stagger, but they stayed on their feet.

"Carol!" Veronica raced to her side. So many places bled, Veronica didn't know where to start.

Adam knelt, gaze scanning the area while he removed his belt. "Cinch this around her right leg."

Blood pooled under Carol's leg. "Shrapnel must have nicked her femoral artery."

"Williamson Medical Center is close. I'll get the SUV. Be alert, Vonnie. The person who planted the bomb is nearby."

Veronica worked fast to cinch the belt around Carol's thigh. People moved closer to see what was happening. "Back up. Somebody call 911 and get the fire department out here."

When Carol moaned, Veronica laid a hand on her friend's shoulder. "Don't move. We're taking you to the hospital."

"Bomb."

"Yep. Hope your car insurance is up to date."

A slight smile curved Carol's lips. "Don't know if bomb damage is covered in my policy."

Adam backed down the aisle and stopped several feet away from them. He ran to Carol, crouched. "I'm going to carry you to the SUV. I'll try not to jostle you too much, but we can't wait for an ambulance. You're bleeding out from a cut to the artery in your leg."

"Do it."

He bent, scooped her into his arms, and raced for the SUV. Veronica scooped Carol's purse from the ground and followed. She climbed into the backseat with her friend.

"First aid kit is in the cargo hold." Adam climbed behind the wheel. He drove from the parking lot as Veronica grabbed the kit.

She found gauze pads, ripped open two packages, and pressed against the cut. Although Carol was still bleeding, Adam's cinched belt had slowed the flow.

"Nica."

Veronica glanced at her friend's pale face. "Save your strength."

"If I don't make it...."

"You will. Can't let the traitor win, Carol."

Adam activated his Bluetooth. "Zane, call Williamson Medical Center and tell them I'm bringing in a bomb victim with a cut to her femoral artery. We're en route and should arrive in seven or eight minutes."

"Veronica?"

"I'm okay," she said. "It's my friend, Carol."

"Does she have family I should contact?"

"David," Carol whispered.

"Her boyfriend, David Young," Veronica said. "He's a contractor with Southland Construction. Hold on a second." With one hand, she dumped the contents of Carol's purse onto the floor of the SUV. Thankfully, Carol's phone survived the blast. She looked up David's name and rattled off his number for Zane.

"Got it. I'll contact him immediately. What about the DEA?"

"No," Adam said. "They'll find out soon enough. Is Jake Davenport available?"

"I'll check. Why?"

"We need someone we trust with Carol. Veronica can't provide protection. Since Jake's a medic, he's the perfect bodyguard."

"I'll inform Maddox, then send Davenport. He should arrive in thirty minutes."

"Copy that." Adam ended the call as he accelerated onto the interstate.

"Don't need a bodyguard," Carol protested.

Veronica added another gauze pad. "Someone in our office could have planted that bomb. You need an outsider we trust to keep you safe. Jake Davenport will do that. His sole priority will be your safety." She smiled. "Plus it helps to have a medic handy to interpret the medical jargon spouted by doctors. Look at it this way, Carol. If Jake stays with you, the only thing David needs to be concerned about is supporting you."

The DEA agent sighed, nodded.

To keep her friend's attention focused, Veronica said, "You and David have been dating for a couple years. Are you talking about getting married?"

"He hasn't proposed yet."

Why was he waiting? The contractor was crazy about Carol. Maybe she'd nudge him if she had the chance. She wasn't averse to playing Cupid for two friends. David was a great guy and Carol deserved the best. "Why not?"

"Don't know."

"When he proposes, will you accept?"

"In a heartbeat."

Hmm. Maybe David needed to know how she felt before he popped the question. Veronica glanced through the window as Adam made a sharp left turn. Thank goodness. The medical center was two blocks away. "Almost there, Carol. You're going to be fine."

"Thanks, Nica." Her eyes closed as Adam skidded to a stop at the emergency entrance. A medical team raced from the hospital with a gurney.

Veronica opened the door and scrambled out of the way. Carol was whisked into the hospital and out of sight. Carrying her friend's purse, she followed at a slower pace with Adam.

Adam pulled his phone from his pocket and checked the screen. "David is on his way. He's in Franklin on a job so he should arrive soon."

"Good. David will be a big morale boost for her." She glanced at the admitting nurse. "I guess I can start the paperwork. Carol won't mind if I get her insurance information from her wallet."

"Do what you can. As soon as Jake arrives, we need to go. You can't afford to be detained, Vonnie."

Much as she hated to admit it, Adam was right. If the DEA hauled her in for questioning, the session wouldn't go well. Not only was she connected to Dane's death, now she was on the scene when Carol's car blew up.

Taking the clipboard with the forms, Veronica started filling out information. As she finished the last of the forms, a dark-haired man dressed in dusty jeans and dirt-streaked t-shirt ran through the ER doors.

"David." Veronica stood.

"Nica, what happened? Where is she?" The muscular construction worker swept her into a tight hug. "Please tell me she's alive."

"The doctor hasn't given us a report yet."

"Us?" His gaze shifted to Adam.

The Fortress operative held out his hand. "I'm Adam. Sorry to meet you under these circumstances."

"What happened to Carol? I talked to her an hour ago and she was fine. Was she in an accident?"

Oh, boy. She didn't blame Zane for not telling David about the bomb. Unfortunately, that meant she had to pass the bad news along. "Come sit down." Once seated, she told David the bare facts.

David's jaw clenched. "Who did this? Is it connected to one of her cases?"

"We don't know, but the DEA will investigate. We take an attack one of our agents personally." She reached over and squeezed his hand. "While the attack might be related to one of Carol's cases, the truth is I think the bomb was planted because of me."

He stared at her, disbelief clear in his eyes. "It was her car, not yours."

"I'm afraid someone is trying to get to me through my friends." And now Adam had the biggest target of all painted on his back.

## CHAPTER SEVENTEEN

Adam watched David Young carefully as he processed the news that Veronica might be the reason his girlfriend Carol was in the hospital. So far, the construction worker showed no signs of aggression.

"How severe are her injuries?" David asked.

"We don't know for sure." Adam wanted the other man's attention off Veronica. "From what we saw, shrapnel from the car cut her in several places. The blast threw her several feet. She might have internal injuries."

"What did the EMTs say about her?"

"We brought her here. We couldn't afford to wait for an ambulance, David. Carol has a cut to the femoral artery of her right leg. She was bleeding heavily."

The other man buried his face in his hands. "She could die."

"She was here within ten minutes of the blast and she's in good hands. All we can do now is wait." Movement in the hallway caught Adam's attention. Jake Davenport. He crossed the room to his friend's side. "Thanks for coming so quickly."

"No problem. Tell me what happened." The medic listened as Adam described the bomb blast and the injuries he'd noted. "Good thing you were close to medical help."

"Should we have waited for the EMTs?" He'd weighed that option and chosen to move her despite the real possibility of internal injuries.

"You did the right thing, Adam. I would have made the same choice."

He breathed a sigh of relief. "Let me introduce you to Carol's boyfriend." He stopped beside Veronica. "David, this is Jake Davenport. He's a medic with Fortress Security. He'll help you interpret the medical jargon and provide security for Carol."

David's eyes narrowed. "Carol is still in danger?"

"Better to be safe," Jake said. "Your job is to aid Carol in recovering and provide security inside her room. I'll take care of the hallway."

As soon as David realized that he was included in the security arrangements, he squared his shoulders. "No one will hurt her while I'm with her."

"Good." Jake nodded. "We're her security detail. That means one of us is with her at all times. I'll be trading off with another bodyguard from Fortress when I need to sleep. I'll introduce you each time so there's no doubt who you can trust. No one is allowed in her room without one of the Fortress people inside. The place will be swarming with feds soon. We can't trust any of them with your woman's life, David. There's a good chance one of them is involved in this plot."

"Are you kidding me?" The construction worker's face reddened. "One of their own agents might be to blame for this?"

"It's possible," Adam said. "There has already been an attempt to kill Veronica today."

"This is insane. They're supposed to be the good guys."

"Most of them are. The problem is we don't know which one has gone rogue if an agent is to blame."

A man in scrubs and a white coat walked to the entrance of the waiting room. "Rossi family?"

David leaped to his feet. "Here."

"I'm Dr. Whitson. You must be David Young. Ms. Rossi has been asking for you. She's on her way to surgery. We need to repair the artery in her leg as well as dealing with a ruptured spleen. She has other injuries, but those two are the most pressing. Someone will update you as soon as she's out of surgery." And he was gone.

"Those injuries are common with bomb blasts," Jake murmured. "She has a good chance, David. Why don't you come with me? We'll buy some bad coffee from the vending machine and talk. It will be a while before she is out of surgery."

"Yeah, all right." David turned to Veronica. "You want anything?"

"Actually, I need to go."

Shock covered his face. "Carol is your friend. You're leaving her when she's in a fight for her life?"

"I'll put her in more danger by staying. Plus, to be honest, the DEA wants to talk to me about Dane's death. In fact, they think I might be responsible. I didn't do it, but if I stay, I'll be unable to prove my innocence or find out who planted the bomb in Carol's vehicle."

"Go. Find the creep who did this and take him down."

"I will." She squeezed his forearm. "You have my word."

Adam escorted Veronica from the hospital through a different exit. He doubted the feds were on the grounds yet, but he didn't want to chance one of them detaining her. He wanted more information before he and Veronica went head-to-head with them.

Back in his SUV, Adam glanced at Veronica as he cranked the engine. "You up for a field trip?"

"Aren't we going to see Graham?"

"I had planned on it before the bomb. What are the chances of him going to the hospital to wait for word on Carol?'

She sighed. "Excellent. He's been friends with Carol longer than I have. We'll have to wait to talk to him."

"He has to go home eventually. We'll stake out his place and wait for him to return home."

"Where are we going, then?"

"There's a small lake not too far from here."

"Perfect. I love to be anywhere near the water."

He shifted the SUV into gear and drove from the parking lot. "I'll make a note of that for future dates."

"This is a date?"

"It will be. I have to make a stop first." Adam took the side roads to the Cool Springs area and parked in front of an ice cream shop. "You want to come inside or wait here?"

"We stopped for ice cream?"

"Yes, ma'am. My sister says it's the only thing that cures the blues."

"Your sister is a wise woman. I can't wait to meet her." Veronica opened her door, paused to look back over her shoulder. "You're an observant man, Adam Walker."

Pleased he'd managed to distract her, Adam purchased two different flavors of the sweet treat and drove her to the lake. They found a bench and sat to enjoy the sunlight, ice cream, and each other's company.

When they finished the ice cream, Adam tossed the trash into a nearby garbage can. "Want to walk for a few minutes?" He held out his hand.

"Thank you, Adam."

He laced his fingers through hers. "For what?"

"Knowing this was exactly what I needed."

They walked in silence for a few minutes. "Is there a chance someone has a vendetta against Carol?" he asked.

"Of course. We have a long list of people who would like nothing better than to see all of us six feet under."

So did he. Knowing she had enemies made him long to stand in front of her, something he couldn't do, not if he wanted a real, lasting relationship with her. Veronica was a capable woman with lethal skills. "Do you know if she has a physical list of enemies?"

"I doubt it. If I can get into the office, I could check her case files."

"Would someone be on duty?"

"Not usually. If we go after midnight, we should be safe enough until three or so. Some of the agents are early birds. So is Dane's assistant."

"Assistant?"

"Risa Shoemaker. She's worked for Dane for years." Veronica left the walkway and stopped at the edge of the lake. "This is so beautiful and peaceful. Thank you for bringing me here."

Adam moved behind her and wrapped his arms around her waist. "Why don't you buy a house near water?"

She laughed, leaned her head against his shoulder. "As an employee of the government, I don't make enough money. Property on a lake or river is too expensive for my skinny budget."

"If money weren't an issue, would you live near water?"

"In a heartbeat. I could get used to this."

He pressed a kiss to Veronica's temple. So could he, especially if she was part of the view. "Beats sand and scorpions."

She turned and looped her arms around his middle. "You were deployed to the middle east?"

"More times than I want to remember."

"What was your job in the military?"

"Marine Force Recon."

Veronica's head jerked up. "Special Forces? I should have known."

"How?"

"There's something about you. The members of the military I've dealt with are all skilled professionals. Those in Special Forces are in a different category altogether."

"Many of the operatives at Fortress are Special Forces. Maddox only hires the best." He gazed into her eyes. "When we clear your name, what will you do next?"

"I don't know. If you had asked me that question two weeks ago, I would have said go back to work for the DEA. Now, I can't answer that question. Would it matter to you what my answer is?"

"Of course. I don't like the way the DEA is handles your assignments. You need a partner you can trust at your back. I'm concerned that after we clear you, your fellow agents might never fully trust you again. On the selfish side, I don't want to wait weeks or months to see you, to hold you."

"And if my choice is to go back?"

"I'll deal."

"My last boyfriend broke up with me because he couldn't handle my frequent absences."

He didn't want to think about her former boyfriends. Adam cupped her face between his palms. "I'm not him. I'll miss you like crazy when you're gone, but I won't force you to make a change on my account." Didn't mean he couldn't encourage her to look at all the options. Unless he missed his guess, Maddox would do a thorough background check on Veronica in preparation for offering her a job with Fortress. "Wouldn't be fair since my job sends me all over the world as well." He didn't go alone, however. He always had a team at his back.

He kept his kiss light, aware they were in a public place and he needed to stay alert. When he eased back,

Adam was gratified to note Veronica's eyes were unfocused, her breathing accelerated.

"You have definite skills." She tightened her embrace briefly, then released him.

"How much time do we have before your friends know my name?"

"Not long, tomorrow at the latest. Even if they don't make the connection from the incident in Green Hills, they will from the surveillance footage at Cool Springs and the hospital. I'm sorry I dragged you into this, Adam."

"My choice," he reminded her. "If necessary, I'll tell them I'm your bodyguard."

"It's the truth."

"Part of it. I'd rather they know we're together, that you're not a job to me."

"You'll be even more of a target. They'll rip your life apart."

"I want them to know you aren't standing alone, that I have your back. Let them dig, Vonnie. They won't find anything. The military will block their access to my service records and missions. Zane has the rest covered."

"If you decide to pause our dating relationship until I'm cleared, I'll understand."

"Not happening." He turned her back toward the SUV. "Come on. I have a craving for a steak and potatoes. There's a small grocery store near here that has the best steaks in the area. According to Claire, their fruits and vegetables are second to none."

Veronica's jaw dropped. "Do you always think of food this often?"

He shrugged. "Fast metabolism and the long, hard workouts. Like you, we have to stay in top shape to do our jobs." Adam scanned the area for potential threats. A couple female joggers, a dog walker, two teenagers. He didn't see anyone waiting in the vehicles in the parking lot.

Adam unlocked the SUV and helped Veronica inside, then drove to the grocery store. Thirty minutes later, they left with more than steaks and potatoes. He smiled as he stored the food bags in the cargo area. Lily would be thrilled with Veronica's choice of chocolate cake and vanilla ice cream. When he'd asked her if the dessert was too much after their mid-afternoon treat, she had lifted her chin and told him there was no such thing as too much dessert.

Adam called Remy and invited him and Lily to dinner. "Tell Lily that Veronica chose dessert."

Remy laughed. "If it has chocolate, she will be a happy woman."

"Is there any other kind of dessert?" Veronica asked.

"Not according to my wife. See you soon."

When they parked at the back of his house, Lily hopped out of the Doucet SUV, a look of anticipation on her face. "Where is it?"

Remy rolled his eyes and Adam chuckled at her question. "In the cargo area."

She rubbed her hands, her eyes sparkling. "Can't wait to see what it is."

Each of them carried a bag into the kitchen and unloaded the food. Lily did a fist pump in the air when she saw the chocolate cake.

"That was my contribution," Veronica said, and the two women exchanged high fives.

"I'll heat the grill." Adam scooped up the brush to clean the grill and walked outside. Remy trailed after him.

"What happened?" Remy asked, voice soft.

Adam summarized the sequence of events for his friend. "We're visiting Graham Norton after midnight."

"Want company?"

That's what he liked about working for Fortress. With rare exceptions, your teammates had your back even at home. "Sure."

"Heard anything from Jake?"

Adam shook his head, glancing through the French doors to the woman caught in the middle of a waking nightmare. "I planned to call while we were out here."

"Go ahead." Remy took the brush from his hand. "I'll clean the grill while you check on Carol. When you're finished, I'll move our SUV to a more secluded spot. If I were the feds, I'd pay you a visit in the next few hours."

"Veronica thought it might be tomorrow."

"The victim is one of their own. Trust me, they won't wait."

"The safe room is behind the mirrored wall in my closet." He gave Remy the code. "If the cops show up, I want Veronica in there with Lily."

"Hiding her will only work for a short period of time, Adam. Eventually, she has to talk to the feds."

"I know. Not tonight." He clapped Remy on the shoulder and walked to the bench under the large oak tree in his backyard.

Jake answered on the first ring. "She's in recovery. The doctor said she'll be back to normal in a couple months."

"That's great news. Who relieves you tonight?"

"Curt Jackson."

Adam relaxed against the bench. Excellent. Curt Jackson was a fellow Marine who was part of Jon Smith and Eli Wolfe's Zoo Crew. The man was as tough as they came and looked as though he ate nails for breakfast. "Thanks, Jake."

"Glad to help. You just keep your woman safe."

His woman. Adam liked the sound of that. "That's the plan." To get to Veronica, they'd have to go through him.

## CHAPTER EIGHTEEN

Veronica glanced out the window to see Adam had moved to a bench under a tree, phone pressed to his ear. Although she longed to race outside and listen to updates, she forced herself to pay attention to the salad she and Lily were creating. As distracted as she was at the moment, Veronica counted herself lucky she hadn't sliced a finger with the knife.

The other woman was fun to be around. Instinct told her, though, that the operative was just as trained and tough as her husband and Adam. Something about the economy of motion and her state of alertness. Might be the circumstances. After all, she and Remy were on bodyguard duty along with Adam.

"How did you meet Remy?"

Lily grinned. "We went on a few missions together. He's one smooth talker. All the Doucet men are. Anyway, I drew the short straw and was sent on a mission with him when a friend of his from childhood went missing. That's when I found out what Remy is really like. Just because he's smooth doesn't mean he's not sincere. I fell head over heels in love with the man in less than a week." She paused. "Well, maybe I was starting to fall before then, but it took that week for me to realize that I loved him."

She was quiet a moment, weighing whether or not to ask the question begging to be asked. "Is it difficult to work with your husband?"

"We don't have a problem working together. Remy lets me do my job without being overprotective, but he keeps close tabs on me." Lily tossed the tomato she'd been chopping into the salad bowl. "I watch his back, too."

Veronica's head snapped up. "Maddox sends you out on missions together?"

"He thinks we're a great team. Because we're together all the time, we anticipate each other in ways the other operatives can't. Are you thinking about leaving the DEA?"

She paid close attention to the cucumber she sliced. "I'm considering a change. I haven't told Adam I'm looking a different direction, though."

"He won't hear it from me. The pay and benefits are good with Fortress. Maddox takes care of his people."

"I understand he values his employees." Not that she'd experienced the same care from her own agency, and that included Dane, who she had considered a friend. "Why did he sit at my bedside?"

"Two reasons. One, he feels he owes you for the lives of his wife and daughter. Two, he was also taking care of Adam. He knew Adam wouldn't sleep without someone to watch over you."

"Why didn't Adam's teammates help?"

Lily peeled a carrot. "He doesn't have a team at the moment. The team he led when he was captured in Belize fell apart in his absence. One of the men was so interested in stealing the leadership, he didn't bother keep to track of Adam, basically sold him out. Adam's sister, Claire, was kidnapped in an attempt to force Adam to talk, but she escaped and contacted Zane. Armed with your information,

Z organized the rescue and went with us to free Adam from Collins' clutches."

"Why doesn't he have a new team?"

"He focused on rehab and went on missions with other teams. Maddox and Adam have been vetting potential team members. So far, Adam isn't satisfied with the options."

"What about you and Remy? Are you part of a permanent team?"

Lily's movements stilled. "We've worked with several teams."

"Do you want to be on a permanent team?"

"It's best to know your teammates. We've managed so far, but we want people we trust at our backs."

Remy opened the French door. "We're ready for the steaks. The potatoes are almost cooked."

Veronica handed the container of marinating steaks to the operative. She grabbed an empty plate along with another pair of tongs to turn the meat, and carried them outside.

She laid them on a cloth-covered table for Remy, then walked across the grass to Adam who still had his phone pressed to his ear. As she approached, he scooted over on the bench to make room for her. He was speaking with his boss.

Adam wrapped his arm around her shoulders and drew her close to his side. She loved that he didn't try to keep her from listening to his conversation, as though he wanted to share this part of his life with her as well. A minute later, Adam ended the call.

"Have you heard from Jake?" she asked.

"Carol is expected to make a full recovery. She'll be off the job for a couple months."

That news was so much better than what she expected. She'd feared her friend wouldn't make it out of the operating room alive. "Your quick thinking saved her life, Adam."

"We saved her life, Vonnie. We're a good team."

Once the food was ready, they decided to eat outside on the patio. If she was an outsider looking at the four of them, she'd assume this was a gathering of friends who didn't have a care in the world. She only wished that were true.

After stacking the dishes in the dishwasher, Adam suggested they watch a movie.

"Sounds good," Remy said. "What are our options?"

"Twister, Sahara, any of the Mission Impossible flicks, or we can go futuristic with one of the Star Wars films," Adam said.

After debating, they decided on Twister. Veronica scooted close to Adam and settled back to enjoy one of her favorite movies. In her mind, nothing beat those natural disaster stories.

Near the end, Adam's watch and phone signaled alerts. Remy paused the movie, his gaze on Adam.

"Company." He stood and walked to the kitchen, the rest of them on his heels. He turned on the large security panel, tapped a few keys and zoomed in on an approaching car. He hissed out a breath. "Feds."

Veronica's gut clenched even as she pressed her hand against Adam's lower back. "We knew they would come."

"I wanted to give you another night to rest before we faced them."

"It's not your fight, Adam."

He slanted a heated look at her. "Wrong. We do this together or we don't do it at all. In fact, I'm for the second option."

"How far out are they," Remy asked.

A glance at the screen, then, "Quarter mile." Adam turned to Veronica. "I'd rather you didn't talk to the feds tonight, Vonnie, but it's your choice."

She blinked. "How can I avoid them?"

"I have a safe room. You and Lily can wait in there until they're gone."

He'd already thought this out, she realized. Maybe planned to take the choice from her, then thought better of it. She understood the need to protect her rode him hard. "Hiding will delay the inevitable."

"I know. I want you to take them on when you're at your best. Will you go to the safe room with Lily?"

Veronica considered her options and knew there was only one choice she could live with. She cupped his cheek. "I can't hide."

He stared at her without speaking for a heartbeat, then nodded his head, accepting her decision. "They question you here with all of us present. The only way you leave this house with them is if they have an arrest warrant. If they do, you don't say a word to anyone until your lawyer arrives."

"I don't have one."

"Yes, you do. She represents Fortress and its operatives. She will be happy to represent you." A wide grin. "She hates the feds."

"Why would she represent me, then? I'm a fed."

"You're *my* fed."

Guess that made a difference. Hope the lawyer believed the same. Veronica had a feeling she might need one before this mess was unraveled, the real culprit caught.

"If we're entertaining the enemy, we need coffee," Lily said. "Think chocolate cake would soften them up?"

That brought a round of laughter and a flurry of activity to get ready for their unwanted visitors. The coffee dripped into the carafe when another alert sounded. Their visitors had arrived.

Veronica rubbed her palms on her thighs, hoping she wouldn't be spending the night in jail.

## CHAPTER NINETEEN

Adam stood in the doorway as the nondescript car stopped in his driveway. Two men dressed in dark suits, white shirts, and dark ties watched him as they covered the distance to his porch, their eyes wary.

They were right to keep an eye on him. A minimal background check told the feds that he was a well-trained soldier and any fool could see he was involved with Veronica.

"Adam Walker?" the taller of the two agents asked.

"Who are you?"

"Clay Forrest, DEA."

Adam shifted his gaze and question to the other man without a word.

"Art Crosby, DEA."

"IDs." After examining the contents of the creds wallets, he asked, "What do you want with me?"

Forrest took the lead. "To ask you questions about Veronica Miles."

"What about her?"

"You admit you know her?"

"Why deny the obvious? You wouldn't be here unless you identified me from a video feed while in Veronica's company."

"Let's go," Crosby said, his eyes assessing Adam. "We'll conduct the interview in our offices."

On their home turf? Not a chance. "Talk to me here or not at all."

"We could arrest you and take you in," he spat out. "You've been seen with a person of interest in an investigation."

Remy walked up to Adam. "Ready," he murmured.

"Who are you?" Forrest demanded, his eyes narrowed.

"Remy, a friend of Adam's."

Adam introduced the two agents, then stepped aside. "Go straight back. Coffee is ready in the kitchen." He knew the minute the agents caught sight of Veronica. Both men froze.

He eased around Forrest and Crosby, leaving Remy at their backs. Lily stood beside Veronica, a mug of coffee cupped in her hands. The women had sliced the rest of the chocolate cake and stacked several small plates along with forks on the counter.

Forrest's hands fisted. "Miles. I'm surprised you're here."

"Really? After someone trashed my home, you expected me to go back there and pull the covers over my head while one of our own sets me up for a hard fall?"

"Whatever fall you take you deserve," growled Crosby as he bore down on her. "Why did you do it? How could you turn on us?"

Adam glided in front of the furious agent, neatly cutting him off from his target. "Back off, Crosby."

"Are you threatening me, Walker? Please, tell me you're threatening me. I have a pair of handcuffs just your size."

"Stating facts, Agent Crosby. I don't threaten." He just delivered. These men weren't touching Veronica without a court order.

"Sit," Lily said. "Do you take your coffee black?" She set her mug on the counter and walked to the coffee maker where four empty mugs waited.

"Yes, ma'am." Forrest's gaze focused on Lily. "I'm Clay Forrest with the DEA. This is Art Crosby."

"Lily. Sit and we'll talk. Would you like a slice of chocolate cake?"

"This isn't a social gathering," Crosby snapped.

She poured the steaming liquid. "Your loss. The cake is fabulous." When the mugs were full, she covered the cake again, then distributed one mug to each person.

Adam and Veronica sat on one side of the table, Lily and Remy on the other, leaving the two agents to sit at the ends of the table.

"Where have you been for two weeks, Veronica?" Forrest asked.

"In Mexico on an assignment from Dane."

"Got any proof?"

"Check the name Valerie Wilder. The flight records will show me entering the country two weeks ago."

"I already did. There's no record of your re-entry into the US."

"I flew her into the country on a private jet." Adam sipped his coffee before setting the mug aside. "She was not physically able to fly commercial."

A snort from Forrest. "You look healthy enough to me, Miles."

"Los Diablos held me captive for several days. They weren't good hosts."

From the expressions on the men's faces, they didn't believe Veronica. She glanced at Adam, resignation in her gaze. "Help me show them."

"Baby, you don't have to do this."

"Maybe if they believe one thing I've said, they'll be more inclined to believe the rest."

Although he didn't think so, he rose when she stood and turned her back to Forrest and Crosby. She remained motionless while he raised the back of her shirt far enough for them to see rows of neat stitches Sam that used to close the slash marks.

Because Sam documented the injuries and showed the pictures to Adam, he'd been prepared for the stitches. The photos had revealed older scars on her back that were almost silver under the light's glare. His heart turned over in his chest, suspecting the cause of the marks on Veronica's back. The thought of someone hurting her made him want to pound the person who abused her.

Once he released the hem of her shirt, Adam couldn't stop himself from wrapping his arms around her waist and holding her for a moment. When her body relaxed against his, he dropped a soft kiss on the side of her neck, and seated her again. He glared at the two stunned agents as he sat beside Veronica. "Satisfied?"

"Los Diablos aren't known for keeping their prisoners alive unless they want something from them." Forrest pulled a notebook and pen from his pocket. "What did they want from you, Miles?"

"Information."

"About?" Crosby snapped.

"DEA operations in Mexico and our agents. They knew too much."

"Los Diablos is aware of our ongoing operations and the agents involved?" Forrest's pen hovered over the paper. "Specifics?"

"My interrogator questioned me about the missions by name and the agents involved in each one. We have a leak."

"Yeah, you," muttered Crosby.

Adam covered Veronica's hand with his. "If she had leaked the information the interrogator wanted, Veronica would be dead. They wouldn't have needed her."

"How did you escape?" Forrest asked.

"Adam and his friends."

"A rent-a-cop and his buddies faced down a vicious cartel and rescued you?" Crosby sneered. "Come on. Tell me another lie I can use to toss you in prison."

Remy set his mug down on the table with a thump. "Do you know who we work for, Crosby?"

"Some private security firm. They're all over the place. Any two-bit thug can get hired by them."

Lily rolled her eyes. "We're with Fortress Security, and Brent Maddox, the CEO, wouldn't hire you if the president himself recommended you."

The agent's face turned red. "Why not? I'm a well-trained federal agent."

"You're closed minded and don't listen. Maddox only hires the best and that doesn't include you."

Forrest stayed Crosby's rebuttal with an upraised hand. "We're straying off topic." He stared at Veronica. "Fortress Security operatives rescued you."

"That's right."

"How did they know you were in trouble?"

"Dane told one of my contacts I was missing and to send in Fortress. From what I understand of the timeline, Dane was killed a few hours later."

"So the Fortress operatives did this out of the goodness of their hearts?" Skepticism rang in his voice. "Like they're protecting one of my agents without a contract?"

"We owed Veronica," Remy said. "She provided the information for us to rescue Adam last year."

Forrest's gaze shifted to Adam. "You were held captive?"

"An undercover op gone bad in a different country."

"You passed on classified data," Crosby accused Veronica.

"The information had nothing to do with DEA operations. I stumbled across his location while on another mission and passed it to Fortress through a go-between."

"And for that Fortress spent thousands of dollars to save your worthless hide?"

Adam stood, placed both palms on the table, and leaned toward the belligerent agent. "Last warning, Crosby. You're in my home on sufferance. One more insult to Veronica and I'll escort you to your vehicle where you will stay until your superior is finished."

"Adam." Veronica pressed her hand to his lower back.

"He isn't allowed to insult you, Vonnie, not after what you suffered to protect him and your co-workers." He broke eye contact with the insufferable agent and speared her with his gaze. "Not after what you endured to protect me."

"What does that mean?" Forrest asked. "How did you protect Walker, Miles?"

Veronica held out her hand to Adam. When he sat again, she said, "A third of the interrogation was about DEA activities in Mexico. The other two-thirds centered on Adam. The interrogator knew more about him than I did."

"Yet here you are, in his house, apparently involved in a relationship with the man." Forrest's eyes narrowed. "How long have you known Walker?"

"The first time I laid eyes on him was in that death chamber."

"You didn't have any contact with him before then?"

She shook her head.

Adam drew in a slow breath. He knew where the questions were headed. Would Veronica believe him or the two agents determined to blame Adam instead of looking inside their own agency?

"Have you considered Walker might be the reason for your captivity?"

## CHAPTER TWENTY

Veronica laced her fingers through Adam's. "He would never do that. Adam is a good man, one of honor and integrity, and I trust him."

"You just admitted you don't know him," Crosby pointed out.

She shrugged. "Some knowledge doesn't take a lifetime to learn." Veronica knew to her bones Adam Walker would die before he betrayed her. She had faced death to keep him safe. During the past year, she'd come to care about the Fortress operative. The past few days had only served to deepen her feelings.

"When did you return to U.S. soil?" Forrest asked.

"Four days ago."

"Where have you been all this time? Why didn't you check in? You violated protocol, Miles."

"I was in a private medical clinic receiving treatment, then came here to recuperate."

"I wouldn't let her check in," Adam said. "It wasn't safe."

"Why do you say that?"

"There's a leak in Veronica's network. Otherwise, Los Diablos wouldn't have taken her so easily. She's smart and takes precautions to keep herself and her identity safe. If Dane trusted his own people, he would have sent in a DEA team to rescue Veronica. He didn't. He asked Fortress for help, knowing we would get her out of there or die trying."

"I want confirmation you were at the private clinic for treatment," Forrest told Veronica.

Her stomach knotted. Sorensen's life and that of his family was at stake. It was one thing to risk herself. She wouldn't endanger the doctor who treated her with kindness despite his grumpy attitude. "I can't do that, sir."

The agent bristled. "Why not?"

"The doctor's identity can't be compromised. He has enemies like we do, and a family to protect. I won't be responsible for his children losing their father and perhaps their own lives. If I give you the information, what guarantee do I have the name of the doctor and his clinic won't be leaked to the wrong people?"

Forrest didn't answer her question. What could he say? Someone in their office talked to the wrong people.

"What do you know about Dane's death?" he asked.

"Not much. I was in Mexico as a guest of the cartel at the time."

"Which you can't confirm," he reminded her. "Look, Miles, I'll level with you. Things don't look good for you."

"Tell me something I don't know." The manufactured evidence of her betrayal was damning by any standards.

A glance at Adam before Forrest turned his hard gaze back to her. "Dane has documents in his email that incriminate you as the leak and traitor. Wouldn't surprise me if you arranged for your handler to meet an untimely end."

Man, hearing those words hurt more than her father's belt and fists had. "Hard to arrange anything from a concrete and stone cell."

"You could have set the plan in motion before you left the country."

"Dane was my friend and mentor. Even if he made me angry, the worst I would have done was resign from the DEA."

"Maybe you arranged his death in the heat of the moment, then was sent to Mexico. You weren't in a position to cancel the assassination."

"Wow. You don't think much of me as an agent, do you? A car accident is a risky way to try to kill someone. He could have survived the accident. Then where would I be?" She shook her head. "No, If I'd wanted Dane to die, I would have shot him at point blank range and gotten rid of the gun. He trusted me. I could have killed him before he realized what was happening. But I didn't kill him or arrange for anyone else to do it in my place. Dane was a good friend who won't see his son's face." That hurt her almost as much as knowing she would never see Dane again or hear his booming laughter.

She lifted her chin. "I will find out who killed him, sir."

"We have enough to take you in, Miles."

"No, sir, you don't. Otherwise, I'd already be in cuffs. Those documents in Dane's email are from an anonymous email address and they were generated on the day after I left for Mexico."

"How do you know that information?" he snapped.

Veronica smiled.

"You could have written them ahead of time, then set them to send after you left," Crosby pointed out with a nervous glance at Adam.

"Why incriminate myself? Contrary to what you believe, I'm not stupid. If I wanted to implicate anyone for being a traitor, I would have pointed the finger at you."

Crosby scowled, shifting his weight, as though he was coming after her for that insult.

Adam pointed his finger at the agent. "One cross word and you're out."

The agent blew out a breath. "You were with Carol when her SUV exploded."

Veronica thought about how to answer questions without hurting Carol. "I wanted to talk to her about Dane."

"You couldn't do that at the office?" Forrest asked.

"Not without dodging fists, bullets, and handcuffs. I saw her in the food court and decided to take a chance."

"What happened in the parking lot at the mall?"

Veronica summarized the events. "Sorry I can't be more help. Adam and I didn't touch Carol's SUV as you've already seen in the security footage. We arrived before she did and followed her out. Someone else tried to kill her." Perhaps to tell Veronica anyone around her would be a target. Her fingers tightened around Adam's. He was in danger because of her.

The agents went through everything three more times. Standard questioning procedure, but her energy dropped to almost nothing. How was she supposed to do a stakeout with Adam if she couldn't stay awake?

Adam stood, drawing Veronica to her feet. "Veronica needs to rest. She's still recovering from her ordeal. If you have more questions, talk to her tomorrow."

Forrest looked as if he would argue until he studied her face. He stood. "Pending the conclusion of our investigation into allegations you leaked classified information, I have to ask you to turn in your badge and duty weapon."

Lily gasped, outrage plain on her face.

Veronica had expected the demand. Didn't make it hurt less to hand over the hard-earned badge and weapon she'd carried for five years. Would she hold them in her hands again?

"We'll be in touch tomorrow, Miles."

"Call Fortress and leave a message," Adam said. "Veronica will call to arrange a time and place to meet."

The agents frowned. "Why can't we contact her directly?" Crosby asked.

"Her safety is at stake and you have a leak. Do you blame her for not being readily accessible?"

"Make sure you respond in a timely manner, Miles," Forrest said. "Otherwise, we will come back with a warrant for you and your boyfriend. If you want to keep your man out of jail, be available."

As soon as Veronica's co-workers left, she turned and walked out the back door. She sat on the bench she and Adam occupied earlier. Veronica buried her face in her hands. Never in a million years did she think she'd be forced to give up her badge. Voluntarily hand it over because she was walking away from a long career with the DEA? Sure. Not this humiliation. And to have it happen in front of an audience, especially Adam, made her cheeks burn and her eyes sting. His opinion of her mattered.

Though she hadn't heard a person approaching her, someone sat on the bench. Without looking, she knew her supporter was Adam.

A second later, his muscular arm wrapped around her shoulders and drew her against his side. "I'm sorry, Vonnie," he murmured. "We'll clear your name."

Instead of replying, she turned and pressed her face against his throat. Her heart hurt so much she could barely breathe.

Adam wrapped his other arm around her, hand cupping the back of her head. Occasionally, he pressed a kiss to her temple, but didn't insist she talk. Veronica needed time to control her emotions before she tried talking. Otherwise, she would end up a sobbing mess.

She beat down her father's voice in her head telling her she'd be a failure no matter what she tried to do. He was wrong. She was an excellent DEA agent. She would be again unless she moved on to something else and didn't occupy a bed in a federal prison.

Veronica shuddered. Cops did not fare well in jail. That wouldn't happen, she reminded herself. Adam and his friends at Fortress wouldn't allow it. Her lips curved upward. If the worst happened, she wouldn't be surprised if Adam flew her out of the country and stashed her somewhere safe until he cleared her name.

Adam's grip on her tightened. "We'll get through this."

When she could talk without her voice breaking, Veronica said, "I need to borrow a Sig."

"Sure. Choose whatever you want from my weapons room."

She gave a soft laugh. "Your weapons room? Oh, man, I'm dating the perfect man for me."

He cupped her face. "I have a confession."

Cold seeped into her bones. No. She couldn't have misread him that much. "Tell me."

"After I learned of your role in my rescue, I kept loose tabs on you. Nothing that endangered you. Zane asked R.J. if you were safe and passed the information to me. We didn't contact anyone else."

"Fair enough. I asked about you, too."

"Yeah? During the past year, I began to care about you, Vonnie." His thumb brushed her bottom lip in a gentle caress. "I didn't set you up. I couldn't. You mean too much to me."

She closed the gap between them and kissed him, the kiss one of aching tenderness. "Thank you for telling me, but I already know you didn't do this."

This time, he initiated the kiss. Unlike hers, Adam's kiss was a claiming. Hard, deep, hot. Perfect because underneath the claiming was gentleness and care.

When he lifted his mouth from hers, he said, "We have three hours before we leave." He drew Veronica to her feet. "Choose your weapon, then go rest."

He walked to his bedroom closet and pressed two spots on his mirror wall. A click, and the mirror moved away from the wall and revealed a steel door. Adam keyed a code into the security panel and opened the door.

The room lit up at their entrance, revealing four security screens which showed Adam's house inside and out from every angle. Veronica's eyes widened. Incredible.

He crossed the room to another steel door. Again, he keyed in a security code. This time, she saw his weapons stash. "Oh, man. Look at this. Do you get to use these on missions?"

Adam flashed her an amused glance. "Not on every mission, but I have used them."

Veronica entered the room and scanned the weapons. Nice. Really nice. Her own weapons collection wasn't as extensive as his. She didn't have his salary, either. She found another Sig and picked up the weapon, checked to make sure the chamber was empty. "May I borrow this one?"

"Sure." He opened a cabinet and handed her a couple magazines along with a box of ammunition. "Anything else?"

She shook her head. "Thank you."

"You need to rest." He led her from the safe room and closet. "I'll wake you when it's time to leave." Adam kissed Veronica and nudged her inside her bedroom.

Veronica toed off her shoes and lay back on the bed with a sigh. Later, a tap on her door woke her. Adam stood in the doorway.

"It's time, Vonnie."

## CHAPTER TWENTY-ONE

Remy parked his SUV a block from Norton's home and turned off the engine. In the back seat, Adam opened his Go bag and removed the comm system Fortress issued to its operatives.

He handed Veronica his backup system and showed her how to attach the webbing.

"This is much better than what we use," she said.

"Maddox keeps us supplied with the best equipment he can find." Lily smiled over her shoulder.

Adam attached his own comm system. "Everybody ready?" After receiving positive responses, he said, "Let's find out what your wannabe boyfriend knows, Vonnie."

They approached the house from the rear, climbed over the fence and hugged the shadows of the bushes and trees in Norton's yard. Adam held up his fist, signaling the others to wait while he checked the garage for the agent's vehicle.

He peered through the window. The moonlight gleamed on a truck parked inside. He retraced his steps. "Dark-colored pickup is there."

"That's his vehicle," Veronica said.

So the target was home. Good. "Remy, Lily, wait for my signal."

The two operatives ran in a crouch for the back of the house along with Adam and Veronica. Adam motioned for them to disable the alarm. When they returned, he slipped around the side of the house and approached the porch with Veronica where they would call the agent sleeping inside. Remy and Lily were to pick the lock and slip inside when Graham Norton opened the front door. Adam wasn't taking a chance with Veronica's safety.

Once Remy confirmed the alarm was disabled and the back door was unlocked, Adam motioned for Veronica to call Norton with the phone on speaker. A moment later, a sleep-thickened voice answered.

"Graham, it's Veronica."

"Nica, where are you? I've been worried."

"I'm at your front door. Can we talk?"

"I'll be right there."

She slid her phone into her pocket and eyed Adam. "I want this resolved, but I don't want a friend to be guilty."

"You're strong. You'll handle whatever is thrown at you." Adam palmed his weapon and held the Sig by his side. "Remy, Lily, be ready."

"Copy."

Inside the house, a low light turned on and Norton fumbled with the lock. A tall, broad-shouldered man softening around the middle flung open the door, his dark hair mussed from sleep. He squinted to see Veronica better on the darkened porch. Adam had unscrewed the lightbulb to give them a few seconds to see whether or not the agent arrived with a gun drawn. Norton was empty handed, a surprise to Adam. He would have been armed if awakened in the middle of the night.

"Nica, where have you been?"

When the agent reached to grasp Veronica's arm, Adam stepped into view and nudged Norton's hand aside.

Veronica's co-worker scowled. "Who are you?"

"Graham, let's go inside," Veronica said. "I'll explain everything."

Not taking his gaze from Adam, Norton backed up, clearing the doorway for them to enter.

Adam indicated for Veronica to precede him. Remy and Lily were in the house, weapons trained on the DEA agent in case he made a move on her.

"Nica, what's going on?" Norton demanded. When Veronica turned toward him, fury burned in his gaze. "Who hurt you?" He glared at Adam. "Did this clown put his hands on you?"

"No, Graham. Adam would never hurt me. Please, can we sit down?"

He motioned for them to take the couch. "What happened? Have you reported the assault?"

"Dane sent me to Mexico. Los Diablos captured and interrogated me."

He dropped into the recliner, his jaw slack. "You're lucky they didn't kill you. What did they want to know?"

Veronica summarized her time in the hands of the cartel. "I need your help. Someone in our office is framing me for Dane's death."

"What? That's crazy. He was our friend."

"Has anyone asked questions about Veronica the past two weeks?" Adam asked.

"Before I answer your questions, how about answering some of mine. Who are you?"

"Adam Walker."

Norton stilled. "Walker? The operative Nica helped rescue last year?"

"That's right."

His attention shifted to Veronica. "Why are you with Walker?"

"He and his friends returned the favor by rescuing me in Mexico."

The agent frowned. "None of us knew you were in trouble. Why didn't Dane send us in? We would have gotten you out of there."

"He asked Fortress to go after Veronica," Adam said. "There's a leak in your office, Norton."

"What are you talking about? There's no leak."

"How else would Los Diablos have known about our missions and the agents involved in them?" Veronica asked. "Plus, Dane has documents that implicate me as the leak."

"I don't understand any of this." Norton jumped to his feet and paced. "How do you know about the documents?"

"I have a friend with computer skills," Adam said. What an understatement. Zane was a top-notch hacker, one the government would pay big bucks to have in their employ. Unfortunately for them, Z wasn't a fan of having the government watch over his shoulder.

"This is unbelievable." He rounded on Adam and Veronica. "Why didn't you call me or Carol, Nica? We would have helped you."

She sighed. "I did contact Carol and now she's in the hospital."

Norton grimaced. "Yeah, I tried to see her, but she has a guard on her door. No one except Forrest got inside to talk to her."

"The bodyguard is with Fortress," Adam said. "If someone inside your organization is involved in what's happening to Veronica, we can't trust the DEA or anyone from another law enforcement agency in that room alone with her while she's vulnerable. You're not safe, either."

"Why am I at risk?"

"Because you're my friend," Veronica said. "You and Carol were the most likely people aside from Dane who wouldn't rest until you found out where I was and why I was accused of selling out the DEA. You are the most dangerous now that Carol is unreachable. You're a target,

Graham. I shouldn't have contacted Carol, but I wanted to tell her to be careful. Now I'm telling you the same thing. Be careful. They almost killed Carol. I don't want you to be next."

"Don't worry about me. I can take care of myself." He studied her face a moment. "Are you really okay, Nica?"

"Los Diablos weren't kind to me, but I will heal. Adam is taking good care of me."

"You could have come to me. I would do anything you needed." He sighed. "But you've always been hung up on this guy, haven't you?"

"I never meant to hurt you, Graham."

He held up his hand. "I know. You've been honest about how you felt from the beginning. What do you need from me? I'll do anything I can to help."

Over the comm system, Remy said, "Company in front."

Adam turned off the light.

"What's happening?" Norton stepped to the side of the picture window.

"You expecting anyone else?"

A snort. "I wasn't expecting you."

"You have a bulletproof vest in the house?"

He nodded.

"Get it and your weapon. There are two SUVs out front, four men in each." Adam glanced over his shoulder. "Remy, you and Lily circle around. Approach from both sides."

"Copy that."

"How many more people are in my house?" Norton demanded.

"Just the four of us." Adam returned his attention to the front of the house. "Veronica's safety means more to me than worrying about you feeling violated because I brought two other operatives. It's good I brought backup."

"You disabled my alarm."

"We planned to bring it back online before we left."

"I could arrest you right now."

"You won't. We want to catch at least one of these clowns to question him. Unless you've been advertising your address to people who want you dead, this is connected to Veronica and maybe Dane."

"So how did they end up here? Did you check your vehicle for trackers?"

"Of course. We weren't followed to your doorstep. So what about you, Norton? Have you been asking too many questions around the office about Veronica?"

He blew out a breath. "Yeah, a bunch. She was missing and Dane was dead. So sue me. I care about Nica." A wry smile curved his lips. "More than she cares for me."

Ignoring that last statement, Adam said, "So you moved higher on the troublemaker list."

"In position," Lily murmured.

"Remy?" Adam asked.

"In position."

"Wait for my signal."

"Copy."

Adam glanced at Norton. "You have a safe room?"

"Adam," Veronica snapped.

"Are you kidding?" Norton gave a short laugh. "Not on my salary."

"Bullet-resistant glass?"

"I wish."

He'd been afraid of that. "Get your gear, Norton."

The agent dashed to the back of the house and returned strapping on his vest. He'd dragged on a shirt and stuffed his feet into boots. "Any movement?"

Adam turned back as the doors of each vehicle opened. "Here they come. Vonnie, cover the back."

She raced to the back door and a second later, Adam heard the lock click into place.

At the front, the group of eight split up. Two raised their weapons and started firing into the house, shattering windows. Two targets raced to the left side to breach the house through the garage. Two others went to the right side toward the bedrooms. The remaining pair of men stayed behind the steering wheels for a fast getaway.

"Fire." Adam squeezed off a shot and while his target staggered, he didn't go down. Crap. "Body armor."

"One target down," Remy said. "Going after the second."

Adam reacquired his target and squeezed off a round to the shoulder. That shooter dropped, writhing in pain. Seconds later, the other shooter in the front dropped. He wouldn't be getting up. Norton had taken him down with a head shot.

"Two targets down," Lily said.

Before he could respond, a crash in the kitchen had him spinning on his heel. "Norton, Lily, watch the drivers." He moved toward the back of the house and Veronica, weapon raised and ready.

"Two new targets breached the house from the back," Remy snapped. "My last target is down. Moving to assist."

Adam eased around a corner and fired at the man preparing to shoot Veronica as she battled his teammate. The wannabe shooter dropped to the floor. Remy raced through the back door and used zip ties to restrain the unconscious man.

On the ground, Veronica slammed her elbow against her assailant's temple and he went limp with a groan. Adam reached down, yanked him off Veronica, and dropped him. After securing him and tossing aside the man's weapon, he held out his hand to Veronica. "Nice job, Vonnie."

She grinned, breathing fast. "Thanks."

"Cops are coming," Lily said over the comm. "Do you want me to detain the drivers?"

He signaled Remy to go, knowing the operative wanted to aid his mate. "Roger that. Remy's on his way. Secure them and wait. I'm sending out Norton. He'll handle the local law enforcement."

"Copy."

Adam raised his voice. "Norton, Lily and Remy will detain the drivers, then stand down. Make sure your cop buddies don't shoot my teammates."

"You got it."

He slid his weapon into his holster and cupped Veronica's cheeks. "You okay?"

"I feel great."

Adam chuckled. "You might not in a few hours. Looks like he got in a few licks."

"I got in more."

He kissed her lightly as the sirens cut off abruptly. Knowing he had maybe two minutes before the police were inside the house, Adam grabbed his phone and took pictures of the men's faces, then sent their prints to Fortress. Slipping outside, he did the same to the thug Remy had restrained at the back door. He would have to wait for the police to identify the rest of them. He planned to ask Zane to check the police reports in a few hours. If he was free to talk to his brother-in-law. He and the others would have to answer questions.

Adam returned to the kitchen seconds ahead of two cops with their weapons drawn. He made sure his hands were visible as did Veronica. "I'm Adam Walker. This is Veronica Miles. You'll need to take my weapon for testing." He turned to the side so the closest officer could confiscate his Sig. "I want a receipt for that." Fat chance he'd be reclaiming the weapon anytime soon. The officer secured Adam's Sig and the one Veronica carried.

"Do you have other weapons?" the second officer asked.

Adam and Veronica glanced at each other and smiled. The police removed the backup weapons and Adam's two knives and Veronica's knife.

The first officer whistled softly before dragging his attention from the small pile of hardware and instructed them to wait out front on the porch with Remy and Lily.

Adam wrapped his hand around Veronica's and walked to the porch with the second officer trailing behind them. Remy had dragged the two chairs on the porch to the darkest corner. Lily occupied one while the other remained empty.

He nudged Veronica to the chair and stood beside Remy as they watched Norton talk to two other officers. "Problems?" he murmured to Remy.

"Not unless you count feeling naked without my weapons," he grumbled. "They're waiting for a detective and the crime scene team."

"I sent off pictures and prints to Fortress on three."

"Same with the drivers and the four we took down. That leaves the two clowns in front."

"Zane will find what we need."

Thirty minutes later, a nondescript car pulled up in front of the house just as the two ambulances were leaving, and two men climbed from the vehicle. When one of the men passed under the glare of the street light, Adam nudged Remy.

"About time we caught a break," Remy muttered.

The detective glanced up, his gaze automatically going to the darkened corner where the four of them waited. He said something to his partner and strode up the driveway and the porch stairs. "I should have known. Can't you stay out of trouble, Doucet?"

"Hey, they fired first. We were protecting our principal."

Detective Cal Taylor's gaze locked on Veronica. He held out his hand. "Detective Cal Taylor, homicide."

"Veronica Miles, DEA."

"Ah." A small smile curved his mouth. "That explains your presence here, Walker. So what's the story?"

Adam gave him a rundown of events in rapid-fire fashion.

"Any of you need the ER?" Taylor asked. When the response was negative, he shook his head. "Of course not. Don't know why I bothered to ask. I need you to go through this again, individually. Going through the crime scene will take me some time."

"I need Veronica in a more secure location," Adam murmured. "And your buddies confiscated our weapons. You also need to keep an eye on Norton. He's a target as well."

"Copy that. Go to Fortress headquarters. I'll meet you after I finish here." Taylor waved his partner over and explained that he was sending the operatives and Veronica ahead to Fortress for security reasons, then indicated for them to go.

During the ride to Fortress, the computer tech on duty sent Adam an email with the results of the print and facial recognition scans. The results made his blood run cold.

## CHAPTER TWENTY-TWO

Veronica glanced at Adam. Whatever he read on his phone had upset him. He wrapped his arms around her and held her as close as he could in the confines of the SUV. She noticed Remy and Lily exchanging puzzled looks.

Since he wasn't ready to talk, Veronica relaxed against Adam and hoped he would take comfort from her presence. Perhaps he would tell her what was troubling him when they were alone.

When they reached Fortress, they returned to the conference room. As they walked through the building, she noticed the place wasn't quiet. She could hear people talking, a copier running, and telephones ringing. No surprise, she supposed. Nights were busy for the DEA, too.

Inside the room, Adam dimmed the lights and went to the wall of windows in silence. Remy turned to Veronica, his eyebrow raised in silent inquiry. She shook her head, not having an answer to his unspoken question. She didn't know what was wrong, but she wanted to find out.

Remy held out his hand to Lily. "Come on. Let's find some water and soft drinks. We'll be in this room a while."

After the operatives left, Veronica stood beside Adam. "What's wrong?"

A sigh. "Come here."

Veronica stepped into the circle of his arms and wrapped hers around his waist. "Tell me."

"I'm the reason you were taken captive in Mexico. It's my fault you were beaten and tortured, Vonnie."

"Why do you say that?"

"The tech staff sent back the results of the fingerprints on the men who attacked at Norton's house."

"And?"

"They are known members of Peter Collins' organization."

She frowned. "Wait. Isn't that the kingpin who held you captive? I thought he was dead."

"He is. Someone picked up the mantle of leadership."

"I thought Fortress took his organization apart."

"We did. We haven't seen anything to indicate they're operating in the drug business. I'll check with Maddox when he arrives in a few hours."

"I'm already here," Maddox said from the doorway. "You owe Rowan another favor, my friend."

Veronica released Adam and turned to face his boss. "How did you know we were involved in an incident?"

"Taylor called me."

She blinked. "You know the detective?"

"He was my teammate in the SEALs and works occasional missions for me."

Remy and Lily walked into the room, arms loaded with bottles of water and soft drinks. They set everything on the table and dropped into seats beside Maddox.

"Taylor gave me the condensed version," Maddox said. "I want the full story." They took turns giving the report. When they finished, the CEO rubbed the back of his neck. "Did they track you to Norton's place?"

"No, sir," Remy said. "We checked the SUV for tracking devices and we weren't followed."

"Someone is watching his house or there's a camera monitoring the place."

"Too dark to check for surveillance on Norton's place, boss."

"Do we know who these clowns are?"

"We sent prints to the tech division. They belong to confirmed members of Peter Collins' organization," Adam said.

Maddox scowled. "We haven't heard his group resurrected for business. Have you, Veronica?"

"A whisper here and there. From what I observed, there wasn't an uptick in drug activity in the area the last time I was in Belize."

"How long ago was that?" Adam asked, his stomach knotting at the danger Veronica had faced on her own.

"Six months. The Collins name is still mentioned with equal measures of respect and fear."

"Is there anyone left in the organization who could take command?" Remy asked.

Veronica dredged her memories for a moment. "The only person who comes to mind is Lilah Collins."

Adam twisted in his seat to stare at her. "Lilah? She was never involved in the old man's business. She was a spoiled rich kid who didn't know where her father's money came from."

"Apparently, she learned fast." Veronica sighed. "Maybe she's the reason Interrogator questioned me so closely about you."

"Why go after Adam?" Lily asked. "He didn't kill her father."

"Lilah doesn't know that," he pointed out. "She knows I was undercover, my friends pulled me out of there, and her father died on her wedding night. She can't know which of us took the shot that rid the world of Peter Collins."

"Does she know what he did to you?" Veronica's face burned. "How he hurt you? You almost died, Adam." If he had, she wouldn't have met the honorable man who was capturing her heart.

Her breath caught. Oh, man. What had she done? She couldn't be falling in love with Adam Walker. Could she?

He gripped her hand. "But I didn't die, and if she is the driving force behind what's happening to you, then she knows I survived her father's torture."

"She wants revenge," Remy said. "We need to let Zane know. He and Claire are prime targets." His gaze shifted to Veronica. "If she is responsible for the attack on Norton, she knows about you, too, sugar. When she realizes you're more than a friend to Adam, she will redouble her efforts to capture you."

"Call Zane, Remy. Veronica, is there a chance Los Diablos is tied to Collins' organization?" Maddox asked as Remy left the conference room.

Veronica groaned. "The timing is right, but I didn't connect them. Do your tech people have names of the cartel's members?"

"We have some. We'll run them against those in the Collins organization, see if we get a hit." He stood, selected a soft drink. "Better hydrate while you can. Taylor will arrive soon."

Remy returned, his face grim. "Eli Wolfe is on his way to Zane's place. Jon is on night watch out there. I've already alerted the rest of the Zoo Crew with the exception of Jake and Curt to head that direction. They'll relocate Claire and Zane to a safe house. They will be fine, Adam. No one will touch them or Veronica. We have your back, buddy."

A nod from Adam.

"Zane said when they're settled, he will start searches on Lilah Collins, her father's organization, and Los Diablos. If she turns out to be our problem, Fortress will take her down and destroy that organization for good."

Adam glanced at Veronica. "What are the odds that Lilah is behind your problems with the DEA?"

"Decent. Maybe Zane will be able to trace Lilah to the anonymous emails in my handler's inbox."

"She has plenty of cash to get the job done." He turned to the others. "We can't focus only on Lilah, though. Someone on the inside knows too much. Lilah couldn't make all the necessary connections inside the DEA without help. Veronica isn't careless." His lips curved. "I ought to know since I had a hard time finding information on her for my own sake."

"The only way Los Diablos knew to connect Veronica to Adam was the leak in the DEA," Lily said, her expression thoughtful. "If we pinpoint that leak, we learn the identity of the person behind the attempt to destroy Veronica."

"Once we have the confirmed ID, we will destroy the organization." Maddox's gaze touched on every person in the room. "No one goes after my people without consequences."

Footsteps in the hall, then Detective Taylor and his partner, Lonnie Treadwell, walked into the conference room. "Got coffee?" Taylor asked as he dropped into the chair beside Maddox. "Soft drinks and water won't do the job."

"You need coffee strong enough to drop a bull elephant in his tracks?" Lily grinned.

"Sounds perfect."

She rose. "I'll make a fresh pot."

"You arrived quicker than I expected," Maddox said.

"DEA took over the scene."

"Who was the agent in charge?" Veronica asked.

"Clay Forrest."

"He's the head of our field office."

"He also has an ego that won't quit."

"Why are you here? He won't let another agency interfere in his investigation."

Taylor smiled. "He doesn't have a choice. Someone higher than Forrest told him to play nice with local law enforcement. We decided he works the crime scene and I conduct the interviews."

"I'm surprised he let you do that much," Adam said.

"You know him?" Taylor asked.

"Unfortunately, I talked to him at my house last night."

"He's not worried about anyone but himself," Remy added.

"What have you learned since you left Norton's place?"

Between the four of them, they updated Taylor on the latest information and supposition. He sat back in his chair, disgust evident on his face. "From a sheltered, pampered daughter to head of a drug cartel?" His shook his head. "That's quite a reach."

"Everything fits," Remy said. "The only obvious connection between Adam and Veronica is the mission in Belize. They didn't cross paths before that point."

"Or after," Adam said. "My first time to see Veronica was in Mexico. I asked Zane about her to see if she was safe. He contacted R.J. Walsh."

He sounded uncomfortable admitting the depth of his interest. Veronica took his hand in hers. "I also contacted R.J. about Adam, to check on his recovery."

Taylor nodded. "I know Walsh. He's a good man although I understand he's hit a rough patch with his marriage."

Maddox grunted. "Gambling."

The detective dragged a hand down his face. "Not what I wanted to hear. All right, let's go back over what happened at Norton's house," he said as Lily returned with a tray containing a carafe of coffee and mugs. "You start, Adam."

By the time they finished recounting the night's events several times, Taylor's face was grim. He glanced at Veronica. "You didn't hear me say this." He turned his attention to Adam and Maddox. "If Lilah Collins is behind this, Fortress needs to clean out that viper's nest in Belize or none of you will be safe."

## CHAPTER TWENTY-THREE

Adam had to hand it to Taylor. The man was thorough; and his partner, Treadwell, was right behind him. By the time the detectives were finished with the question-and-answer session, Veronica was visibly drooping. So were the rest of them. Lack of sleep and adrenaline dump was kicking all of them.

"I'll send copies of the statements to your email, Adam." Taylor stood. "Read, sign, and send them back. Anything else happens, I want to know about it."

"Copy that."

Maddox rose, shook the hands of both detectives. "Job offer is still open, Cal."

Treadwell's eyes widened, his attention shifting to his partner.

"Not yet."

"Soon?" the CEO pressed.

A slight nod was his response.

Satisfaction gleamed in Maddox's eyes as the two men left.

No one said anything until the elevator doors closed.

Maddox eyed the four of them. "We need to move fast. I have a few calls to make to clear the mission since the original skirmish with Collins was sanctioned by the government. First, though, you need at least six hours of sleep. I'll coordinate with Zane. We'll dig while you rest." He turned to Adam. "A word with you, then I'll send you on your way."

Veronica's hand tightened on his. Adam squeezed back. He appreciated her concern and support, but this was his home turf.

"We'll wait in the lobby," Remy said and escorted the women from the room, closing the door.

Maddox eyed him for a moment. "How serious are you about Veronica?"

Adam lifted his chin, couldn't explain to his boss what he didn't understand himself. "Why?"

"It's obvious your objectivity is compromised."

His jaw tightened. No. He wouldn't allow Maddox to use that argument to assign someone else to Veronica's security detail, not with his boss's recent history. "Didn't stop you from doing what was necessary to protect Rowan and Alexa."

His boss inclined his head in acknowledgment. "Do we have a shot at recruiting Veronica?"

"Before this debacle with the DEA, I would have said no. Now, I think the chance of success is better than half." Maybe more. Watching her interact with her co-workers and Fortress had been enlightening. Veronica was a perfect fit for Fortress. More important to him than anything else, she would have people she could trust at her back. That wasn't the case with the DEA, might never be true now that suspicion had been cast on her character and integrity. Didn't matter how the information that she wasn't a traitor was disseminated, someone would miss the truth. He didn't want this woman to be a casualty of friendly fire.

"If we recruit her, do you have an opinion on which unit I should assign her to?"

"What do you think?"

"Could you work with her?"

"No question."

"It's time for you to choose a team, Adam. Have you given more thought to possible candidates?"

"You know I have." They had discussed the topic at length.

"Care to share your conclusions?"

Adam shook his head. "Not yet."

"Fair enough. When you're ready, I expect a list of names."

"Yes, sir."

"Get some rest. I'll contact you in a few hours."

He stood. "We need to restock our weapons, boss. Metro police confiscated everything we had on us."

"Go to the weapons vault, get what the four of you need."

"Thank you, sir." Adam rode the elevator to the lobby. "Weapons vault," he said to the others as he held the doors open.

"Weapons vault?" Veronica looked puzzled.

"Fortress keeps a large stockpile of weapons on hand for operatives to use. We can restock our hardware from the vault."

She frowned. "Why not replenish from our own stash?"

"Safer to stay away from both houses. We attracted a lot of attention in both places."

Once the elevator doors closed, Remy said, "Do you have a place in mind for us to stay?"

"The Garden Hotel in Murfreesboro."

"Oh, good choice." Lily's cheeks turned an interesting shade of pink.

"You've been there."

"For our anniversary." A good memory from the expression on her face.

The elevator stopped below ground at the weapons vault. Adam slid his security card through the scanner to access the hallway. "Choose anything you want." He paused. "Within reason."

"No rocket-propelled grenade, huh?"

The three operatives chuckled. "Between the three of us, we already have a few of those."

"Oh, man." Veronica sighed. "Sometimes I wish that was standard equipment for the DEA."

The four of them chose handguns and knives to replace those confiscated by the police.

"Just think, Veronica. You would have access to these weapons all the time if you joined Fortress." Lily nudged her as they re-entered the elevator. "Come on. You know you want in."

"It's tempting," Veronica admitted.

Adam kept his expression neutral although inside he was anything but neutral. He longed to weigh in on the discussion, but the decision had to be her choice. "No pressure. Just remember you have options."

While Remy drove toward Murfreesboro, Adam called the hotel and reserved a suite for them.

An hour later, he swiped the key card to open the suite door on the second floor. "Choose a room, Vonnie. Remy and Lily will take the other one. I'll bunk on the couch."

"I'll take the one on the right."

"Who's taking first shift?" Remy asked.

"I will." Adam was wise enough not to mention how tired Lily looked.

A nod. "I'll relieve you in three hours." The couple went into the second bedroom and closed the door.

"I feel guilty leaving you on the couch." Veronica laid her hand over his heart. "I should sleep out here. You would be more comfortable on a bed."

"I've slept on far worse than a luxurious couch." His arms circled her waist. "Someone has to stay out here in case we have a breach."

"I can do that."

"You are more than capable," he agreed. "However, you're still recovering from the hospitality of Los Diablos. You're not up to full strength yet. Plus, you are the principal, not the protector, on this mission."

Adam captured her lips with his, spent several minutes indulging in Veronica's taste. By the time he lifted his head, he knew he needed to send her to bed. His self-control was almost gone. "Go rest. I'll be here if you need me."

"What did Maddox want with you?"

"I'll talk to you about that later. You have my word."

"Your discussion concerns me?"

He nodded. "We'll talk." Another kiss, this one whisper light. "Go, sweetheart. I'm trying to remember I'm a gentleman. Help me out."

Veronica gave him a dazzling smile and went to the bedroom.

Adam blew out a breath after the door closed behind her. Whew! Veronica Miles just did it for him. No matter her mood or how tired she was, he loved being around her, loved her smile. Watching her sleep made him go soft inside. Listening to her voice soothed as much as stimulated him. And her eyes? Oh, man, he could drown in those beautiful eyes. But what a way to go.

He sat on the couch and stretched his legs out in front of him. He sounded like Remy, Zane, and Maddox over their wives and they were crazy in love with their women.

Adam froze. Was he in love with Veronica? He drew in a slow, deep breath, knowing he was in so deep it was too late to stop the slide. Over the past year, he began to care for Veronica. During the past few days, he'd fallen for the woman who might break his heart. If she didn't feel the same about him, Adam didn't think he would recover with his heart intact. And that confirmed what he already suspected. What Adam had with Jessica was nothing compared to this runaway freight train.

He wanted to tell Veronica he loved her, but the timing couldn't be worse. They'd be an amazing team. If she would take him on with all his baggage. Not many women could handle what he did for a living. Veronica could. If he was lucky, she would agree to be his partner on the job and off.

Two hours into his shift, Zane called.

"You and Claire okay?"

"We're safe. We're in the Garden Hotel in Murfreesboro."

He grinned. "First floor?"

"Yes, why?"

"Remy, Lily, Veronica and I are staying on the second floor."

Zane chuckled. "Good choice. Why are you staying here?"

"Veronica's home and mine have been compromised. Too many people know both locations. After that fiasco at Norton's, I wanted to give Vonnie a chance to rest without worrying who would come after her next."

"I don't blame you. Listen, R.J. is trying to locate Veronica. He called and left three messages within fifteen minutes, saying it was urgent that she contact him immediately."

"Did he say why?"

"Afraid not."

Of course he didn't. Nothing about this situation was easy. "Vonnie has only been asleep two hours. I hate to wake her."

"I understand, but R.J. doesn't raise an alarm for no reason."

"All right. Text me his number. I'll find out what's going on before I wake her. Anything on Lilah Collins?"

"She's still in Belize, living in her father's mansion with her husband. She also set up a foundation to benefit children down there. Lilah has gone from being a spoiled rich kid to a skilled money manager."

"Any indication she's picked up her father's business on the side?"

"Nothing conclusive yet. I'll let you know what I find."

"Copy that."

When the text came through, Adam called the number. No answer. He frowned. Was the SEAL so paranoid he wouldn't answer a call from a number he didn't recognize?

He sent R.J. a text and waited. One minute, two, five. The longer the silence lasted, the more his gut tightened. The door to Remy and Lily's room opened and Remy walked out.

Sitting beside Adam, Remy motioned to the phone. "What's going on?"

"R.J. has been trying to contact Veronica. I called and texted him, got no response."

"Not good. What do you want to do?"

"Fly with Vonnie to the Bahamas for two weeks."

A grin. "Sounds good to me. Lily loves the beach."

"We need to check on R.J."

"Do we wake the women or risk cold shoulders when we return?"

Adam snorted. "I'm smarter than that. Vonnie would tear a strip off my hide."

"Good thing you know that, Walker." Veronica entered the living room, fully dressed, including her Sig.

"And you should know better than to ask that question, Remy," Lily said as she walked into the room. She unscrewed the top on a bottle of water. "Where are we going?"

"R.J. Walsh's place," Adam said. "He's with Trident. He's a friend of Zane and Veronica's."

"He's also a friend of Rio Kincaid's who connected me with R.J. in the first place. R.J. is one of my contacts." Veronica shoved her hair away from her face. "I tracked Adam's progress through him because Rio can be difficult to contact."

"Grab your Go bags and we'll head out." Adam waited until Remy and Lily had left the room. "Did you sleep?"

"More than you." Veronica eyed him critically. "You need some downtime."

"Has to wait." He grabbed his bag and headed for the door as Remy and Lily returned. "Stairs. We don't want to scare the guests." They looked like what they were. Mercenaries. Not exactly the kind of people you expect to see early in the morning at a luxury hotel. They didn't need a skittish guest sounding the alarm and garnering a heavy police response. Adam's gut told him they couldn't afford to delay.

The forty-minute drive seemed interminable. In reality, Remy traveled the distance from the hotel to R.J.'s house in record time considering the traffic. As Remy parked in the driveway, Adam tried one last time to contact R.J. Still nothing. They didn't have a choice. If R.J. was still alive, Adam prayed his reflexes were still sharp enough to abort a shot at one of them.

"Want us to go around back?" Lily asked.

He'd considered splitting up on the drive here. "No. He's paranoid. If he didn't hear his phone for some reason, I don't want him to think we're surrounding the place. He knows me and Veronica. It's best if you stay with us."

On the porch, Adam rang the bell. When he didn't hear movement inside, he knocked on the door. "R.J., it's Adam Walker. Open the door."

After a few more seconds passed, he picked the lock and turned the knob. Inside, the house was silent except for a wheezing sound coming from the living room.

Adam signaled Remy and Lily to search the house. He and Veronica swept to the right, weapons drawn. At first he didn't see anything in the dim light. Then his gaze fell on the figure sprawled on the floor.

"R.J." Veronica shoved her Sig into her holster and hurried to the fallen SEAL. "Adam, I need more light."

He turned the three-way switch to a higher setting and light flooded the room.

"He's been shot twice and lost a lot of blood," Veronica said. Her face said the man had lost too much.

Adam grabbed the house phone and placed a call to emergency services, reporting the incident to the dispatcher. Without disconnecting, he set the phone down where the dispatcher's recording wouldn't catch his conversation with Veronica and the others.

Veronica glanced at him. "I need towels."

Remy and Lily returned to the living room. "I'll get them," Remy said. "House is clear."

"R.J., can you hear me?" Veronica gripped the operative's hand. "Talk to me. Who did this to you?"

Adam crouched on the other side of him. "Sit rep," he snapped. Just as he'd hoped, R.J. stirred, opened his eyes. After dragging in a ragged breath, the injured man said, "Risa."

## CHAPTER TWENTY-FOUR

"Risa shot you?" Not possible. Dane's assistant, the sweetest woman Veronica had ever met, hated guns. If she did own a weapon, why shoot R.J.?

R.J. grimaced, closed his eyes, and went limp.

No. Just no. Not another death. "R.J." She pressed her fingers to his neck, feeling for a pulse. A weak one. At least he was alive.

Remy returned, handed her a stack of towels. Veronica applied pressure to R.J.'s wounds to stem the flow of blood long enough for the EMTs to render aid.

In the distance, a siren sounded, drawing closer by the second. "Vonnie, we can't be here when help arrives," Adam said.

They couldn't find the shooter if they were locked behind bars. Still, she hated to leave the man when he was critical. No one should be alone in that condition. "I can't leave him, Adam. I know it's not smart, but I can't do it."

He gave a slight nod, accepting her decision without question. What a gift he'd given her. "I need your weapons."

"Why?"

"If we stay until the EMTs arrive, we'll encounter local law enforcement. We shouldn't be armed to the teeth."

Veronica handed him two Sigs and the holsters. When she reached for her knife and sheath, he held up his hand.

"R.J. has gunshot wounds. Keep that." He stood. "I'll store your weapon in my Go bag." He signaled Remy and Lily to follow him outside.

When they returned, the three were armed with knives. Veronica had to smile. The police would take one look at them four of them and wonder why they weren't armed with handguns. She hoped the police didn't search the SUV. The weapons stash in the vehicle would raise eyebrows. If they confiscated the weapons from the Fortress vault, Maddox would not be happy.

Adam updated Maddox and Zane about R.J. He ended the call as the ambulance parked in the driveway.

A moment later, EMTs hurried into the living room with their equipment. The next few minutes were chaotic as they worked on R.J. before they finished, a patrol car rolled up.

Adam clasped Veronica's hand. "Come on. I'm sure the police will have questions for us."

"Good idea. This house is a crime scene. The police will move us outside to answer questions anyway."

As they left, the EMTs moved R.J. to the stretcher. A policeman scanned the four of them for visible weapons.

"You called in a shooting?"

"That's right. I'm Adam Walker. This is Remy and Lily Doucet, and my girlfriend, Veronica Miles."

"You friends of the victim?"

"Veronica and I are acquaintances. Remy and Lily never met him."

"Vic's name?"

And so the questions began. Veronica knew they would be asked the same ones more than once when the detectives arrived. Under normal circumstances, she would have been patient with the questions, knowing the process was necessary. But these weren't normal circumstances. Someone was targeting the people she cared about.

"Wait over there, please," the policeman said. "Two detectives will arrive soon to ask you questions."

Veronica walked to the far side of the porch and sat on the white swing beside Adam. Lily and Remy sat on the wicker loveseat. Lily curled into her husband's embrace, looking relaxed and unworried by the events of the past few minutes. Appearances were deceptive. One look at the operative's alert gaze as she scanned the area continuously belied her apparent unconcern.

Adam wrapped his arm around Veronica's shoulders. "How are you holding up?" he murmured.

"Afraid for another friend."

He pressed a kiss to her temple. "This is not your fault, baby."

"I know. Doesn't make me feel better." She tilted her head back. "Makes me concerned for your safety, Adam."

"We'll watch over each other."

She laid her head on his shoulder. "I don't want to lose you." Just the possibility of that made an invisible band around her chest constrict. Would her confession scare him off? Probably not. Adam Walker didn't scare easily.

"You won't." He opened his mouth to say something else, but stopped.

"Adam?"

He trailed his fingers down her cheek. "What I want to say has to wait. This isn't the right time or setting."

What did that mean?

Another car parked in front of the house. Must be the detectives. She sighed, dreading the next session of questions and answers. She needed to be sharp and right now, her brain operated at snail speed. "I wish I could curl up with you on a couch and fall asleep watching a movie."

"Sounds like a great plan. We'll get there."

After a quick conversation with the first policeman on scene, the detectives approached them. The questions from Henley and Cotton continued for two hours, long enough to strain Veronica's patience.

"You asked the same questions several times over and we provided the same answers," Adam said, his tone curt. "We can't give you more details. If you think of different questions, call the number I gave you."

"We want to search your vehicle."

Adam's smile lacked humor. "Not unless you have a warrant. You are welcome, however, to test our hands for gunshot residue. You won't find anything because we didn't fire a weapon at R.J."

"But you have them or access to them."

He inclined his head. "We couldn't do our jobs otherwise."

The detectives glowered at them although they remained silent.

Veronica and the others stood and walked off the porch. "Having to follow rules bites," she said after they were safely inside the SUV.

"That it does," Remy agreed. He drove from the property and headed toward the hotel. "I'm not sorry to be with Fortress instead of the NYPD."

Inside the suite, Veronica turned to Adam. "Take my bed. You need to sleep."

"I'll be fine."

Stubborn man. She pressed her fingers lightly against his jaw. "Adam, please. You promised we would watch out for each other. You need rest." Deciding to press a bit more for his sake, she leaned up and kissed him. "Do it for me." She felt his muscles relax before he nodded.

"Come get me if there's a problem."

"I promise."

The Marine pressed a hard kiss to her mouth, then glanced at Remy in wordless communication. He got a nod in response before he went to Veronica's room.

When she turned, both Remy and Lily were grinning at her. "What?"

"If I hadn't just seen that myself, I wouldn't have believed it." Lily shook her head. "Adam has a will of iron and yet you convinced him to put himself before you for a short time."

"Hey, he's a logical guy," Remy protested. "He knows he needs sleep in order to protect Veronica."

Lily shook her head. "He thinks he's Superman."

Not Superman, just a man who looked after his circle of friends. He cared deeply about people he let into his life. Although she hadn't met his sister Claire yet, Veronica knew he would lay down his life for her in a heartbeat, as would her husband.

She glanced at the Doucets. "Sleep. I'll take the first watch."

"You're still recovering," Remy said.

"Now who's being stubborn? It's a three-hour shift and I have research to do."

"If you become too tired, knock on the door and I'll relieve you." He held her gaze a moment. "I'm trusting you to be honest with me and yourself."

"You have my word." She waved him on.

Left alone, she grabbed Adam's laptop from his Go bag. He'd given her the password earlier and told her to use his computer when she wanted to do searches. Zane had tweaked the computer so that searches didn't leave electronic footprints. She didn't see how that was possible, but apparently Fortress's tech guru was something of a miracle worker.

She went to the DEA database and searched Risa Shoemaker's name. Not enough information. Risa had worked at the Nashville DEA office for six years. She'd been hired ten months before Veronica. Dane insisted she was the best assistant in the agency.

She dug into Risa's background, flinched at what she read. Man, if she'd known about Risa's rough childhood, Veronica would have been friendlier. Oh, she'd never been mean, just not warm and fuzzy. A snort. Right. Like she was ever warm and fuzzy.

Risa had been dumped by her single mother on her grandparents who were harsh disciplinarians. More than one visit to the hospital after a discipline session. Veronica scowled. Might as well call it was it was. Abuse. Her grandfather tried to beat her into submission. She didn't blame the woman for leaving the day she turned eighteen.

After working two jobs year round to put herself through college and graduating with a business degree, Risa applied at the DEA and was assigned to Dane.

No weapons permit. No run-ins with the law, not even a traffic ticket. Risa Shoemaker was squeaky clean. Why would R.J. point a finger at Risa? Didn't make sense.

Veronica needed to talk to R.J. If he was still alive. Maybe Zane could find out for her. He seemed to know everything. She called Zane.

"Everything okay, Veronica?"

"We're fine. Adam, Remy, and Lily are asleep. I'm researching Risa Shoemaker."

"Why are you looking at Carver's assistant?"

"When I asked R.J. who shot him, he managed to say Risa's name before he passed out."

"What do you need from me?"

"My computer hacking skills are mediocre. I need to speak to R.J. again. Can you check the hospital computer to see how he's doing? Calling won't help because I'm not a relative and I can't use my badge since I don't have one at the moment." There went that pain in her heart again.

"I heard. We'll clear your name, sugar."

"Thanks." She heard keys clicking in the background. A moment later, a sigh sounded in her ear. "Zane?"

"I'm sorry, Veronica. R.J. died on the operating table."

## CHAPTER TWENTY-FIVE

Adam opened his eyes at the six-hour mark, wide awake and alert. Military training had perks. Waking up alert without an alarm was one of them.

He rubbed his jaw. Needed to shower and shave. Otherwise, his beard would scratch Vonnie's sensitive skin when he kissed her. Much as he hated to admit it, his girl and Maddox were right. He had needed six hours of rest.

What about Veronica? Had she slept while he'd been down? He grabbed his bag and went to shower. Adam returned dressed in fresh clothes and anxious to see Veronica. He walked into the living room and stopped short. Where was Veronica?

Lily handed him a bottle of water. "Food is in the refrigerator. We ordered room service two hours ago."

"Where's Vonnie?"

She inclined her head toward the patio. "She's been out there a while. Wouldn't eat."

Adam watched Veronica a moment, noted the slumped shoulders. "What happened?" Why didn't they wake him? If the woman he loved needed him, he wanted to be available for her.

"R.J. didn't make it."

Food could wait. Veronica couldn't. He opened the patio door and sat in the chair beside hers.

Adam laced his fingers with Veronica's, but allowed her to sit in silence. This side of the hotel faced a greenway and gardens on the hotel grounds, a spectacular view. If you were looking for a view to soothe your heart, this was a good one.

A few minutes later, he said, "Lily told me about R.J. I'm sorry."

"He was a good man, despite his addiction."

"Small comfort, but Trident will take care of his family."

"I'm glad." She turned to him, then, her eyes reddened, her cheeks tear-stained. The sight tore at his heart. He never wanted to see that look in her eyes again, but he couldn't prevent life from hurting Veronica. "The family shouldn't have to worry about R.J.'s gambling debt."

"Agreed. I'll have Maddox contact the head of Trident. They'll take care of everything."

Her fingers tightened around his. "You look better."

"At the risk of hearing 'I told you so' for a long time in the future, you were right. I needed sleep. I could have kept going, though."

Veronica's lips twitched. "Of course."

He felt like he'd accomplished a great feat by lighting a spark of humor in her eyes. "I'm starving and I hate to eat alone. Join me?"

That brought a full-blown smile. "Adam Walker, you can't convince me eating by yourself worries you."

He grinned. "Come on. Lily tells me you didn't eat. I slept for you. Eat for me."

"Not the same thing," she pointed out. "I won't waste away if I skip a meal. I've done it often enough in the field."

"You shouldn't. It makes you weak, and in our business you never know when you'll have a chance to take in fuel again." He drew Veronica to her feet. "What did you learn while I slept?" No question in his mind that she had utilized the time well.

When they walked inside, Lily returned to the bedroom she shared with Remy. The other operative must be resting.

"Risa doesn't have a weapons permit."

"She could have bought a weapon off the street."

"True, but I don't see that. She hates guns and refused to handle them in the office. I also found out she had a terrible childhood."

He remained silent while he reheated two plates of food. "Like yours?"

Veronica froze. "You researched me?"

"No." He wouldn't go behind her back except to save her life. "Observation, Vonnie. Will you tell me after we eat?"

Her eyebrow rose. "Why after?"

"Simple. You will stop eating and I don't think you've gained an ounce since we left Mexico. The cartel didn't feed you, did they?"

"I told you their hospitality was lacking."

He climbed onto a stool at the breakfast bar and nudged one of the plates in her direction. "Talk to me about something fun while we eat. We'll change to serious topics later."

"What kind of fun topic?"

"Where is your favorite place to vacation?"

Immediately, her shoulders relaxed. "The beach. I've been to several, but my favorite is Orange Beach on the Gulf coast. There's something special about that place. The sand is perfect, the breeze warm and sultry. There are several beachfront condos with kitchens and an amazing view of the ocean. The whole place is full of life and energy. By the time I leave there, I feel like I've been at a spa for a week. I'm relaxed and mellow, and best of all I can sleep at night."

He grinned at her. "So you tolerate it?"

"Are you kidding? I'd live there if I was independently wealthy and wouldn't become bored by the second week." She paused. "Okay, maybe by the third week. Want to run away to Orange Beach with me?"

Startled, he stared at her, and noted the twinkle in her eyes. The lady was teasing him. Little did she know Adam would take her up on the offer in a second as long as they had matching wedding rings on their fingers. "Name the date and time and I'll go with you." He leaned over and kissed her before polishing off the rest of his meal.

"You're next. Where is your favorite place to vacation, Adam?"

"The mountains."

Veronica wrinkled her nose. "You mean one of those rustic hunting cabins in the middle of nowhere with trees for company and no indoor plumbing?"

"Ha. Not even close. I like comfortable beds, hot water, and more than one channel to watch on television. My preference is Gatlinburg. I stay in a chalet and enjoy all the amenities plus amazing food and museums. I also enjoy buying weird gifts for Claire."

"Have you been there since she and Zane married?"

"Nope. I spent most of that time rehabbing from my injuries." He tilted his head. "Want to run away with me to Gatlinburg?"

"Name the date and time. I think it would be fun."

"I'll hold you to that." When he finished his meal, he was pleased to see Veronica's plate was empty as well. Adam stacked the plates and utensils in the dishwasher.

He held out his hand. "Come with me." He walked to the garden and found a secluded bench in the corner. The twilight was deepening swiftly toward night and the breeze had increased. The bench he chose had two high walls at their backs so neither of them would worry about someone sneaking up on them.

He draped his arm across her shoulders and hugged her to his side. "Tell me about your childhood, Vonnie."

"It's not pretty."

Stalling. Figuring she might talk if he didn't stare at her, Adam encouraged Veronica to lean her head against his shoulder. He watched the fountain in the center of the garden, letting her decide if she wanted to let him in this far. Man, he hoped so. He didn't want secrets between them that weren't work related. His ran his hand lightly up and down her arm, willing himself to be patient.

"I grew up in a small town," she said after a while. "Three traffic lights and two stop signs the year I was born. We rated a few more of each by the time I entered high school. We had 10,000 people when I left at eighteen. On the outside, my family looked like the perfect American family. Big house, two cars, a dog, two kids, stay-at-home mom, and an important father. The appearance was deceptive. We were anything but perfect." She dragged in a ragged breath.

"Take your time."

She huddled closer.

Adam twisted and wrapped his other arm around Veronica, basically surrounding her. "I've got you, baby."

"While on the outside, the house looked beautiful, the inside was ugly. Oh, not the furniture or the decorations. My father would never allow his home to be anything but a showplace that might have graced the cover of a magazine. Inside that house, though, was a war zone. Dad was a gentleman to the outside world. Inside our home, he was a tyrant. Everything had to be to his exacting standards. Of course, that was impossible. No one could meet his standards."

He already knew where this conversation was headed based on Veronica's back, but made himself ask the question anyway. "And when you didn't meet the standard?"

"He punished the offender without remorse." A mirthless laugh escaped. "He never has an ounce of regret because the punishment is justified in his mind."

Adam forced his body to remain relaxed while inside he was anything but relaxed. No one had the right to do that. "Your father beat you with his belt, didn't he?"

She tensed.

"I noticed the scars when you showed Forrest and Crosby the whip marks. They were too far away to see the old scars."

"Dad is very fond of his belt."

When Adam met the man, he'd make certain Veronica's father understood if he ever touched his daughter again in anger, he would answer to Adam. He took care of those he loved and now that number included Veronica Miles. "What about your brother?"

"Charles left as soon as he turned 18, six years before me. He joined the military and never returned. Dad keeps up with his career, proud of his true American hero son. That's all he talks about."

"What about you? You're with the DEA. That's cause for bragging rights as well."

A snort from the woman in his arms. "Chandler Miles has nothing but disdain for law enforcement, all branches."

"Including you?"

"Especially me. Because I'm with the DEA, I must be on the take or enjoy killing people. He said I would never amount to anything good."

Fury rolled through Adam. "What does your father do?"

"He's a judge."

"But he doesn't like law enforcement?"

"He says we're all corrupt thugs."

"On what does he base his opinion?"

"The cops in my hometown are in his hip pocket. Flash a little green their direction and they overlook anything, even a 911 call from a terrified, sobbing 13-year-old who didn't clean her room to her father's specifications and bled from his latest beating."

Veronica's words cut into Adam's heart.

"The responding officers didn't bother to check on me, just clapped him on the shoulder like a good buddy and stuck out their hands for cash to look the other way. After my father finished the second round of punishment, I couldn't attend school for a week."

He tightened his grip on the woman in his arms. How could a father do that to his child? "Is he still living?"

"He's too ornery to die."

"Do you ever go home?"

Veronica's head lifted from his shoulder. "Sometimes, but only for a few hours and always when he's at work. My mother won't leave him. Now that he doesn't have me or Charles for a punching bag, he's turned on her."

"Next time you go home, I'm going with you."

Her eyes narrowed. "People will notice if he disappears."

"Who said anything about him disappearing? I'm going with you, Vonnie."

"What if we're not dating anymore?"

He hoped to have his ring on her finger by that time. "I still want to go. No matter what happens between us, we'll still be friends and you need someone at your back if you run into your father. Will you let me be your backup?"

"Not necessary, but it's fine if you come with me."

Excellent. He'd research Chandler Miles before meeting him. They had spent enough time thinking about Veronica's past. It was time to deal with the host of problems in the present. "We need to talk to Risa Shoemaker." Adam had a feeling Risa was the key to everything.

## CHAPTER TWENTY-SIX

When Veronica and Adam returned to the suite, Remy and Lily were waiting for them. "Zane called," Remy said. "He invited us to their suite for coffee and information. Claire mentioned something about ice cream."

Adam shook his head. "My sister has a serious weakness for sweets." How she managed to stay healthy was a mystery, but she was rarely sick.

"Oh, ice cream." Lily smiled. "What are we waiting for?"

With a chuckle, Remy clasped his wife's hand and led her to the door.

The four of them walked downstairs to the first floor where Adam knocked on the door to the Murphy suite. A moment later, Zane opened the door and moved back for them to enter.

"Adam!" Claire's black hair flew behind her as she raced across the living room and threw herself into his arms. "I'm so glad to see you."

"Sis, it's only been a week since you saw me last." Nevertheless, he hugged his sister tight. "You okay?"

"Never better." She beamed at him. "Please, sit down. I'll call room service in a minute and have them send ice cream. Any preferences?"

Once Claire called in their choices, she sat in the recliner, Zane by her side in his chair. "You must be Veronica. I'm Claire, Adam's sister. Thank you for helping us find Adam last year."

"I'm glad I could help."

"You have information for us, Z?" Remy asked.

"I do have some information about your case and something more personal." He paused, glanced at Claire. "It's your news, baby."

"Ours," she corrected.

Adam tensed. What was going on?

"I'll sit on the patio for a few minutes," Veronica said as she stood.

"Stay, please," Claire said. When Veronica sat again, Claire's smile widened. "We wanted you to be the first to know Zane and I are going to have a baby."

Lily jumped up and rushed over to hug Claire. "Oh, man, I get to be an aunt. Congratulations, Claire." Next, she leaned over and kissed Zane's cheek. "You'll be a great father, Z. I'm happy for you both."

Remy bussed Claire's cheek and clapped Zane on the shoulder. "We get dibs on babysitting."

"You may be sorry you volunteered."

"Not a chance. When is the little Murphy due?"

"End of November."

As the buzz of conversation flowed around him, Adam crouched beside Claire and hugged her. He couldn't believe his baby sister was going to have a child of her own. Oh, man. He so wished Nana could have lived long enough to hold her great-grandchild. She would have loved that. "Congratulations, sis. If it's a girl, I'll make plans with Z to scare off suitors until she's thirty."

Claire laughed, hugging him tight. "No, thanks. Zane will be plenty scary with that big, bad Navy SEAL thing he has going."

"Marines are more scary than frog boys."

"I heard that," Zane groused.

A short while later, someone knocked on the door. As one, all except Claire drew weapons. Lily and Veronica stepped in front of Claire. Adam signaled Zane to stay where he was. He went to the door with Remy and checked the security peephole. Bellhop uniform and a cart with several dishes of ice cream.

He motioned for Remy to stand to the side and opened the door.

"You ordered ice cream?"

Out of sight of the bellhop, Adam slid his weapon into his holster and grabbed his wallet. "That's right." He pulled out a tip. "Thanks." The bellhop left and Adam rolled the cart into the suite.

Once the dessert dishes were empty, Claire poured coffee from the carafe for everyone else. She chose bottled water for herself.

"What information do you have for us, Z?" Adam threaded his fingers through Veronica's.

"I dug into Risa Shoemaker's background." Zane proceeded to give a concise report, most of it Adam already knew from the information Veronica told him.

"Her finances?"

"No big deposits in her account and nothing to indicate she's living beyond her means."

Veronica frowned. "So it's not her."

"The electronic footprints say the saboteur is definitely her," Zane said. "I can't find a motive. Have you two knocked heads about anything?"

"Are you kidding? I'm barely in the office more than a day or two a month, if that. The only communication I have with her beyond that is email, and that's rare. I don't know what I did to make her mad."

"Maybe you didn't," Claire said.

"Then why would she sabotage me?"

"Maybe it's someone in her circle of friends or family."

"Someone who accessed the office when she was there," Remy said. "What do you know about her family?"

"I doubt she's had contact with them, not after the way she grew up."

"A boyfriend or husband?"

Veronica shrugged. "I don't know. I spoke to her a minute about generalities each time we talked. Dane was anxious to debrief me or send me to another assignment."

"Did you run across the name of a boyfriend or husband?" Adam asked Zane.

"No husband, but she's in a new dating relationship with Raul Escobar."

"Wonder if he has ties to Lilah Collins or her father."

"Let's find out." Zane grabbed his laptop from the pocket at the back of his chair.

While he typed on his computer keyboard, Adam turned to his sister. "Where are your bodyguards?"

"The Zoo Crew is spread around the hotel. Eli and Jon are at dinner with their wives. They left two minutes before you arrived and should be back soon."

Good. He wanted Zane to have backup, especially now that his sister was carrying Adam's niece or nephew. He had never pictured himself as an uncle. He'd get some ideas from Remy, an uncle many times over. The Doucet brothers had several children each, which made Aiden and Marie Doucet, Remy's parents, very happy.

"Got it." Gaze glued to his screen, Zane said, "Raul Escobar is a very common name, but there is one on the list of Peter Collins' employees. His name appears again in connection to Lilah."

"We need to know everything about this guy."

"I'll have Jon give me a hand."

Excellent. Jon Smith, a world class sniper, was also as skilled with a computer as Zane.

A knock was followed by the sound of a key card unlocking the suite door. Jon Smith and Eli Wolfe walked in.

"Where are your better halves?" Remy asked.

"On their way to my house for the night," Eli said. "Brenna and Dana are watching sappy movies and eating popcorn without us."

"I see you're broken up about that."

"If it was a John Wayne film fest, I would be miffed. Don't tell Brenna, but missing a romance movie doesn't bother me."

"Anything new?" Jon asked Adam.

"Veronica Miles, this is Eli Wolfe and Jon Smith." Adam said. "Veronica's problems are coming from Risa Shoemaker, Carver's assistant. Risa has no motive for setting up Vonnie, but she has a new boyfriend with ties to Peter Collins and his daughter."

Jon turned to Zane. "What do you need, Z?"

"An extra pair of hands."

"I'll get my computer."

"Guess I have the watch, then." Eli walked to the French doors.

"Want some company?" Remy asked.

"Sure. I'm ready for more humorous stories about your nieces and nephews."

Remy and Lily followed the SEAL to the patio. While Jon waited for his computer to boot up, he glanced at Veronica. "You healing all right?" he asked, his voice soft.

Adam tightened his grip on Veronica's hand. The SEAL zeroed in on what mattered most, Vonnie's recovery. He wasn't surprised. Jon had been captured by a human trafficking organization, then beaten and drugged repeatedly before Eli found him. It took the sniper months to recover from the ordeal. Rumors floated around Fortress that he still hadn't fully recovered and that was the reason he and Eli were selective in their missions.

Adam wasn't convinced. From observing Jon's interaction with his wife, Dana, he thought the sniper's reluctance to be parted from his wife had more to do with her recovery from a similar ordeal rather than for his own sake.

"I'm recovering," Veronica said. "Dr. Sorensen and Adam have helped me stay on track."

A nod, then to Zane, "What's this clown's name?"

"Raul Escobar."

"I need to know everything you can find about this guy," Adam said. "Either he's the culprit behind Vonnie's problems or he turned Risa against her."

He nodded. "Z, you want me to take the financial side or the personal side?"

"Personal. I'm already working on his financial accounts."

While they worked at their keyboards, Adam encouraged Claire to talk about her wedding photo shoots. Before long, Veronica was laughing at her funny bridezilla stories.

"Sounds like they're insane," Jon commented without looking up from his work.

"Sometimes I think they might be." Claire smiled. "Most of the time, though, it's a product of serious pre-wedding stress. When I meet with them after the wedding to choose their photo packages, they're like different people."

"Raul Escobar is no choir boy," Jon said. "He's suspected of killing several people, but the cops either couldn't pin anything on him or they didn't bother to try. I'd say Collins made the problems disappear with a hefty bribe. According to what I've seen, he was one of Collins' key people."

Adam frowned. His name wasn't familiar. If this man was a major player in the cartel, Adam should have known about him. "Why didn't I know him? I knew Collins' key people."

"Escobar's assignment was in Mexico and the U.S. He wasn't in Belize when you were undercover." He paused. "Escobar is married to Maria Elena Vargas. I doubt his wife knows about Shoemaker because she's currently living in Belize."

"I feel bad for Risa," Veronica said. "Escobar is using her to gain access to me. Is it possible Escobar killed Dane?"

Jon's fingers hovered over the keyboard, unmoving. "You think his death wasn't an accident?"

"How many times in our business do we have real coincidences?"

He inclined his head. "Never. Everything is connected."

"Exactly. Dane was a skilled driver. He used to drive stock cars before he joined the DEA, had driven since he was a kid on the race tracks. I don't believe he lost control of his car."

"Seems unlikely. Might be helpful to examine his car."

"I'll call Taylor, see if he can locate the car." Adam stood. "May I use one of the bedrooms for a minute?"

Claire pointed to the room on the left of the suite. "Tell Cal I said hello."

He closed the door behind him and called the detective. "I need some information."

"Shoot."

"I want a look at Dane Carver's wrecked vehicle."

"Why?"

"The DEA agent used to be a race car driver. Seems unlikely that he would lose control of his car."

"Accidents do happen."

"Sure. This man is connected to Veronica and several people connected to her have been hurt or killed in the last few days. You want to tell me that's a coincidence?"

"Something else happened since Norton's attack?"

Adam explained about R.J.

Taylor whistled softly. "Give me a second. How's your girlfriend?"

He gave a quick update, then said, "She's incredible."

"Planning to keep her?"

A snort. "My Nana didn't raise a fool."

A burst of laughter. "Good. Looks like Carver's white Tahoe is at the towing company's yard. You want me to check it out or clear the way for you and your girl?"

"You have enough going on. Besides, I'd like to see the Tahoe myself."

"I'll take care of it tomorrow first thing." He shared the name and address of the towing company, then said, "Be careful, man. Everybody around your girl has a target on their backs. I'd hate to learn from Maddox that you were another casualty of this hunt."

## CHAPTER TWENTY-SEVEN

Veronica studied Risa's house, at least what she could see in the dim light. White siding, dark shutters, beautiful landscaping. A sweet setup, like Risa. Or more what she thought Risa was like.

She couldn't believe Dane's assistant tried to ruin her career and perhaps kill her and her friends. And maybe Veronica's ability to read people wasn't as good as she thought.

"Ready?" Adam asked, his hand outstretched.

"Let's do this." She laced their fingers together and walked with him to Risa's door. Veronica glanced at their entwined hands. She had always felt she didn't need a man, especially after her less than ideal childhood. She didn't need Adam, either, but she liked being with him, particularly liked how they were together, a great team on the job and off. She pressed the bell.

A minute later, the locks disengaged and the door swung open to reveal the brunette with a surprised smile who worked at Dane's side for years. Was this sweet face the face of a killer?

"Veronica! I didn't know you were back. What are you doing here?" Risa's gaze shifted to Adam. She took an involuntary step backward. "Who is this?"

"My boyfriend, Adam. This is Risa Shoemaker, the woman who keeps us on track."

The other woman shook Adam's hand. "Please come in. I suppose you want to ask me questions, Veronica." She closed the door behind them. "Let's go to the kitchen. I'll make coffee."

"Don't go to trouble on our account," Adam said.

"It's not a problem. I could use something warm. All this craziness surrounding the office is frightening. I'm not like the agents I work with. I don't know how to handle what's happening." Risa led them to the quaint farmhouse-style kitchen where she measured coffee and water, and turned on the coffee maker. "I want to hide and forget any of this happened, pretend Dane is on an extended assignment somewhere. But I can't. Things will never be the same without him."

"Risa, what do you know about Dane's death?"

She sat at the table and waved them to two chairs across from her. "Not much. The police said it was an accident, that Dane lost control of his SUV."

"Didn't you think that was strange?" Veronica leaned her forearms on the table. "Dane was an excellent driver."

"It was odd, but accidents happen to the best drivers. Maybe someone cut him off or he swerved to miss an animal that darted into the street."

An easy explanation that just didn't fit the man Veronica had known for five years. "Do you really believe that?"

Unease settled on Risa's face. "You don't?"

"Dane used to be a professional race car driver."

"I didn't know about the race car driving. Dane didn't share much about his past."

Protecting his privacy and Cissy's was a top priority for Veronica's handler. He had been afraid a misstep on his part would lead enemies straight to his wife.

"How long have you been back, Veronica? Did you hear about Carol?"

"We saw her SUV explode."

Shock filled the other woman's gaze. "Were you hurt?"

Veronica shook her head. "Adam and I weren't injured. We drove Carol to the hospital."

"That was you? Good job. With Dane gone, losing someone else in the office would have been awful."

Risa poured coffee into three mugs, then carried them to the table on a small tray. "I have cookies, too."

"The coffee is fine, Risa. Thank you for the offer, though." Veronica sipped the drink. "Did you hear what happened to Graham?"

Dane's assistant set her mug down with a thud. "He's all right, isn't he?"

Veronica thought about Risa's reaction. Fear, almost panic at the possibility that Graham was dead, too. Perhaps Risa had more than a passing interest in the DEA agent.

"He's fine," Adam assured her. "Someone tried to kill him. A team of ten men came after him early this morning."

"Are you sure he's okay?"

"Positive. You can call him to confirm."

"I will. What's happening, Veronica? I don't understand why there have been so many attacks on our people."

"They're not the only ones. I was taken prisoner in Mexico by the cartel I was sent to track."

Risa's face blanched. "Are you all right? Did they hurt you?" She winced, held up her hand. "Never mind. Of course they hurt you. I know enough from listening to you and the others talk how vicious and cruel they treat their prisoners. How did you escape?"

She and Adam had talked over their strategy on the way to Risa's. Even though she had objected to Adam exposing himself to more danger, he'd insisted she use his name in their discussion with Risa. "Adam rescued me."

Brow furrowed, Risa asked, "Are you from another DEA office?"

"I'm with Fortress Security, Risa."

"How did you know she was in trouble? None of us knew where Veronica was and with Dane dead there was no way to find out."

"Dane sent a message through a friend to Fortress. That friend is now dead, too."

She moaned. "I don't understand what's happening." A pause. "Wait. I'm glad to know all this information, but why did you come to me?"

"Someone framed me as a mole in our office, Risa. Dane had emails showing supposed proof of my guilt."

"That's crazy! You're not a traitor. No one would believe that."

Although it felt good to hear someone else believed her innocent, Risa's support wouldn't be enough to regain her badge and weapon. "Forrest does. He took my badge and weapon, Risa. I want them back." If she resigned from the DEA, she wanted to walk away on her own terms. "To do that, I have to find out who's doing this and why."

"How can I help? We need you, Veronica, especially now."

How did she accuse a woman she'd worked with for years of being a traitor? She glanced at Adam.

He covered Veronica's hand with his, squeezed. "Risa, a friend of mine traced the emails about Veronica to you."

Risa's jaw dropped. "Me? I would never do that. I have no reason to hurt Veronica." She turned her gaze toward Veronica. "You believe me, don't you?"

"I want to, but there's no question the information came from you."

"It wasn't me."

"Do you have visitors at work?" Adam asked.

"Well, sure. Not many. A friend or two stops by occasionally for lunch."

"No family."

"Never."

Not surprising given her family background. "Who visited you after I left for Mexico?" Veronica cupped the coffee mug between her palms. The timing fit because the emails were sent right after she left.

Risa's cheeks turned pink. "My boyfriend."

"I didn't know you were dating anyone."

"We've been together a few weeks."

"Raul Escobar."

She frowned. "How do you know Raul's name?"

"We're investigating everyone connected to Veronica," Adam said. He pulled out his phone, tapped the screen, then turned it around so she could see the picture. "This is what we learned about your boyfriend."

She stared. "Who is that woman with Raul?"

Veronica reached over and covered Risa's hand. "His wife, Maria Elena."

Risa jerked her hand free and covered her face. "No. You're lying. Why are you trying to hurt me?"

"Risa," Adam said, his voice soft. "Look at me."

She raised her tear-drenched gaze to his.

"I know this is hard to hear. Fortress computer experts did two separate searches. There's no doubt. Raul is married and has four children."

"Why did he lie to me?" Tears streaked down her face.

"He used you, Risa," Veronica said, hurting for the other woman. "That's his loss. You're a special woman, one any smart man would be happy to have in his life."

"Yeah?" Risa uttered a watery laugh. "Why haven't I met this smart man, then?"

"Maybe you have."

"Who?"

"Graham."

She shook her head. "He's hung up on you."

Noticed that, did she? "He's not the man for me. He's known that for a while." And he might be more aware of Dane's assistant now that Veronica had made it clear she wasn't interested in him. Especially after she nudged him in Risa's direction. Now that she considered it, they would be great together.

"Risa, was Raul alone in your office for any reason?" Adam asked.

She started to shake her head, stopped. "Wait. I had to take a package down the hall. The mail guy dropped it off in the wrong office. Raul waited for me at my desk. He said he had a phone call to make."

"So he had access to your computer. How long were you gone?"

"Maybe fifteen minutes. The package was for a lady who doesn't know how to have a short conversation."

"Did you log off your computer before you left?"

"I always do when I leave the office. It's habit."

"Do you have your password written down?"

She hung her head. "I have to change passwords every two weeks. I kept forgetting the new one."

"Where do you keep it?"

"Taped to the bottom of the mouse pad."

Adam glanced at Veronica. "Raul would have had time to find it, log into prepared dummy accounts, and send the emails from Risa's computer. Five, ten minutes at the most."

"But why would he do this?" Risa asked. "Why make me look like a whistleblower?"

"This isn't about you, Risa." Adam set aside his empty coffee mug. "It's about me."

"You know him?"

He shook his head. "I've never met him. However, I worked undercover in Belize to bring down Peter Collins."

"He's head of a drug cartel."

"He was. He's dead. Collins found out I was a plant and tortured me for information. He would have killed me if Veronica hadn't given Fortress my location. They saved my life with her help."

"What does that have to do with Raul?"

"He worked for Collins and now is employed by the drug lord's daughter, a woman who wants revenge for my role in bringing down her father. Raul wanted information on me. Collins never knew my real name. Somehow, word leaked that Veronica had a hand in my rescue. That's why she was kidnapped and interrogated for information on me."

Risa turned her stricken gaze on Veronica. "It's my fault. I'm the reason you were hurt. Veronica, I'm so sorry. I never meant for that to happen."

"Pillow talk, Risa?"

"I didn't use your name or Adam's. I swear. I just thought you did such a good thing by helping an American in trouble."

"Did you volunteer the information or did Raul ask you specifically about the situation?"

"He said he heard agents discussing an operation in Belize to rescue a missing American. He pressed for names, but I know better than to talk specifics."

"Vonnie?"

"I don't see how that's possible, Adam. I wasn't under DEA orders to hunt for information on your location. I stumbled across it by accident. That's when I contacted R.J."

"We had a leak at Fortress during that time, but I know my real name didn't get out because Collins was still using my undercover name during the interrogations."

Veronica was silent while she worked through the possibilities. "R.J. He knew I was the one who located you. Perhaps he talked too freely about my role and word leaked."

"Is it possible Carol or Graham talked?"

Oh, man. That would be the most simple explanation. "They both knew. Maybe they mentioned the information and the secret landed in the wrong hands."

"I want to help," Risa said. "I brought a snake into our lives."

"Can you contact Raul?" Adam asked.

"Of course. I have his cell number."

"Call him. See if he'll come here. We want to talk to him."

"As long as I have a chance to tell him how despicable he is."

"I'll make sure you have the opportunity."

Thirty minutes later, Risa's doorbell rang.

## CHAPTER TWENTY-EIGHT

Risa stepped back to admit Raul to her house. From the shadowed hallway, Adam watched the dark-haired, dark-skinned man enter the living room and sweep Risa into a tight hug. He frowned when she turned her head away from his kiss.

"What's going on, babe? You sounded upset on the phone."

"I am. Sit down, Raul." She waved him to the couch, sitting so he turned his back to the hall.

Perfect. Adam and Veronica eased from the shadows, weapons drawn, waiting.

"Why are you sitting over there? Are you mad at me?"

"You could say that. Why did you do it?"

"Do what?"

"Why did you use me to hurt Veronica?"

He stiffened. "What did you say?"

"You sent emails to Dane, framing Veronica as a traitor. You made it appear as though I sent them. I would never hurt Veronica like that. She wouldn't turn on the agency or her friends. It was you."

"Honey, who has been feeding you lies about me? I'll talk to them, straighten things out."

"Not lies, the truth. How could you do that to me? I thought I meant something to you."

A harsh laugh exploded from Raul, the sound conveying his disdain. "A weak woman like you? Not likely."

Hurt followed quickly by anger crossed her face. "You admit to sabotaging Veronica?"

"Sure. You won't live long enough to tell anyone."

At those words, Risa smiled. "I think they might have something to say about that."

He snorted. "You think I'd fall for that old trick? You really are a fool, Risa. I'll be glad to stop wasting my time with you."

Adam pressed the barrel of his Sig against the back of Raul's head. "Hands up, nice and slow."

Raul froze. "Who are you?"

"The man you've been searching for." He pressed the gun harder. "Hands, Raul. I won't tell you again."

He slowly raised his empty hands. "Now what?"

"Lock your hands behind your head and stand up."

"You will regret this."

"Not nearly as much as you will."

Veronica rounded the back of the couch, weapon aimed at Raul, placing her body in front of Risa's. "You can leave now, Risa. Go out the back door."

The other woman glanced back with her hand on the knob.

Raul scowled at Risa with hatred in his eyes. "You set me up," he said, his voice just above a growl. "I won't forget your betrayal. Be watching for me, baby. I'll be back for you."

"Go, Risa," Veronica said. "No detours."

"Are you sure he won't mind?"

"I cleared it with him. He's expecting you."

A moment later, she was gone, headed to Graham Norton's place where he would keep her safe.

Adam zip tied Raul's hands together. "Into the kitchen."

"Planning to feed me?"

"Move." He shoved the thug into a chair in the center of the kitchen and secured him with more zip ties and duct tape. The thug wouldn't get free unless he had help or a knife. He didn't have either.

"Hey, man, I need to use the restroom. Untie me."

"Too bad."

"That's cruel."

"Ask me if I care."

"What do you want from me?"

"Information."

A snort. "You're out of luck. I ain't talking. Who are you?"

"Adam Walker."

All expression vanished from Raul's face.

Adam smiled. "I'm flattered. You recognize my name."

"You're a dead man."

"Not even close. As you can see, your boss didn't manage to kill me and you won't be that lucky." A knock sounded at the front door. Adam flicked a glance at Veronica. "Watch this clown." He would have sent her to the door, but she didn't know Curt Jackson.

"Leaving me with your woman?" taunted Raul. "Not smart. I'll kill her before you return."

"If you believe that, you're more stupid than I thought." Veronica would gut him before the arrogant man had a chance to lay a hand on her. His woman was as tough as they came.

He checked the peephole. "Thanks for coming, Curt." Adam could interrogate Raul. He'd done enough of it in the field, but Curt had better training in the art and was more effective. Adam wanted fast results.

"No problem. Where's our boy?"

"Kitchen. Veronica is watching him."

Curt paused, glanced back over his shoulder. "Veronica Miles is here?"

Adam raised an eyebrow as he stared at his friend.

"What? That woman is legendary in our circles."

"Yeah, she is. She's also mine." Good grief. He would be beating his chest like Tarzan before long. If Veronica heard him claim her in that way, she might take him down a notch or two herself. She was more than capable of doing the job.

Curt held up his hands. "Sorry, bro. I've looked forward to meeting her." He followed Adam into the well-lit kitchen where Veronica had closed the blinds.

By the time Curt walked into the kitchen, his entire facial expression changed. Coupled with the thousand-yard stare he had down pat, his cold demeanor sent chills down Adam's spine, maybe because he knew Curt's capabilities.

Raul's face lost every trace of color at the sight of Curt Jackson. Guess it wasn't Adam's inside knowledge. Old Raul was a thug, no match for a professionally trained interrogator.

"Raul says he won't answer our questions," Veronica said.

Curt smiled. "We'll see. The information you want is still the same?" he asked Adam.

"Copy that."

He slid his gaze to Veronica, gave her a genuine smile before saying, "You should wait in the other room or, better yet, outside."

Her jaw dropped. "Why?"

"Deniability. You can't tell what you don't know."

She was silent a moment, then left the room.

As soon as she was clear, Adam grabbed a chair, turned it around backwards, and draped his arms across the back. "Last chance, Raul."

The man spit at him.

Curt circled around behind Raul, nodded at Adam.

"Who sent you, Raul?" He already knew, but wanted confirmation.

No response.

The operative behind Raul lifted his hands and pressed against a sensitive pressure point. Raul gasped, his eyes widening. He clenched his jaw, fighting to squash his response to the pain.

Waste of time. Curt would increase the pressure, raising the pain to an excruciating level.

"Answer the question and the pain stops," Curt murmured.

Raul's response was a vile curse.

The operative shifted slightly. A moan escaped the restrained man, sweat beading on his forehead. His skin blanched as Curt increased the pressure on the nerve. "Be smart, Raul."

A jerky shake of Raul's head. He tried to get away from Curt's hands, couldn't because of Adam's tape job. Ah, the wonder of duct tape. All Fortress operatives carried rolls of the stuff. They found the tape useful. One of their operatives even duct taped his shoulder wound until he could seek medical help.

Adam rose, grabbed his mug and poured another round of coffee for himself. Returning to his seat, he took a couple of sips. "Save yourself some pain, man. I already know the name. I want confirmation."

"Yeah?" Raul's lip curled. "Prove it."

"Collins."

"Peter Collins is dead."

"His daughter isn't."

The thug's gaze dropped. "She's a pampered princess. You ought to know that. You worked for the old man long enough."

He was lying. "Thanks for the confirmation."

"I didn't say anything."

"You didn't have to. Let's move on to something more interesting." Adam set aside his coffee. He hoped Veronica was far enough away that she wouldn't hear the next part. He wanted to live long enough to marry her. "Who hurt my woman?"

"I don't know your old lady."

Curt shifted slightly. Raul screamed in pain. When he fell silent, Curt murmured, "Answer the question."

"You answer a question," he spat out. "Who is your woman?"

"Veronica. She was captured and tortured for days on Collins' orders. I want the name of the man who hurt my woman."

"I don't know. I've been in the U.S. for months."

Adam shook his head. "You're making this harder on yourself, Raul. It's not necessary. You really want to suffer for an organization that won't lift a finger to help you?"

Another curse from their captive.

"I want the interrogator's name." He stared at the thug. "I'll learn that name no matter what I have to do to get it, including going after your family."

Raul scowled, trying to brazen his way out. His eyes gave him away. "You lie."

"Your family lives in Belize, about two miles from the Collins compound. You have four children. Two beautiful little girls, two handsome boys. Your wife, Maria Elena, is a great mom who will soon be a widow if you don't tell me the name of the man who hurt my girlfriend."

Another increase in the pain level had Raul screaming again, then sobbing as he squirmed, trying to relieve the pressure and pain.

Adam signaled Curt to ease up, knowing the nerves would throb and ache, a constant reminder of what he'd endured and might yet experience again. "Tell me his name and the pain stops."

"He'll kill me."

Satisfaction filled Adam. So this clown did know Interrogator's name. "I'll kill you if you don't. She's mine to protect. He signed his own death warrant. If I get to him first, you won't have to worry about him coming after you."

"Will you come after me?"

Adam just smiled. "Name."

He remained silent.

Curt lightly touched his back.

Immediately, Raul tensed up. "No, don't."

"Name," Adam repeated.

"Tony Silverman. He's the interrogator Collins kept on retainer."

"Why should I believe you, Raul? I never heard this man's name mentioned while I was in Belize."

"No one knew his name."

"How did you find out? You're not second in command at the organization."

"Lilah's husband knew. He's been part of the organization for years, in charge of the west coast operations. He was hand-picked by the old man to marry his daughter."

"So who's in charge of the organization? Lilah or her husband?"

"They both are. She's the public face of business with the Collins Foundation while he runs the rest. But Lilah has as much say about her old man's other business as her husband."

"What about Los Diablos? What's their connection to the Collins organization?"

"We have a deal with Los Diablos. They are our sole distributors."

"So you found out Veronica would be in Mexico and sent Los Diablos after her." Adam's soft voice caused the other man to flinch.

"I was doing my job. She's connected to you. The boss wants you found and brought back to Belize."

He smiled. "I'm going to make your job easy, Raul. I'm going to go to Belize and take care of unfinished business."

"What about me?"

"You will be my guest for a while." While Adam texted Zane, Curt filled a hypodermic needle with a drug to knock out Raul.

"What are you doing?" Raul fought against the duct tape and zip ties. "Don't kill me. I told you what you wanted to know." By the last word, the thug was screeching.

Curt administered the drug and within seconds, the thug was unconscious.

"Did you kill him?" Veronica hurried into the kitchen, her gaze locked on Raul.

"No, ma'am. He's taking a nap." He smiled, held out his hand. "Curt Jackson. It's nice to meet you, Veronica."

"You're with Fortress?"

He nodded. "I've been helping Jake Davenport protect your friend, Carol."

"How is she?"

"From what I understand, she might go home in a few days. Of course, her activity level will be restricted for a while. Jake says she's doing great."

"Thank goodness." She eyed Raul again. "What will we do with him? We can't turn him loose. He'll run to Lilah Collins."

"Zane is sending two operatives to pick him up." Adam dropped a light kiss on her mouth.

"What will they do with him?"

"Take him to a black site and encourage him to spill his guts about everything while they record it. That along with the documents Zane and Jon will provide proving you were framed will get your job back if you want it."

Relief flooded her face. "Let's take care of Lilah Collins and her crew, including the interrogator. I'm sure you plan to protect your woman from future pain."

Adam's cheeks burned as Curt laughed. When Veronica smiled at Adam and winked, he tapped her nose. "Very funny, Miles. Once we take care of the Collins organization, I imagine there are government agencies who would like to chat with him. According to Zane, Raul is associated with several crimes here and abroad. You and Risa don't have to worry about him anymore."

"I'm more concerned for Risa than for me."

When the operatives arrived, they covered Raul with a blanket, carried him to their SUV, and tossed him in the cargo area. Curt returned to the hospital. Veronica called Graham and told him Risa could return home, that she was safe.

That done, Adam held out his hand to Veronica. "Let's go back to the hotel and get some sleep. In the morning, we have a mission to plan."

## CHAPTER TWENTY-NINE

Adam walked with Veronica, Remy, and Lily into the Fortress conference room and pulled up short when he saw the center of the table piled high with breakfast food. A table at the far side of the room held several kinds of juice, coffee, water, and sodas. "What's this?"

Maddox turned, waved them to the plates. "Help yourselves. We have a lot of work to do."

"You have enough food to feed an army."

"The Shadow unit is joining us. Nico made it a point to tell me they were coming hungry."

"That's because we just got off the plane," Nico said as he walked into the conference room followed by his teammates. "You didn't give us a chance to go home and freshen up before we came here."

"Load your plates and sit. Durango is joining us via video conference any minute."

"Why are so many people involved in this meeting?" Veronica asked.

"We're going to take down Los Diablos first, then go after the Collins organization." Maddox's gaze swept over all of them. "By the time we're finished with both groups this time, there won't be anything left but ashes. No chance of a resurgence."

"Please tell me you didn't start without us." Eli Wolfe walked in with his partner, Jon. "Claire threatened to stalk us with her camera if we dared order any food in the suite this morning."

Adam scowled. "Who is with my sister?" He would personally knock heads together if the SEALs left his sister unprotected.

"Kill the death glare, Walker. She came in with Zane. They'll be here soon."

"Load your plates and sit," Maddox said. "Durango will be joining us when Zane arrives."

"I'm here." The Fortress tech guru rolled into the room and set up at the end of the table with the comm system and his computer with frequent glances toward the door.

"Is Claire okay?" Adam asked, concern tightening his gut. Normally, she was with Zane if they were in the same vicinity. For some reason, his sister was nuts about the frog boy.

"She'll be along."

Zane didn't look too worried so she must be all right. Still didn't make Adam feel better. He wanted to see that his sister was doing fine with his own eyes.

A couple minutes later, Zane said, "Durango is ready." An image of each member of Durango filled the screens on the wall.

"Why didn't you invite us down?" Quinn Gallagher asked. "You must be getting soft, boss. I don't remember you putting out that kind of spread for us when we were in town. I thought we were your favorite team."

The other operatives in the room hurled various insults at Gallagher.

Maddox grinned and, in a lull, said, "There is an excellent reason for this spread, but you have to wait until one more person arrives for an explanation."

"Now you have my curiosity raised," Josh Cahill said, the Delta unit's leader.

"You can wait with the rest of them." He glanced toward the door. "Here's the woman I've been waiting for." Maddox swept Claire into a hug. "All right, sugar, the floor is yours."

So that's what the spread was for. A celebration of Claire's pregnancy. Adam relaxed deeper into his chair.

"Hi, guys," Claire said to the Durango team.

"Claire, it's great to see you," Rio Kincaid, the team medic, said with a smile. "How's Z treating you?"

"Like I'm a princess."

"He better if he knows what's good for him." The quiet words came from Alex Morgan, Durango's sniper. He was one of the best shooter's Adam had worked with.

"If he slips up, let us know. We'll pay him a visit." Nate Armstrong's Cajun drawl was distinctive. The EOD man was in a class of his own.

"Sweetheart, tell them the news before they hatch a plot to teach me a lesson," Zane said.

"Brent was kind enough to let me hijack your meeting for a minute so I could tell you all at one time that Zane and I are going to have a baby."

Cheers broke out in the conference room and in the meeting room in Otter Creek where Durango was based.

"Congratulations to both of you," Josh said after the pandemonium died down.

"Thank you." Claire smiled. "I'm leaving now. My stomach isn't settled enough to tolerate the smell of food this early in the day."

"My sister, Serena, drank chamomile mint tea or Coke when she was pregnant with Lucas. She said those were the only things that worked for her when she had morning sickness."

"I'll try those." She cupped Zane's face and kissed him, then waved at the others as she left the conference room in a hurry.

Zane's face reflected his worry. "Maybe I should go after her. If she's sick, she might need help."

Sam, Shadow unit's medic, set her plate on the table. "I'll go. The boss needs you more than me right now."

The members of Durango took turns razzing Zane while the others in the conference room filled their plates and settled around the table. Adam handed Zane a plate. "Need your strength, Z. I doubt Claire will let pregnancy slow her down any."

His brother-in-law sighed. "That's what I'm afraid of. I might need to attach a turbo booster to my chair to keep up with her."

"Let's get started," Maddox said.

"Do you have permission to treat this as a mission?" Adam asked.

His boss slid him a look. "What do you think?"

That's what he figured. Brent Maddox was persuasive, especially when defending his people. The boss hadn't forgotten what Adam went through the year before or what Veronica had endured to protect him. "Objective?"

"Government will be arranging cleanup. Our job is to capture or eliminate the leaders, and destroy the organizations. The president wants the flow of Los Diablos' fentanyl into the U.S. stopped."

Beside Adam, Veronica started. "The President of the United States is your employer?"

"In this instance. Of course, you don't know that."

She held up her hand. "I didn't hear a thing about President Martin."

"Adam, bring everyone up to speed," Maddox said.

He gave a rundown of events without interruptions. Once he finished, the questions began.

"We're in," Cahill said. "St. Claire's team is in place here at PSI. They'll cover in our absence. What do you need from us?"

For the next few hours, the group studied maps of the target areas and diagrams of the buildings. "Pack heavy," Maddox said as they were wrapping up. "Fortress doesn't have any friends in the Chihuahua province. We'll take two planes. Josh, does PSI have a two teams ready for low-level field work?"

"Yes, sir. What did you have in mind?"

"We'll leave part of our equipment on the planes. I need one team with each plane to guard our gear and transportation."

Cahill leaned closer to the monitor. "You're going, sir?"

"You think I'd let you have all the fun? The four teams will operate with their own leaders. Someone has to coordinate the efforts of the teams and pick up the slack. That's my role. One other thing. We need to take care of business in the next 72 hours and get back here. My daughter has a karate tournament. If I miss it, all of you will be explaining to Alexa why her father missed her first match."

Nico flinched. "We'll get you back in time, boss. No one wants to upset that little charmer."

A nod, then Maddox turned back to the screens. "Josh, the plane will be wheels down in Knoxville in an hour. Be ready to move. We'll rendezvous at the airport here."

"Copy that." The screen went black.

"Nico," Maddox said. "Restock your equipment from the vault. Sam, raid the clinic for medical supplies. Be prepared for anything. We leave for the airport in two hours." He turned to Adam. "You need a team to work with on this op. Choose your people, Adam."

That was easy enough. He'd already decided who he wanted for his permanent team. "Vonnie, Remy, Lily, and Jake Davenport."

"Good. Eli?"

"Jon, Curt Jackson, you, and Fox Montgomery."

Nice, Adam thought. That team rocked. No one stood a chance against them. "We need Carol Rossi, Graham Norton, Cissy Carver, and Risa Shoemaker covered while we're gone." He had commandeered Carol's bodyguards for his own team and didn't want to leave Veronica's friends vulnerable.

"I'll assign bodyguards for each except for Cissy Carver. I got word this morning the DEA has relocated her to a safe house along with a doctor. By the time we return, the danger will be eliminated." Maddox eyed the Doucets, Jon, and Eli. "I need to speak to Veronica a moment."

The four operatives left the room, leaving Maddox with Adam and Veronica. Adam was prepared to dig in his heels if his boss asked him to leave the room as well.

"Veronica, once this mission is complete, the president will ask for a briefing during which there's a good chance he'll ask about the personnel involved. This is your last opportunity to back out. No one will think less of you for protecting your badge."

"I'm going with you."

"Are you sure? We aren't bound by the same rules you are. We'll capture if we can. If not, our orders are to eliminate the threat and we won't think twice before we pull the trigger to protect our people."

"I know."

"Do you?" Maddox tilted his head. "You should also know I would choose those options whether or not this op was sanctioned. No one goes after my people without consequences."

"I understand, sir."

"I hope so because when the DEA finds out you're involved in this mission, they will make an issue of it. While the president will grant you immunity for anything you have to do during the course of this mission, your agency won't be as forgiving. You may lose your badge permanently, Veronica. Can you live with that?"

"I appreciate your concern. I want to finish what I started." She glanced at Adam, then focused again on Maddox. "No matter what it costs me, I'll have Adam's back."

"Why are you so insistent on protecting him? Adam is highly trained and he'll have a top-notch team at his back. Why you?"

She raised her chin, stared straight at Maddox. "I'm in love with him. Nothing matters more to me than his safety."

Adam twisted in his seat. Had he imagined the words that he longed to hear? "What did you say?"

"I love you, Adam Walker."

He barely heard Maddox leave the conference room, his attention focused on Veronica. Adam cupped her face between his palms. "Say it again," he demanded.

A small smile curved her lips. "I love you."

"You don't know how happy I am to hear those words." He pressed his lips to hers in a feverish kiss. Adam thought his heart would leap out of his chest. "I love you, Veronica Miles."

She wrapped her arms around his neck. "I hope it's not too soon to tell you how I feel. I wanted to tell you the truth before we left for Mexico since I preferred not to bare my heart on a plane full of mercenaries with big ears and a penchant for in-house gossip."

"Are you sure, Vonnie?"

She blinked. "Why wouldn't I be?"

"Are you sure about taking a chance on a permanent relationship with me? I'm not ready to stay stateside. That time will come, but not now."

"I'm not ready to be stateside, either. Can you handle the fact I'll be in the line of fire?"

"I hate that you might walk into a hail of bullets. You have skills. I trust you and your training." His lips curved. "I'd trust your training more if you were trained by Fortress."

"Is that possible?"

"If you sign on with us, absolutely. In fact, Maddox will insist on it, although the training course is shortened since you have law enforcement experience."

"What would you do during those weeks?"

"Come with you. Our team would train with you as a unit."

"Team?" She leaned back. "I didn't think you had a team."

"If they agree to sign on with me, I want to work with Remy, Lily, and Jake."

Veronica grinned. "I was hoping you'd choose them."

"Are you resigning from the DEA?"

"Would you mind?"

"I can't think of anything better than working with you."

"Will Maddox ask me?"

"Let's find out. Maddox," he called out.

His boss opened the door and stepped inside the conference room with a manila folder in his hand. "You have questions for me?"

"One. Are you offering Vonnie a job?"

"I am." Maddox named a salary that made Veronica's jaw drop.

"Are you serious? That's four times what I make at the DEA."

"One of the perks of going private. But that's not why you're considering the job, is it?"

"No, sir. I can't trust my own people to have my back, no matter how much Forrest spreads the word that I'm cleared. Most of all, I don't want to be assigned to ops out of the country for months at a time. I want to build a life with Adam."

"I understand. Adam is the team leader. I assume you'll want to work with him. Will you have a problem following his orders on a mission?"

"No." No hesitation.

"If you want the job, Veronica, it's yours." Maddox opened the folder and pulled out a document. "Sign here and you become one of mine. If you sign, you need to resign your DEA position before we leave for Mexico." He pulled out a pen and slid it to her.

With another glance at Adam, Veronica took a deep breath and signed her name with a flourish. "I need access to a computer for a couple minutes."

Maddox circled the table and logged into the computer. "Use this one." He moved away while she typed out a quick message, then pressed send.

"Done."

Adam's boss grinned, held out his hand. "Welcome to Fortress, Veronica Miles."

## CHAPTER THIRTY

Veronica hefted her new Go bag over her shoulder with a grunt. The rest of the operatives made the bags look light the way they moved them around without effort. She had to remember she was still recovering from Silverman's torture. In fact, Sam had removed her stitches just minutes earlier and pronounced her healed with a few scars to remind her of the ordeal.

She mentally shrugged. She wouldn't see them. Besides, what were a few more scars? At least these had been earned protecting the man who now held her heart in his hands. That he loved her after such a short time astonished Veronica. Then again, both of them had been in the background of each other's lives for a year. Maybe their feelings weren't so surprising.

Either way, she was grateful her feelings were reciprocated. Confessing her love for Adam would have been mortifying if he hadn't felt the same. Maddox had probably suspected. Why else would he push her to tell why she was willing to sacrifice her career for Adam?

She slid a look at the operative who walked beside her. "Do I get my own rocket-propelled grenade now?"

He laughed, his eyes twinkling. "I already slipped one into your bag, Vonnie."

"Sweet."

"Yeah, it is, but I hope I don't have to teach you how to use it on the run."

"Ha. We're Fortress. We don't run."

"She learns fast," Remy said with a smile.

Adam glanced at the other operative. "Maddox wants to form a new team. You interested?"

The Cajun eyed him a moment. "Depends. Who's the team leader?"

Oh, boy. Veronica looked from Remy to Adam. Did Remy want to lead his own team? He didn't seem to mind following Adam's lead when they were at Graham's house. In fact, he appeared low key about everything. Maybe she misread him. Easy enough to do since she had only known the Doucets for a few days.

"I am," Adam said.

"Lily and I come as a package deal."

"I didn't expect otherwise. I want the package."

Remy looked at his wife. When she smiled, he turned back to Adam. "We're in."

"Yes!" Veronica grinned. "Working with you will be fun."

"Wait. You're working with Fortress?" Lily asked.

"I signed the papers with Fortress and resigned from the DEA an hour ago."

"That's great news. Who's the fifth member of the team, Adam?"

"Jake Davenport if he agrees."

"Good choice. Jake's a great medic and a crack shot." Remy put his bag and Lily's into the back of his SUV, then reached out a hand to take Veronica's bag. "Here he comes now." He inclined his head toward the truck turning into the parking garage beneath Fortress headquarters.

Jake parked a short distance away. "Sorry I'm late. Got caught in traffic on I-65. There's always an accident or construction going on." He jogged over with two bags in hand, already dressed in what Veronica realized was the standard Fortress work uniform, black cargoes, black shirt, and boots, a uniform she was also wearing for the first time.

Veronica tilted her head. "Why do you have two bags?" she asked the medic.

He patted the larger of the two bags. "Mike bag with medical supplies. The other is my Go bag." Jake stored his gear in the back with the other bags. "Where are we headed?"

"Climb in," Adam said. "We'll talk on the way."

Before Adam started his explanation, Veronica turned to the medic. "How is Carol?"

"Great, but worried about your safety."

She sighed, relieved to hear the agent was improving. "Carol is a good friend." One Veronica would miss working with.

"She says the same about you. So, Adam, what's the mission?"

Adam gave Jake the short version of the upcoming operation.

A soft whistle from the medic. "Ambitious. How many teams are we taking?"

"Four on the ground. Two with the planes." He spent the travel time to the airport relaying details. "When we're airborne, I'll show you the schematics. Jake, Maddox wants me to form a new team. Remy, Lily, and Vonnie have already agreed to sign on with me. I'd like you to be our team medic. Think about it while we're on this op. Let me know after we return."

Jake smiled. "Don't have to think about it. I would be honored to work with all of you."

"I'll let Maddox know we're officially a team. Expect training time in Otter Creek as a team while Veronica takes the short training course for operatives."

"Oh, man." Lily sighed. "The only good thing about going to PSI is visiting with our friends. Durango and St. Claire's team are tough task masters. They are going to run us ragged."

"Look at it this way," Remy said. "At least you'll have Nate cooking for you."

She brightened. "That's right. Veronica, you'll love the food. Nate is a professional chef."

Definitely beyond anything the DEA provided. "Please, call me Vonnie."

Remy parked in a section of the airport parking lot reserved for Fortress. They exited the vehicle as another Lear jet landed and taxied their direction. "Durango and the PSI trainees are right on time."

"What does PSI stand for?" Veronica asked.

"Personal Security International. It's the Fortress bodyguard training center. We also conduct search and rescue training on site, including K-9 teams."

Good grief. Maddox covered it all. No wonder he was constantly hiring new operatives.

While the jets refueled and the pilots went through their pre-flight routine, one of the PSI teams relocated to the second jet and the rest of the teams boarded their respective planes. In less than an hour, Veronica found herself strapped into a seat beside Adam across from Remy, Lily, and Jake as the plane barreled down the runway.

After the jet was airborne, Adam went over the schematics and maps with Jake. When the medic learned what he needed to know, Adam said to his team, "Take advantage of the flight time to sleep."

That's when Veronica realized the other two teams were already asleep, except for Jon Smith who worked on his computer. Wasn't he comfortable sleeping in close quarters with his co-workers? She leaned close to Adam and whispered in his ear. "Does Jon ever sleep while flying?"

"He will catnap if Eli is awake to keep watch. In three hours, he'll wake Eli, then sleep a few hours himself." He reached overhead and grabbed a couple pillows and blankets, handed one of each to Veronica. "Try to rest. The next three days will be fast and hard."

Although she thought the effort would be fruitless, she reclined her seat, but she was too keyed up to sleep. Maybe there was a book on board that she could read while the others slept.

"Come here," Adam murmured. He turned and wrapped his arms around her so she was able to rest her head on his chest.

The next thing Veronica knew, Adam nudged her to tell her they were about to land in Mexico. She sat up, stretched. Incredible. She'd thought sleep would be impossible. Apparently all she needed was for Adam to hold her.

The plane landed on a private airstrip. The operatives on the four mobile teams grabbed their gear and exited the plane. Four Suburbans were parked in the grass at the end of the tarmac. Two men stood in the shadows of the trees, waiting. One of the men lifted a hand to Maddox in silent greeting.

The Fortress CEO strode across the distance and shook hands with the men. After a short conversation, the strangers disappeared into the trees and Maddox returned. He addressed the four teams. "Keys are in the ignitions. We leave at ten-minute intervals to avoid attracting unwanted attention. Check in when you reach your assigned coordinates. We'll take down the four targets at one time.

We don't want Los Diablos to have any warning. If they get wind they're under attack, they'll scatter and be that much harder to take down. I'd rather use the Shadow unit for other operations than ferreting out the remnants of Los Diablos."

Veronica marveled at the thought of taking down all of Los Diablos' drug factories plus the place where she had been held and interrogated for days. If this was a DEA operation, the chances of a successful operation being planned and executed this fast was next to nil. Then again, Maddox didn't have to work his way through mountains of red tape to make this mission happen.

Adam's team was second to leave the airstrip. Sandwiched between Adam and Jake, Veronica paid attention to the route Remy drove with Lily serving as navigator. She didn't think her driving back to the plane would be necessary, but Veronica would rather be prepared for the unexpected. That's how she'd stayed alive while working alone for weeks. Things went wrong on operations, no matter how well you planned. You either adjusted or you died.

Half a mile from their assigned coordinates, Remy drove off the road and parked the SUV deep in the surrounding trees and underbrush. No one would see their vehicle from the road. To be sure civilians or the enemy didn't disable their ride, they camouflaged the vehicle with branches and bushes. When they finished, Veronica wouldn't have realized there was a vehicle hidden if she didn't know what to look for.

Once they donned their comm systems, Adam led the way through the trees. A quarter mile from their destination, he held up a fist, signaling them to halt. He glanced at Remy and pointed out the camera hidden in the branches of the tree ahead to their right.

Veronica blew out a slow breath. Good thing she wasn't in charge of this op. She would have missed the camera and tipped off Los Diablos to the presence of intruders. Yeah, she had skills, but Fortress operatives were two or three levels above her. Working with them was going to be a challenge, but fun.

Remy shimmied up the tree and, instead of disabling the camera like she expected, turned the lens slowly in a different direction.

Progress from that point on was slower as the operatives scanned for more cameras. They shifted four more as they walked closer to the place where she'd been held. A few hundred yards from the edge of the tree line, Adam again held up his fist to halt their forward movement.

She edged closer to see what caught his attention. It took her a minute to spot the trip wire strung between two trees. Oh, boy. What next? Adam signaled her and the others to move back, then slid his pack off his back and removed a few tools. Veronica's stomach lurched when she realized he was going to deal with the trip wire himself.

Though she wanted to protest her boyfriend taking such a huge risk, Veronica would have to suck it up and deal. Adam wouldn't tackle the trap unless he knew how to handle himself. That was something she had noticed over the past week. Yes, he had skills. He was also wise enough to delegate the assignments based on a team member's strengths. If he thought one of the others could handle the trip wire better, he would have shifted the responsibility.

Still, she didn't take her eyes from Adam as he worked to trace the wire and deal with the bomb attached. When Adam motioned them forward, Veronica took her first free breath in several minutes. It was one thing to know Adam's job was dangerous. Seeing the danger up close and personal brought another level of fear for his safety.

They crept forward, crouching at the edge of the trees. Adam texted Maddox that they were in position. While they waited for the other teams to set up, the five of them watched the activity around the beautiful stone mansion. The place looked like a home you would see on the cover of a home magazine.

Ironic that the peaceful place held a chamber of horrors. Veronica's stomach twisted into a knot. Remembering those long hours in Silverman's hands made her want to hurl.

The Fortress operatives had skills she wasn't sure she wanted to know, but she knew if they could obtain information they needed without hurting someone, they would choose that option. Raul hadn't given them a choice. If Curt hadn't obtained the information, Risa would have died.

A flurry of activity caught her attention. A dirty van raced toward the house and skidded to a stop in the driveway. Two thugs hopped out and came around to the side, yanking open the door. They dragged out a bound and gagged prisoner.

Even at this distance and in the dimming light of day, she recognized the prisoner fighting for his life.

## CHAPTER THIRTY-ONE

Adam felt Veronica's body stiffen as he watched the tableau play out in front of him. "Vonnie?" he murmured.

"That's Carlos, my informant. I have to help him."

When she inched forward, Adam stopped her with a hand on her shoulder. "Not yet. The other teams aren't in place. If we go in early, we endanger everyone."

"Carlos doesn't have the training to withstand an interrogation. He won't make it. I can't let that happen, Adam. He has a family."

"Silverman may not be here. Darkness will fall soon and we can free Carlos."

"That might be too late. I can't take that chance."

"Vonnie...."

"Hear me out," she interrupted. "I understand the team can't move yet, but I can go in alone to help Carlos."

"They will catch you, baby."

"That's the point. These guys know my face. They know not to touch me until Silverman returns."

"I haven't forgotten the guard who wanted to rape you."

"You killed him."

"There may be others who enjoy hurting women. What if Silverman is there? You know what he's capable of first hand." He captured her chin with his hand. "I know you want to help Carlos, but we can't move until nightfall, no matter how much you want to change the timetable. As team lead, I'm asking you to trust me and hold position." If she wouldn't obey his orders on a mission, he'd ask Maddox to assign her to a different team for her safety and his.

The battle raged in her gaze a moment, then she nodded. "I'm sorry, Adam. I know better than to question the team leader or change the game in mid-play. It won't happen again."

He nudged her shoulder. "I don't expect you or my team to be puppets."

The goons forced a still struggling Carlos into the house and slammed the door.

Adam's phone vibrated. Shielding the screen, he checked the text from Maddox. Excellent. He activated the mic on his comm system. "We go in twenty." His team acknowledged the order. Twenty minutes. Adam hated Carlos might pay the price for helping Veronica. His girlfriend had survived three days of torture. Her informant could handle a few minutes of discomfort.

He asked Zane for a satellite image of the mansion and the surrounding estate. The result came a minute later. Adam studied the series of images, including the guard routes he'd memorized from his first breach of the place.

His lips twisted. Nothing had changed. The storeroom was still the best way into the basement where Carlos was likely to be. Once his team took care of business in the basement, they would clean out the nest of vipers. The hoods wouldn't expect enemy attack from inside the house. Adam hoped Silverman was on site. If not, he'd track down the interrogator and take him out personally.

Four Fortress tech gurus were aiding the teams with thermal images of the target buildings. Zane was assigned to Adam's team. He trusted his brother-in-law more than any member of tech support.

At the twenty-minute mark, Adam signaled his team, the darkness deep enough to hide their movement across open ground. He covered the distance to the same window, using the same bush to hide him as the pair of guards swept around the corner and walked the path in front of the house.

Once they disappeared around the other side of the house, Adam activated his mic. "Go. One minute before they reappear." He raised the window and slipped into the darkened storage room, followed quickly by Veronica, Remy, Lily, and Jake.

He texted Z and had him patch into their comm signal through Adam's phone. When his brother-in-law was in the communications loop with them, Adam said, "Thermal image update."

"No change in the last fifteen minutes."

"Copy. We're ready. Vonnie's informant was brought in twenty minutes ago. Location?"

"Down the hall, third room on the right."

Just as Adam expected. Carlos had been taken to the same room where Veronica was held. He eased the door open a crack, checked that the corridor was clear. He signaled his team and, with his weapon raised and ready, slipped into the corridor.

Veronica followed on his heels to the torture chamber while the rest of his team swept the other rooms. All were clear except one. Remy quickly subdued another guard.

Through the comm system, Zane said, "The informant has been suspended from the ceiling and there is one other person in the room, circling."

Veronica's jaw flexed.

"Copy. Remy, Lily, start setting the explosives. Jake, cover the stairs. Vonnie, with me." Adam didn't want the others to sweep through the upper floors without him and

Veronica. According to Z, the mansion held fifteen occupants plus two guards outside.

Adam tried the knob. The door was unlocked. He glanced at Veronica as he screwed on the suppressor. She nodded. He held up three fingers and counted down in silence.

He eased open the door enough to listen to what was going on in the room.

"Now, Carlos, let's have a chat, shall we? Tell me where I can find the pretty American woman you helped. Give me the information I want and you return to your family. That's a good bargain, isn't it? She's not worth your pain and suffering, my friend. Where is she?"

"I don't know. She's a photographer. She travels all the time. I never know when I will see her."

"That's not what I wanted to hear."

"It's the truth," Carlos protested, his voice rising.

"You must have some way of contacting her. Give me that and I'll be satisfied. I'll send you home."

In his ear piece, Zane murmured, "Silverman has his back to the door."

Adam pushed the door open wide enough to slip through the opening, Veronica a step behind. He moved to the right while she shifted left. Both had their weapons drawn and aimed at the man who had tortured Veronica.

Without turning around, Silverman said, "I told you never to disturb me when I'm working. What is it you want?"

"I hear you've been looking for me." Veronica walked into Silverman's line of sight, keeping his attention focused on her.

"My dear Veronica. How nice of you to join us. Come to save your friend?" He shook his head. "Waste of time, my dear. I'm disappointed. No matter. We'll spend a lot of time getting reacquainted."

As Silverman turned, Adam tackled him from behind and took him to the floor. The interrogator bucked, trying to throw Adam off his back and to attack. When that didn't work, he threw an elbow back and clocked Adam in the temple.

For a moment, he saw stars in front of his eyes. That momentary distraction was enough for Silverman to slither free. As he started to rise, Veronica snapped off a roundhouse kick to his rib cage, the crack of ribs sounding loud in the stone room.

The ruffian scowled at Veronica. "You'll pay for that," he said, fighting to draw in breath.

She smiled and executed another kick, this one to his temple. Silverman dropped without another sound.

"Nice job," Adam murmured as he zip tied and duct taped the unconscious man.

Veronica hurried to the wall near the door and lowered the iron frame from which Carlos was suspended. "Are you all right, Carlos?"

He nodded. "Thank you for rescuing me, but you shouldn't be here. Los Diablos are looking everywhere for you. They want information they think you have."

"I know." She freed him. "There's a storage room down the hall to the left. Climb through the window and hide behind the bush until the guards pass. Once they're on the other side of the house, run to the woods and flag down a ride at the road."

"What about you?" Carlos nodded at Silverman. "If he wakes up and finds you gone, the other members of Los Diablos will scour this area like locusts. You must protect yourself."

"I'm not alone, Carlos. My teammates are with me. After we're finished, you won't have to worry about Los Diablos again."

"Be careful, my friend." And he was gone.

Zane murmured, "Fifteen minutes to complete your mission."

After slapping tape over Silverman's mouth, Adam and Veronica returned to the hallway as Remy and Lily approached.

"Finished," Remy said, pointing with his chin to the bomb attached to the wall outside the torture chamber, one of several strategically placed bombs. The team would set more after they took care of the members of Los Diablos in the residence.

"Z, location of targets."

"Take the stairs. Turn right. Six people at the dining room table. Two others are roaming guards, one on the first floor, one on the second. The remaining four are asleep on the second floor."

"Copy."

Adam signaled the others to attach their suppressors, then he led the way upstairs. Near the landing, footsteps approached the staircase door. He held up his fist, then aimed his Sig at the door.

The knob turned. A beefy man, dark-skinned with black hair, pushed open the door and walked into the stairwell. Adam fired one shot to his heart. The thug dropped and Adam shoved him out of the doorway and moved into the hall. The sounds of glasses and eating utensils clinking against stoneware drifted their direction.

"That was the roaming guard on the first floor," Zane said.

One less to worry about.

"Two entrances to the dining room," Zane continued. "If part of the team goes through the living room and turns left at the corridor, you'll come up on the far side of the room. The table is situated so that you won't be shooting each other."

"Copy. Jake, head for the second floor. Take out the roaming guard as quietly as you can." Adam signaled

Remy and Lily to take up position on the far side of the dining room. Between the four of them, they should be able to take care of the occupants of the table. Hopefully, one of them would be the head of Los Diablos.

A minute later, Remy clicked his comm system to indicate he and Lily were in place. Adam glanced at Veronica, received a nod. He activated his mic and counted down. On his mark, the four Fortress operatives commenced firing.

## CHAPTER THIRTY-TWO

At the first shot, the cartel members leaped to their feet. Chairs hit the floor. A glass dropped from nerveless fingers and shattered. Within thirty seconds, the men who had been eating around the table were dead, their bodies on the floor or fallen across a chair or the table.

"Go, go," Adam said and sprinted for the stairs with Veronica right behind him. The noise of the battle would have alerted those on the second floor to trouble, and Jake was alone against the remaining cartel members.

As he neared the top of the staircase, the sound of suppressed gunfire reached his ears. Adam peered into the hall, spotted Jake aiming at a tango who had emerged from his room with his weapon drawn.

A movement to his right caught Adam's attention. Another man was drawing a bead on the medic from behind. Adam fired as Jake dropped the goon he'd targeted. "Room to room," Adam whispered into his mic. They needed to take out the rest of the Los Diablos personnel, blow the house, and get back to the plane. "Z, time."

"Seven minutes."

"Jake, watch our six."

"Copy."

"Remy, Lily, go left. Vonnie and I will go right."

Adam motioned for Veronica to take the first room while he took the second. Veronica's weapon discharged seconds later. In the room Adam prepared to breach, feet raced toward the door. He motioned for his girlfriend to drop to the floor. As soon as the ruffian opened the door, Adam slammed the butt of his Sig on the back of the creep's head. Veronica leapt to her feet, and used zip ties and duct tape on the thug, then Adam dragged him back into his room.

One more room to clear. Veronica pressed her back to the wall on one side of the door while he took the other. He reached for the handle. A noise inside made him freeze. "Z," he whispered. "I hear a baby."

His brother-in-law growled. "Hold." Seconds later, "The mother must have been holding the child. There are three people inside, one a baby."

"Position?"

"The baby is on the bed with an adult. The second adult is standing in front of the two with a weapon pointed at the door."

Not what he wanted to hear. A stray bullet could injure or kill the child. "Copy. Vonnie, aim for the heart." He would take the head shot to make sure a gun battle didn't rage with a baby close.

From the side of the doorway, Adam kicked open the door. Immediately, bullets peppered the wall across from Adam. In concert, Adam and Veronica took their shots, and hit the man in the heart and head.

Adam glanced at the man now spread-eagled on the floor. Satisfaction curled in his gut. Javier Salazar, head of Los Diablos. The president would be pleased this target was down.

The woman on the bed had curled her body around her baby. She was crying, the baby wailing in fear. "Please, don't hurt my baby," the mother begged in Spanish.

"Take your child and get out of the house. If you want to live, don't come back here for any reason," Adam answered. In English, he said, "Jake, take care of the guards outside."

"Copy that."

The woman scrambled from the bed, shoved her feet in her shoes, grabbed a blanket and wrapped her baby. Veronica handed her the diaper bag as Jake said, "Guards are down. The path is clear for the woman and her baby."

"Copy." To the woman, he said, "Go now. Hurry. Stay on the driveway to the road." He didn't want to chance this woman triggering one of the traps in the woods.

She scooped up her baby and raced from the room.

He and Veronica followed her into the hall and met Remy and Lily. "Clear?"

"We're clear."

"Time, Z," Adam said.

"Three minutes."

"Jake, we're setting the rest of the explosives inside the house."

"Heading for the vehicles now."

Remy and Lily raced to the first floor while Adam and Veronica took care of the second floor. With thirty seconds to spare, the five operatives met at the tree line where they'd entered the grounds.

Adam pulled out a burner phone and handed it to Veronica. "You do the honors."

She grinned. "With pleasure." A minute later, the night rocked with multiple explosions. The windows exploded outward, and flames and smoke billowed from the gaping holes.

Nice. Nate Armstrong's bombs were perfect to take down the house without blowing a huge crater or setting the nearby trees on fire. "Let's get out of here. Whatever passes for EMS in this place will be responding soon." Along with the federales who were in Salazar's pocket. Adam led his team into the trees and bushes, following their cleared path.

The Suburban was still covered. Adam, Veronica, and Jake tossed aside the tree branches and bushes. Remy checked the vehicle for tracking devices while Lily dropped to the ground and shimmied under the frame as the others finished clearing the camouflage.

A minute later, Lily wriggled free of the car's frame and leapt to her feet. "Clear."

Remy drove them from the trees and onto the road. He turned toward the airstrip. Three minutes later, flashing lights raced toward them.

Adam reached into the cargo area and grabbed his rifle. He lowered his window, as did Lily. They waited to see if these were EMS workers on the way to the burning home or federales who had no love for Fortress. Emergency vehicles sped past their SUV and raced toward the orange glow in the night.

"Keep to the speed limit, Remy." Adam laid his rifle on the seat beside him. "We don't want to attract attention." More sirens sounded in the distance. Not wanting to distract the other teams, he called Zane. "We're away from the mansion and en route to the plane. Status on the other teams?"

"All the missions were completed and the teams are heading to the airstrip."

"Have you caught chatter on the Internet?"

"A lot of speculation. No facts. A couple people mentioned ghosts which will make Maddox happy. I'm continuing to monitor communications in the area."

"Adam." Remy pointed ahead of them. "We have a problem."

He glanced through the windshield. In the distance, the road was blocked by three vehicles and several heavily armed men. "Zane, contact the pilots. Tell them we're coming in hot. Warn the other teams of trouble."

"Copy that."

Adam ended the call. "Remy, take the next right. The area behind the roadblock is heavily populated."

The operative sped up and, at the last second, took a sharp right, controlling the skid with ease. The SUV surged forward as Remy floored the accelerator.

Adam twisted in his seat to watch out the back window along with Jake. Remy made a left turn followed by a quick right at the next corner. The headlights of the trailing vehicle stayed behind them, inching closer.

Adam frowned. Remy couldn't continue evasive maneuvers long term. They needed to go to the airstrip. Chances were high the other teams encountered the same problem. "Remy, at the next intersection, take a right. The road is a relatively empty stretch all the way to the airstrip. Once it's safe for innocents, we'll deal with the vehicle following us."

"Too bad we don't have Jon Smith aboard," Jake said. "This horrible road will make a shot difficult."

Adam clapped him on the shoulder. "Who needs a world-class sniper when we have rocket-propelled grenades?"

The medic chuckled. "The all-important equalizer. The local government doesn't waste money on infrastructure." He reached into the cargo area and grabbed his Go bag. From inside, he pulled a rocket launcher and two grenades.

"I want to learn how to use that," Veronica said. "How does Fortress teach newbies to shoot one?"

"PSI has a place deep in the mountains for training."

"Trouble up front," Remy snapped.

Adam growled. Another SUV bore down on them at a rapid rate. "Lily, take them out, fast. Jake, you're on the clowns coming up behind us. Vonnie, watch the side roads on the right. Don't poke your head out of the vehicle. Blowback from the RPG. I'll take the left."

They lowered the windows in the SUV. Lily said, "Hold it steady," and shifted to perch on the window frame. She fired a grenade at the fast-approaching vehicle. A split-second later, a fireball exploded and the enemy's vehicle veered directly in front of them.

Lily dived inside the SUV and Remy took evasive maneuvers to avoid a collision with the uncontrolled vehicle.

"My turn," Jake said. He sat on the window frame and, a moment later, the vehicle pursuing them exploded.

Adam wouldn't hold his breath, but he hoped the third vehicle at the roadblock had stayed behind to man the post. "Good job."

They completed the remainder of the drive without interference. Remy slid to a stop at the end of the airstrip beside one of the other SUVs. As they unloaded, an SUV driven by Alex Morgan raced toward them with the third Fortress team on board. Excellent. One more to go.

"Grab your gear. Fortress stirred up a hornet's nest. Won't take long for the federales to start searching private airstrips." Adam opened the cargo area. He reached in, grabbed his Go bag and Veronica's.

"I can carry my own bag," she muttered.

"Remy is carrying Lily's. She's watching our six."

Her head whipped in Lily's direction. Immediately, she dropped back and took up a position a few feet from the other operative to help protect the others.

Adam's lips curved. Go bags were heavy. At the moment, speed was more important than allowing his girlfriend to haul her equipment bag to the plane. He'd rather tap into her strength; Veronica was trained to protect.

As the two women stepped into the plane's cabin, the fourth SUV raced to the end of the airstrip. The operatives bailed from the vehicle, grabbed their gear, and raced for the Lear.

Immediately, the first jet powered up. The operatives from the last SUV rushed up the stairs. Adam closed and locked the door behind them as the engine revved.

Maddox dropped into the nearest seat and activated the intercom. "Get this bird off the ground."

"Copy that."

The operatives stored gear bags and strapped into the seats as the volume of the engine roar increased. The plane taxied down the strip and lifted off as a handful of vehicles with flashing lights poured onto the tarmac.

As soon as they were level, Maddox asked for a report from Adam and the leader of the PSI team. Once they finished, he called Josh Cahill on the other plane and put the call on speaker. "Report."

"Both teams were successful with one minor injury."

"Minor? Who's bleeding like a stuck pig over here?" Quinn Gallagher protested.

"Rio?" Maddox asked.

"Bullet just kissed Quinn's biceps. No stitches necessary. I'm patching him up as we speak."

"Dodge faster next time, Gallagher. Your wife will hunt me down if you are seriously injured on a mission and I want her happy. She's a vital part of our S & R training."

"Yes, sir."

"No injuries to report from this end. The second phase of our operation will go as planned." He turned his head to stare at Adam. "Except for one adjustment. Zane caught a transmission from one of Los Diablos's men, Salazar's second in command. He alerted Lilah Collins to the attack on the cartel."

"What is the adjustment?" Adam's gut clenched. He already knew he wasn't going to like it.

"Zane reserved the honeymoon suite for you and your bride at the same hotel where he and Claire stayed with Remy and Lily."

"Honeymoon suite?" Veronica stared at her new boss.

"Yes, ma'am. Congratulations on your elopement, Mrs. Walker."

## CHAPTER THIRTY-THREE

Veronica sat back, stunned at the news that she was newly "married" to Adam Walker. "Fortress techs aren't the only ones capable of hacking into government records. I assume Zane planted the proper trail."

"Of course. He doesn't miss a trick." Maddox smiled. "Relax. At least you get to enjoy some time in a luxury suite at Fortress's expense. You'll have to spend some quality time in the room in order to give the right impression. Zane will make reservations for dinner at a nearby restaurant. After that, take a moonlight stroll. At some point during the evening, I hope one of Lilah's henchmen will make contact."

Make contact? A fine euphemism for abduction. "How will Lilah Collins know we're in Belize?"

"Belize City isn't the size of New York City. Word gets around fast. Plus, Zane will make sure word leaks that you insisted on honeymooning in Belize because you've always wanted to visit the country."

She frowned. "Wouldn't that seem suspicious? I would never ask Adam to take me to a place where he was held captive and tortured."

"Lilah doesn't know that, Vonnie," Remy said. "She's never met you, doesn't know you love Adam too much to ask that of him. Maybe Adam didn't share his past with his new bride because he didn't want to distress her."

Veronica's cheeks burned. Remy was correct. She did love Adam that much. Didn't mean she wanted to announce she was in love with the amazing operative in this manner. She shifted her gaze to Maddox. "If you ask me to play the role of a high-maintenance diva, we might have a problem."

Adam snorted. "You don't have a high maintenance bone in your body. Lilah wouldn't buy that even if we tried to sell it to her. She has to know what Silverman put you through. No diva would have survived days in his hands and lived to tell about it."

"When did we get married?"

Maddox glanced at his watch. "About three hours ago."

Something in his voice had Veronica's eyes narrowing. "This is all a false paper trail, right?"

"You were right in assuming someone from Lilah's organization would check on the marriage. I wanted the cover story to hold up under scrutiny."

"What does that mean?" Adam asked, his voice sharp.

"It means two operatives made up to look like you and Veronica made a quick trip to Las Vegas and tied the knot using your names and IDs. According to the state of Nevada, you are legally married. And before you complain, someone has already been checking extensively with boots on the ground."

Adam exchanged glances with Veronica, then turned a glare on his boss. "You're stepping all over my plans, Maddox. I hoped to ease Vonnie into marriage. This is like using a sledge hammer to force her acceptance."

On the speaker phone, Josh Cahill said, "Boss, your wife would have had your hide if you pulled this stunt with her. I don't even want to think about what Del would do to me."

While the banter between the Durango unit and Maddox continued, Veronica looked down at herself, flinched. She didn't look like a bride out to celebrate her marriage to the man of her dreams.

"Vonnie?" Adam covered her hand with his. "Talk to me."

She turned, froze. Veronica had never seen that look in Adam's eyes. Uncertainty, as though he wasn't sure of her feelings for him. No surprise, she supposed. She had told Adam she loved him, but there was no way for him to know she didn't toss the L-word around like candy at Mardi Gras. She had never said those words to another man.

Veronica leaned in and kissed him, her free hand cupping his cheek. "I'm not dressed like a woman out to wow her new husband. I look like a refugee from a militia group."

He relaxed, his crooked smile curving his lips. "The plane will land in Belize City about the time shops open. We'll shop before we go to the hotel." He sent a pointed glance to Maddox who watched them with interest. "You can foot the bill for our wardrobe, Maddox."

A chuckle from the buzz-cut blond SEAL. "Consider it my wedding gift to you and Veronica."

Durango's leader said, "Anything else, Maddox?"

"That's it for now. Get some rest. While Veronica and Adam are living in luxury, the rest of us will battle the bugs while keeping an eye on the Collins estate and grounds."

A groan from Gallagher. "Heat and humidity, here we come."

The rest of the operatives chuckled and razzed the other man before Maddox ended the call. "Same goes for you," he said to the operatives on their plane. "Rest while you can. It's going to be a long, hot day while we see if Lilah changed the security surrounding the house. Zane is searching for schematics of the house and looking for upgrades to the security system."

"Tell him to look for changes to the out buildings as well," Adam said. "The guards stayed in those buildings and Collins discussed constructing new tunnels between those buildings and the basement. After Fortress pulled me out of there and blew the original tunnels, Lilah may have made the changes her father considered."

"I'll pass the word."

Within minutes, the cabin was quiet except for the sounds of operatives settling into sleep and Jon's fingers clicking on his keyboard. Veronica watched him for a couple minutes as Adam slept beside her.

The sniper glanced up, raised an eyebrow in silent inquiry.

She needed some water anyway and the small galley was near the front of the plane. Veronica stood.

"Vonnie?" Adam's gaze zeroed in on her. "You okay?"

"Getting water. Go back to sleep."

With a slight nod, he closed his eyes.

She slid past him and walked the aisle to the galley. With a shrug, she grabbed an extra bottle of water. If Jon didn't need the water, he could return it later.

Retracing her steps, she stopped beside the operative who had set his computer aside and waited for her. "Water?" she whispered.

"Thanks." He patted the seat beside him. "Can't sleep?"

"Not yet. Adrenaline."

"It will drop soon." He tapped her water. "Drink while you can."

"Aren't you tired?"

He didn't say anything.

Right. Sore subject. "Sorry. I didn't mean to pry." More silence. Veronica decided to return to her seat. She'd find a way to apologize later for intruding.

"Eli and I were on a mission that went south. We were working with another Fortress team. The sniper from the second team left his position against orders. I was captured. Eli found me a few days later."

"You don't have to say any more. I understand." After what she'd gone through at Silverman's hands, Veronica understood the near paranoia with safety when you were vulnerable.

"Adam is the same."

Her gaze shifted to the man who had captured her heart and found him watching her interaction with Jon. She winked at him and returned her attention to the sniper. "From what I've observed, Fortress operatives don't sleep unless they're in secure surroundings or have one of their own that they trust on guard."

He inclined his head in silent agreement. "He's a good man, Veronica. Will you give him an honest chance?"

If only Jon knew the truth. She was crazy about Adam Walker. "Absolutely."

A nod. "My wife likes him, and Dana isn't comfortable around men."

"Oh?"

"Long story, one that's hers to tell if she chooses to share."

"She must miss you when you're gone."

"She and Brenna, Eli's wife, stay together when Eli and I are working. They're sisters."

Veronica thought about her brother, sighed. Was he safe? She'd been tempted to use her DEA connections to check on him. She'd resisted the urge. Veronica didn't want to know if her brother was a replica of her father. "They're lucky to have each other."

"Do you have siblings?"

"One brother. Haven't seen him since he left at eighteen and joined the military."

Jon drained the rest of his water. "It's hard for those who serve in the armed forces to relate to civilian life. Some don't try to connect with their families, preferring to stay immersed in military life."

"I think the decision to stay away was a deliberate choice that didn't have anything to do with his military service. Our home life was bad." A yawn caught her by surprise. "Sorry. I promise it's not the company."

The sniper held out his hand for her empty water bottle. "Go rest so Adam will sleep. I'll toss the bottle."

"Thanks." She returned to her seat and Adam wrapped his arms around her. She fell asleep with her head resting against Adam's chest, the steady beat of his heart a source of comfort and a reminder she wasn't alone and vulnerable.

It only seemed short minutes passed when the landing gear locked into position with a jerk. Veronica blinked and sat up. Daylight streamed through the windows of the Lear, the tropical sun warming her skin.

Adam strode down the aisle and dropped into the seat beside her. "Good morning. Ready to start our first day as husband and wife, Veronica Walker?"

She smiled. "I'm ready to spend Brent Maddox's money on my honeymoon wardrobe."

Operatives all over the plane burst into laughter as Maddox scowled in her direction.

## CHAPTER THIRTY-FOUR

Adam left his Go bag on the plane in the care of the PSI team tasked with protecting their equipment, felt naked without the equipment he depended on within easy reach. However, he was supposed to be a besotted groom on his honeymoon. Carrying his bag wherever they went would look suspicious and he didn't trust the safety of the hotel to leave his equipment unguarded. Besides, he and Veronica and their teammates would leave Belize in a hurry. He'd rather not have to replace his weapons stash when he returned to the states.

Maddox clapped him on the shoulder. "Don't let your wife bankrupt me."

"You deserve whatever she dishes out for putting her through this." He still couldn't believe Maddox changed the game in mid-play.

"I don't think she's suffering repercussions," his boss said, his tone wry. He edged closer. "She loves you, Adam. Both of you will be able to carry off this role without difficulty. The relationship won't look fake because it isn't."

"Except for the fact I'm not really married to her." He wanted the marriage to be real. If she agreed to marry him one day, he would be the most blessed man on the planet.

"The paperwork is real. You simply had two stand-ins in front of the official."

Adam's jaw clenched. Not the same thing. He wanted to court Veronica and win her hand in marriage the old-fashioned way, not like this. She deserved better. She deserved the best he had to offer, not a sham marriage arranged by a boss with an agenda.

"Adam." Veronica's hand squeezed his arm. "We'll do things our way and wrestle with the legalities later."

"Ready?" Remy asked, his Go bag in hand, Lily behind him with her bag.

His eyebrows soared. "I would never take another couple on my honeymoon."

"We're in the room across the hall from yours. We won't make obvious contact, but we're your backup. We'll follow you wherever you go in case Lilah's thugs take you somewhere besides the Collins estate."

"I'm next door to the Doucets," Jake said. "You have your full team with you this time, Adam."

Unlike the last time he'd been assigned to work undercover in Belize. "Why would Lilah take us to a different location? She owns the people who work for her, just like her old man." Peter Collins had searched hard to find something to blackmail Adam's alter ego and thought he owned Adam, too. He'd been wrong.

"One more thing," Maddox said. He unlocked the small safe near the galley and withdrew two velvet-covered boxes, handed them to Adam. "You'll need these."

Adam opened one box, stared. A carved wedding ring with small diamonds scattered throughout the design. Beside him, Veronica's breath caught.

"It's beautiful."

He freed the ring and slipped it on Veronica's finger. He blew out a breath. A perfect fit. How did Maddox know Veronica's ring size? Adam opened the second box and pulled out the matching carved wedding band for him. This one didn't have diamonds. Thank goodness. He'd never choose a ring that drew attention.

He slipped it on his finger, grimaced. The unaccustomed weight would bug him until he got used to it. What was he thinking? This marriage wasn't real, no matter what Maddox said. Adam wouldn't consider the legal ties binding unless he heard the vows himself.

Veronica nudged him. "Looks good on you. I like it."

Adam moved into the aisle and motioned for her to step out. "Let's roll. We have a wannabe drug kingpin to take down."

"Zane reserved an SUV in your name," Maddox said. "Remy, you have one reserved in your Fortress fake ID. So do you, Jake." He waved them on. "Go be tourists."

Adam escorted Veronica from the airport and found their SUV. Remy and Lily sat in an SUV nearby, pretending to look at a map of the area. Jake was two spaces away, consulting his own map.

"My skin feels like it's crawling," Veronica said.

"Mine, too." He cranked the engine. "At least we have air conditioning in here."

"Is it too early to shop and disappear into the suite?"

"Not to shop. We should eat lunch out, though. Have to make the honeymoon look real." He smiled. "Besides, I have to show off my drop-dead gorgeous new wife to the world."

"And maybe I have to show off my hot husband and warn off the other women."

Through the ear piece in Adam's ear, Remy said, "You do realize I can hear everything you're saying, right? You need some new lines, Adam."

"I think he's doing great," Lily chimed in. "So is Vonnie. You guys sound like sappy newlyweds."

"Would you zip it?" Jake groused. "As the only single person on this team, you're causing me some serious embarrassment. Remy is right, Adam. You need some new lines."

"Hey, I got the girl, didn't I?"

"By some miracle. Remy, does Adam have a tail?"

"Yep, a tricked out SUV. Lily is texting Z the plates."

Nice to know his gut hadn't lied about someone besides a teammate watching him and Veronica. "There's a shopping center three blocks ahead on the right. Jake, veer off and take the next right. The road parallels this one and will lead right to the store where I'm taking Vonnie."

"Copy that."

In short order, he arrived at the shop and parked. Knowing Remy and Lily were close, Adam helped Veronica from the SUV and took his time kissing her. Never a hardship. He would love to kiss this woman for the rest of his life.

"This feels weird," she murmured against his lips. "I don't like knowing someone is watching."

"More than one in the vehicle," Remy said. "Two bruisers. Zane says the car is registered to the Collins estate."

"Can't say I'm surprised." He slid his hand down Veronica's arm and laced their fingers together. "Let's give them what they're expecting."

The next hour passed more pleasantly than Adam had expected. His teammates kept up the smart aleck comments over the comm system. Instead of being irritating, knowing they were close and watching over him and Veronica was freeing. Their banter and relaxed interaction with each other confirmed Adam's gut feeling that this team was the right one.

"Can we eat now?" Lily asked. "I'm starving."

"I'm with her," Jake said.

Adam gave his teammates the name of a restaurant nearby and the directions. "Remy, Lily, go ahead. Jake hang back with us." He paid for their purchases with his Fortress account, glad Maddox was picking up the tab when he saw the total. "Just for future reference, is this a normal shopping spree for you?"

A snort from Veronica. "Are you kidding? I hate shopping and I'm not a clothes horse. I'd rather buy online than in a store any day."

Adam laughed. That was a sentiment he'd heard from Lily more than once over the past year. He had a feeling Veronica and Lily would be good friends.

At the restaurant, Adam noticed several people sneaking looks at him from different tables around the room. Some of them he recognized from his undercover days with the Collins organization. Others seemed horrified and fascinated by the scars he still bore from his time in Collins' torture chamber.

"Ready to leave, love?" Veronica asked, her gaze steady on his.

The band around his heart squeezed tight. She'd seen the stares, knew why he was attracting attention, and it didn't bother her. In fact, Veronica didn't appear to notice his scars. She just saw Adam.

"More than ready." He kissed the back of her hand, wishing they were on a real honeymoon without an audience watching every move.

She leaned over and captured his lips in a lingering kiss. "Come on. We have better things to do than hang around in a restaurant."

After they left the restaurant and parked in the hotel's garage, Adam grabbed their bags from the back of the SUV and carried them to the lobby where he registered and received the suite key card. The hotel had an open floor plan with too many flowers and plants for his taste. It also included an indoor atrium and interior balconies on each of the fifteen floors that gave guests a great view of the greenery below them.

Although most people would appreciate the atmosphere, it reminded him of too many missions in jungles. Made Adam want to wield a machete to hack a path to the elevator. Following an elevator ride to the third floor, he unlocked the door and ushered her inside.

As soon as the door was locked behind him, Adam signaled Veronica to stay quiet. Ten minutes later, he'd gotten rid of four listening devices and two cameras. Veronica hadn't blinked at the bugs, but seeing the cameras made the color drain from her cheeks.

"Won't Lilah and company be suspicious when they realize we got rid of everything they planted to spy on us?"

He chuckled. "I would be a poor operative if I didn't search the suite. Believe me, they would be more suspicious if I hadn't made sure our room was free of surveillance. Remy, anything in your room?"

"Negative."

"Jake?"

"Same."

"Good. Looks like Lilah hasn't made the three of you. Rest. Watch some television. We're going to be the suite for a while."

The afternoon was quiet. Adam's teammates checked in periodically, but for the most part stayed silent. He and Veronica spent the hours getting to know each other better.

Knowing the suite would be checked when they left for dinner, Adam mussed the covers and punched the pillows so it looked as though the bed had been occupied. That done, he turned the television on low to an old movie and drew Veronica down on the couch beside him. She settled against him and there they sat for the remaining hour of the movie.

When the credits rolled, Adam signaled his team. "We're ready to leave. There's an outdoor cafe down the block on the right where Z made reservations for us. We'll walk and enjoy dinner outside. If Lilah is going to take us tonight, it will be there or on the way back to the hotel."

"The three of us will take one SUV and watch from down the block. We've got your back, Adam," Remy said. "Yours, too, Vonnie."

"Zane told me Escobar copped to forcing Carver off the road. He's also responsible for the attacks on Carol Rossi and Graham Norton. Maddox also called. Fortress is in position and waiting for a move by Lilah's cronies. They'll let you know if there's any activity."

"Copy that."

He faced Veronica, held out his hand. "Sweetheart?"

A smiled spread across her mouth. "After I change clothes, I'll be ready to take down the woman threatening my husband."

## CHAPTER THIRTY-FIVE

Veronica spun around, arms spread. "What do you think?" She decided if they might be taken to the Collins estate tonight, she needed to wear clothes easy to maneuver in. Hence the pants and shirt in a dark color, both of them easy to run in if she needed the mobility. She'd prefer to have combat boots on her feet, but compromised with closed shoes that laced so they wouldn't fly off in a fight.

Adam's eyes lit with wild heat. "You look so beautiful that I want to take a bite."

"Aww, come on," Jake complained through the ear pieces. "You're causing my blood pressure to spike."

Veronica laughed along with the others. "Sorry, Jake."

"If that was true, you wouldn't have flirted with Adam for the last six hours."

"You'll survive." She turned to Adam. "I guess we can't carry a lot of weapons on us."

"Not tonight."

"We have extras for you and Adam," Lily said. "You won't be weaponless for long."

"I hope not. I feel under-dressed without my Sig."

"We're heading to the garage," Remy said.

Veronica and Adam waited five minutes before leaving the suite. "Will someone retrieve our belongings?" she asked.

"I doubt we'll have time." Adam pressed the elevator call button. "The room has to look occupied. Lilah's cronies will check."

She sighed. "I like everything I chose. I hope someone appreciates the clothes."

When they walked from the hotel into the tropical night, Veronica drew in a deep breath. Flowers scented the air. People strolled along the sidewalks on both sides of the street. No one seemed in a hurry. Laughter and the chatter of excited voices filled the night. Cars passed them at a sedate pace.

"Two bruisers are following," Remy said. "Half a block behind you. Both look Hispanic. One's on the heavy side, the other tall and thin. The big one's wearing a white shirt, the other blue, black pants. Both are packing. They're not trying to conceal their presence."

Veronica slowed to a stop in front of a store display window and pointed out a couple of items to Adam. He'd want an excuse to see the two men trailing them down the street.

He bent his head as though having trouble hearing her voice with all the noise on the street. Less than a minute later, his hand squeezed her hip in a silent signal to move on.

As they continued to the cafe, Adam said, "Jake, get a picture and send it to Zane."

"Copy that."

"I'd rather be the hunter than the prey," Veronica said.

"Same." Adam steered her into the cafe and requested a table on the terrace. Two minutes later, they were seated outdoors with menus in their hands. Veronica ordered a tropical salad with grilled chicken and sparkling water. The last thing she wanted was a heavy meal that might slow down her reaction time.

Adam's lips curved. He echoed her order. "I'll feed you more later," he said after the waiter left them.

"I'll hold you to that. A steak and baked potato sound perfect."

"I married a woman with good taste."

Through the ear piece, Remy said, "Maddox called. Zane noticed a spike of cell phone activity coming from the Collins estate. It's probably not a coincidence that the two clowns following you around town have been answering phone calls almost constantly in the last few minutes. My guess is they'll try to take you tonight."

"Good." Adam's eyes gleamed with satisfaction. "I'd rather get this over with and start the campaign to win my wife's hand the proper way."

Hearing those words from Adam made Veronica's heart turn over in her chest. He was such a good man, one with more integrity in his finger than her father had in his whole body.

Technically, Maddox was right. She and Adam were married. However, he had been romancing her all day, acting as though he still needed to win her heart. How could she not love Adam Walker?

"Z also got a hit on the facial recognition system. The bruisers work for the Collins organization."

She and Adam exchanged smiles. At least they knew who stalked them. Good to know another party wasn't involved to muddy the waters.

For the rest of their meal, Veronica and Adam stuck to neutral conversation topics although they touched and kissed frequently. She reminded herself the physical interaction was for their audience. Didn't matter. Every time he touched her with such gentleness, Veronica's heart melted a little bit more for the Marine sitting across the table from her. What she wouldn't give for this to be a real honeymoon without danger dogging their steps.

Adam paid the check, then walked hand-in-hand with Veronica along the sidewalk, slowly heading toward their hotel. "Where are they, Remy?" he asked.

"One of them is moving up, fast. The other peeled off to the right."

"He's circling around," Veronica said.

Adam squeezed her hand. "He'll come at you."

"He assumes I'm the weak link."

"He's wrong."

Nice to know the man she would love to marry for real believed in her skills. Ahead one hundred feet was a dark alley. There, Veronica thought. That's where the second guy would come at her. Hated that she had to let the thug think she was unaware. If she'd been that oblivious to her surroundings over the years, she would be dead by now. Her job had never been safe, especially in the countries and neighborhoods where she worked.

She and Adam kept to the same easy pace even as the predator behind them closed in. A shadow shifted at the mouth of the alley. Seventy-five feet. Fifty feet. Ten feet.

"Moving in now," Remy said.

Seconds later, the tall, thin man left the shelter of the alley's shadows and pointed a gun at Veronica.

Adam shifted his weight, then stopped as the beefy guy behind him shoved a gun against his spine and said, "Do exactly what we tell you or your wife dies right here."

Wife, not woman or girlfriend, Veronica realized. They knew she and Adam were married. Maddox had been right. Lilah Collins checked the details to make sure the cover story was true, looking for leverage to control Adam. "What do you want?"

"Come with us."

Adam scowled. "Why?"

"Shut up and move, Walker."

Thin Man wrapped an arm of steel around Veronica's waist and shoved the weapon into her side. "Let's go, lady. You should have chosen a better man. Maybe you'd like a taste of one of us."

Veronica laughed. "You have a death wish. I would kill you before I let you touch me."

He shoved the barrel of the weapon deeper into her side. "We'll see who has a death wish before this night is over."

"Leave her alone." Adam reached for Veronica.

Beefy Man rabbit punched him in the kidney. Adam dropped to his knees, dragging in a ragged breath.

"Adam!" Veronica broke Thin Man's hold and crouched beside Adam, prepared to blow her cover to protect him while he was incapacitated. There was a reason Special Forces soldiers knifed a kidney if a target had to die without making a sound. The pain left the victim unable to utter a sound.

"Vonnie, did he use a knife?" Jake asked.

"No more fists to the kidney," she said for the medic's benefit. "We'll go with you. Just don't hurt him." If she'd been free to do what she wanted, Beefy Man would be rolling on the ground with a broken knee cap. Veronica longed for a chance to take down these two bozos.

"Get him on his feet," he snapped. "Now."

Veronica leaned close. "Adam, can you stand?"

He gave a slight nod.

She hoped he was telling the truth because she couldn't haul him to his feet on her own. She did what she could to aid Adam as he struggled to his feet. When he swayed, Veronica wrapped her arm around his waist to steady him, afraid he'd go down again if she didn't anchor him to her side.

"Adam," Jake said over the ear piece. "If you're seriously hurt, call this off. Maddox and the others are in place. We aren't putting your life at risk."

Out of the corner of her eye, Veronica caught Adam's hand signal to hold position. "Where are we going?" she asked Thin Man to keep the thugs' attention on her and off Adam.

"To the parked black SUV by your hotel."

She and Adam continued walking up the street. By the time they reached the vehicle, Adam wasn't leaning on her as much although he was careful to make it seem as though he still needed assistance.

The vehicle was parked in a dimly lit section of the street. Veronica doubted anyone noticed the forced march to the vehicle at gunpoint.

While Beefy Man pointed the gun at Veronica, his partner used zip ties to cinch their wrists together. Thin man shoved Veronica into the backseat first. Adam followed right behind her.

"One move against either of us and the first bullet goes into your wife, Walker," Thin Man said, then slammed the door and climbed into the front passenger seat. He twisted and pointed the weapon at Veronica.

Nice. She hoped he wasn't the nervous sort. The roads around Belize City weren't the smoothest she'd ridden on.

Veronica watched the landmarks, memorizing their route. Her stopover in Belize the year before was too short to familiarize herself with the layout of the city. If she had made her connecting flight on time or resisted the urge to explore the city last year, she wouldn't have learned Adam's location.

She shuddered. So close. She'd come so close to losing the chance to love this man. Adam pressed close to her side. Veronica turned, noted his upraised eyebrow.

She couldn't say what was on her mind. Instead, she leaned her head against his shoulder, grateful he was alive and they were together.

Adam pressed a kiss to her forehead. Since Thin Man had cinched their hands in front, Adam covered her hands with his, as though offering silent comfort. With subtle movements, the operative maneuvered the small knife in his hand, slowly cutting her zip tie almost all the way through. One good flex would free her hands.

When he pressed the handle against her palm, she returned the favor. By the time she finished, they were driving through the gates of a large estate. The place was alive with activity and blazing lights inside the massive house.

With only seconds before they reached their destination, Veronica closed the thin knife and slid it back into place on the underside of Adam's watch.

Over the ear piece, Maddox said, "Adam, Veronica, as soon as you confirm Lilah Collins is in the estate, we'll move in. When the rest of your team is in position, we'll be ready."

"In place in five," Remy confirmed.

Beefy Man drove the SUV to the back of the house. "End of the line, Walker." He climbed out and opened Veronica's door. "You first, lady. Any trouble from you, and your traitor husband gets a bullet in the head."

She glanced at Adam. He winked at her. Oh, yeah, the operative was cool under pressure. Knowing almost twenty operatives waited for one word from them steadied her breathing. Let the games begin.

## CHAPTER THIRTY-SIX

Adam followed on Veronica's heels, using his body to protect her from the goon prodding him with the barrel of an HK. At least they weren't manhandling Veronica yet. His gut knotted. Eventually, Lilah would send someone after Veronica to make Adam pay for his role in Collins' death.

He glanced around the large kitchen as they walked through. Nothing had changed in the gourmet kitchen where two chefs were on call twenty-four hours a day. Had a craving for an omelet in the middle of the night? No problem. One of the chefs on duty would create a masterpiece for you. Having meals available when he was on guard duty during the night was great. Tonight was no different. Mariko Tanaka turned from the large stove to see who was coming into the kitchen. Her gaze caught his a moment, then she turned away without acknowledgment. Guess Mariko thought he was a traitor, too. "Where are we going?"

"You know the way." Beefy Man laughed. "You spent some quality time in there with Mr. Collins." Another shove in the back. "Get going."

Adam glared at the man over his shoulder, then gave Veronica directions to the basement. Every step they took to the chamber where he'd been held for so many days made the knots in his stomach draw tighter. He wasn't worried so much for himself. He didn't want Veronica anywhere near the place, especially so soon after her encounter with Silverman.

In the elevator, he nudged Veronica to the back corner and positioned himself in front of her. Both hooligans smirked, believing him helpless. So much the better if they believed the lie. Adam's priority was Veronica. He wouldn't let them hurt the woman at his back. She'd sacrificed enough for him.

The reflective doors slid open to reveal another man, one with a familiar face. "Andre."

The man's expression hardened as anger flared in his gaze. Andre stepped back and waved them out of the elevator with his Sig.

Adam kept his body between Andre and Veronica in case the Collins soldier decided to hand out some retribution, using Veronica. Andre opened the door to Peter Collins' favorite room, his torture chamber.

Seeing the room brought back a host of memories, none of them good. Still the same stone chamber, a cold, drafty room with a drain in the middle to wash away the blood from Collins' victims. The only difference this time was two chairs were in the center of the room, side by side.

"Sit," Beefy Man said, punctuating his one-word statement with a shove against Veronica's back.

She stumbled forward and fell sideways into the chair. She yelped when her ribcage connected with the hard frame.

Adam scowled at Beefy Man as he helped her sit up. "Hold on, baby," he whispered.

"In place," Remy said.

"We're ready to roll," Maddox said. "I'd like to grab Lilah, but not at the expense of you and Veronica. We'll give it a little more time, Adam, but if things go south, we're moving in."

Adam sat beside Veronica and leaned over as though he were nuzzling her ear. "Copy." His lips curved when his girl shivered. He made a mental note that the woman he adored had sensitive ears. He brushed his lips over the shell, glad to give her something pleasant to think about in this situation.

No matter how fast Fortress breached the estate and mansion, bullets could riddle their bodies in a matter of seconds, snuffing out their lives. He couldn't lose Veronica and would fight with every skill in his arsenal to protect her.

When he lifted his head, Veronica locked her gaze with his. The utter confidence in him and his skill stunned Adam. Deep in her eyes he saw trust and bone-deep love for him. He gave her a slight nod. They would leave this place alive. He wouldn't accept any other outcome. They had too much to live for. A lifetime of love and happiness. Maybe a family of their own one day.

Thin Man, Beefy Man, and Andre positioned themselves against the wall, out of Adam's reach. They still didn't consider Veronica a threat. Didn't they research her? She was a trained DEA agent, as dangerous as he was.

Adam quartered the room, noted three cameras aimed their direction. Was Lilah or her husband watching? Both? He turned his attention to Andre. "How's your mother?" When he worked undercover, Mrs. Valenzuela fed him several meals. She had believed Adam was a good influence on her only child.

Undercover assignments were his least favorite. Nana had stressed the value of honesty, and in an undercover assignment Adam lived a lie and deceived everyone he came in contact with. He hated lying to Andre and his mother. Mrs. Valenzuela was a sweet woman who didn't understand her son worked for an evil drug kingpin.

The soldier straightened, a grim smile curling his lips. "She asks about you. I don't have the heart to tell her you're a traitor, responsible for the deaths of many friends."

"I had a job to do. Collins planned to weaponize viruses, Andre. Thousands of people would have died if he'd succeeded."

Andre burst out laughing. "You're a fool if you believe that, Walker. The boss was only into powdered dreams, man."

"I found proof to the contrary. He was evil, determined to get rich on the poverty and deaths of others."

A scowl. "Was anything you told me true or did you lie about everything to me and Mama?"

He and Andre had grown close in those months, and that's what burned the other man so much. They were friends and now Andre felt as though he'd been personally betrayed. Because of the possibility their conversation was monitored by Lilah or her husband, he remained silent. The best way to work undercover was to stick close to the truth so you didn't trip yourself up with too many lies. As angry as Andre was, he wouldn't believe much of what Adam shared was true. He warned Andre last year that he needed to leave the Collins organization and find honest work for his mother's sake. He hadn't taken that warning to heart.

"That's what I thought," Andre said, disgust in his voice. "If you weren't already a dead man walking, I'd kill you with my bare hands."

"Enough," Beefy Man snapped. "He ain't your problem anymore."

"What are you going to do with us?" Veronica asked.

"Me? Nothing." A leer crossed his face. "At least not yet. The boss will be down here soon enough. If you were smart, you wouldn't be so anxious to know what's next."

"I'm the one you want," Adam said, wanting their attention off Veronica. "Let her go. I'll do whatever Lilah wants."

"You got no leverage, Walker. You could have been rich beyond your wildest dreams. Instead, you'll go to an early grave."

Frustrated with his lack of success in confirming Lilah's presence in the mansion, Adam subsided into silence.

In his ear piece, Maddox said, "EOD, go. The rest of you be ready. Adam, Veronica, five minutes and we move in without confirmation."

He decided to try one more time. "Who's running this dog-and-pony show since old man Collins ate a bullet?"

"Shut your trap," Thin Man snapped, taking an aggressive step forward. "Did you kill him?"

*Come on, Lilah. Make an appearance.* "You're in charge now?" Adam laughed. "I don't think so. Your boss wants questions answered? She'll have to ask me herself. I don't talk to underlings."

"Not even to save your wife?"

He lifted one shoulder in a shrug. "You want my cooperation, you need leverage. Without her, I don't have a reason to live."

"Don't give them too much power," Maddox warned through the ear piece.

Adam had told them the absolute truth. Without Veronica, his life was meaningless. Hard to believe how quickly the woman at his side had become as essential to him as breathing.

A tall, thin blond woman with glittering eyes walked into the room followed by her sandy-haired husband.

Adam's hands fisted. "I wondered when you would make an appearance, Lilah."

## CHAPTER THIRTY-SEVEN

Adam held himself still as Lilah Collins and her husband Wes walked to within two feet of him and Veronica. As they approached, Maddox gave the order to move. Once the Fortress operatives were in position, EOD would take out the power grid for the mansion and the compound. There were no street lights this far out of the city which meant when the lights went out, the grounds would be pitch black except for emergency lights, perfect for the operatives preparing to storm the place.

"I've been looking for you, Adam Walker." Lilah's smile was cold. "I spent the last year dreaming of this day. You killed my father and turned the happiest day of my life into my worst nightmare."

He didn't refute her assumption that he'd killed Collins. He hadn't been in any shape to fire a weapon a year ago. Peter Collins did his work well.

He wouldn't endanger his teammates, especially Zane who shot Collins. Lilah wouldn't care that his brother-in-law fired the fatal shot to protect Adam and the woman who was now Zane's wife. She also wouldn't care that someone higher up the food chain authorized the shot to protect American citizens. "You wasted your first year of marriage because you're obsessed with revenge? Your father died as a result of his choices."

"How can you say that? He was a good man, a great father."

His teammates needed time to get into position. That meant stalling. "Lilah, I worked for him for months. I know what kind of man he was. You're seeing him through the eyes of a girl who idolized her dad. That was the smallest part of Peter Collins. The largest part of him was a drug kingpin who planned to weaponize viruses and sell them to the highest bidder. Thousands of people would have died."

"Walker is not worth your time, sweetheart." Wes captured his wife's hand and brought it to his lips. "Let me deal with him for you. You agreed to let me take over your father's enterprises. Handling unpleasant tasks related to your father's work is part of the package."

"You make Peter Collins sound like a CEO of a Fortune 500 company," Veronica said. "Your father was a drug dealer, Lilah. He preyed on people's weaknesses and profited from them."

"You don't know anything about him," Lilah snapped.

"I know more than you think. I worked for the DEA. Your father was at the top of our most-wanted list."

The blond turned desperate eyes to her husband. "She's lying, isn't she, Wes? Dad wouldn't have infected people with a virus. Tell them they're wrong."

"He's in this as deep as your father was," Adam said. "He worked for Collins for years. Why do you think your father hand-picked Wes for you?"

"Sweetheart, don't listen to him," Wes said. "Go upstairs. I'll deal with both of them. You brought them to our territory. Now I'll finish the job. Your father was my friend and mentor. I owe Walker." His gaze shifted to Veronica. "While he's tough enough to withstand punishment for days, I don't think his wife will be. She is his greatest weakness."

A mistake to underestimate the woman Adam adored. He flexed his hands. One hard twist and the bonds would break. "You want a fight, Wes? Cut these ties and I'll give you one. Come on. Four against one is overwhelming odds. Just give me your word you won't lay a hand on Veronica."

"Fine. I won't touch her." His mouth curved. "Lilah wouldn't like that anyway." Wes inclined his head toward the two thugs who had abducted Adam and Veronica. "I'll give her to them to do with as they wish."

"No one touches her," Adam snapped.

"How will you stop them? You'll be dead soon."

Two large explosions rocked the night, one right after the other. Seconds later, the electricity went out, plunging them into darkness except for a dim emergency light in the hall.

Adam broke his zip tie and lunged at Wes. Andre cursed and shifted position, trying to get a clean shot. A scream from Lilah was cut off abruptly when Veronica punched her and knocked her out.

"Don't hurt the woman," Wes ordered as he threw a roundhouse at Adam's head.

Adam blocked it, countered with his own jab to Wes's nose. He heard the satisfying crunch, knew he'd broken the man's nose. Wes roared in fury and pain and tried to buck Adam's weight off his body.

Veronica gasped and Adam knew he had to end this tussle with Wes, fast. He clamped his hands around the Wes's head and slammed the back of his head against the stone floor until Lilah's husband went limp. He snatched the man's weapon from his holster.

Leaping to his feet, Adam rounded on Andre who held Veronica in front of him as a shield. "Let her go, Andre."

"Did you kill Wes?"

"He's breathing. My orders are to bring him and Lilah in for questioning." He shifted to the right, weapon trained on his former friend's head. "Don't do it, man. You know I'm a good shot."

"You won't get out of here alive. We'll cut you down where you stand."

"Andre, think of your mother. You're an only child and your father is gone. She needs you. Don't make me do this."

A bitter laugh escaped the other man. "Bringing Mama into this? You really are scum, aren't you, Walker?"

"I'm trying to keep you alive and protect my wife."

Through his ear piece, Remy said, "Adam, we're in the hall. We'll take down Beefy Man and Thin Man. You and Vonnie deal with Andre."

Although he didn't dare take his eyes from Andre, Adam noted the slight nod from Veronica. If he didn't do something, Mrs. Valenzuela would lose her son in the next few seconds.

He shifted to the left, banking on Andre turning to keep Adam in his sights. The move put Andre's back to the door where Adam's teammates were ready to infiltrate the room.

"Andre, Veronica is innocent. All she did was fall in love with me."

"That's not the way I heard it."

"You should know better than to believe everything you hear." He moved closer to his girl and Andre. "Walk away from this life. I can help you, but you have to choose to live rather than die in this place with these scumbags."

Black shadows moved into the doorway. Out of time.

"Now," Adam said.

Veronica rammed her elbow into Andre's stomach and wrenched herself to the side as Adam lunged forward and tackled him. He grasped the thug's wrist in a punishing grip, fighting to gain control of the weapon before Andre shot Veronica or one of Adam's teammates.

When Andre refused to release the grip, Adam shifted his hold, and twisted hard. Andre's wrist bone snapped, and his shout of pain echoed in the room as Adam ripped the weapon from his unresisting fingers and tossed it aside.

"I have him," Remy said. "Check on your girl."

Adam's heart lurched and his head whipped to the right. "Vonnie!"

Jake knelt beside Veronica's still form.

He covered the distance separating them in two strides, his throat tight. "What happened?"

"Knife wound to the side."

No, he couldn't lose her. "How bad?"

"Can't tell in this light. We need to transport her to the plane."

"Maddox," Adam said, "Vonnie took a knife to the side. We need to get her out of here."

"Copy. Take her out the back door to the SUV you arrived in. Secure Lilah and Wes. The Shadow unit will transport them. Cahill, clear a path."

"Copy that," Durango's leader replied.

"Adam, hold the flashlight for me." Jake slapped the light into his hand.

He turned the beam toward Veronica's side, saw the blood flowing from the knife wound. Who had stabbed her and when? Adam thought back through the past few minutes and remembered her gasping. His gaze tracked immediately to Andre who was sitting with his hands secured behind him. "You did this?"

Andre lifted his chin, defiant. "I had my orders, too."

Adam surged to his feet, hands bunched into fists.

"No." Lily planted her hands on his chest and shoved. "He's not worth the trouble. We need to take care of Vonnie."

Remy tore off a piece of duct tape and slapped it over Andre's mouth.

Adam clamped a lid on his fury and shifted his attention to his girlfriend. "Can we transport her without injuring her further, Jake?"

The medic grabbed a white packet from his mike bag and ripped it open. "I'm using a pressure bandage for now. She'll hold until I can work on her."

"Why isn't she conscious?" Had she lost that much blood already?

"Hit her head when she fell. She has a goose egg on the side." He applied the bandage to her side, watched a few seconds, then nodded. "Let's get her out of here."

Adam scooped Veronica into his arms and stood. "Remy, Lily, take point. Jake, watch our six." He left the chamber of horrors without a backward glance.

The operatives climbed the stairs to the first floor. At the top, a Collins thug plunged through the doorway. Remy took him down with a vicious punch to the throat, crushing the thug's windpipe. He stripped the thug's weapon, and shoved him aside. Lily fired her weapon twice in the hall and dropped two more.

"Adam," Cahill said, "Kitchen's clear. So is the path to the SUV. Have your car expert hot wire your ride."

"Thank you, Josh," Lily said, a smile curving her lips. "Nice that you appreciate my less-than-legal skills."

"This is way out of my jurisdiction, short stuff. I'm happy to ignore your criminal tendencies."

Despite his worry about Veronica, Adam shook his head at the interchange between the Otter Creek policeman and Lily.

In the kitchen, Nate Armstrong, Durango's EOD man, was removing a bomb from his pack. He inclined his head toward the back door. "Alex is covering you. Go."

"We're coming out the back door," Adam said into the comm system.

"You're clear," Durango's sniper said.

"Remy, Lily, go."

Remy and Lily left the kitchen. A moment later, the SUV's engine cranked. A smile tugged at Adam's lips. Lily Doucet's skills were legendary in Fortress. Good to know the reality lived up to the hype.

"Go, Adam," the sniper said. "Tangos moving in from the east."

He angled through the door with Veronica and ran for the vehicle with Jake a step behind. He climbed into the back seat, Veronica still in his arms. Didn't make sense, but he couldn't let go of her, almost as though he'd lose the woman he loved if he laid her on the seat.

Jake climbed into the back with him and Veronica.

"Go," Adam snapped.

Remy threw the SUV into reverse, knocking into two more thugs, and raced toward the front of the compound. One of the earlier explosions had blown the gates off their hinges. At the road, Remy turned right and sped down the street until another black SUV parked in the trees came into view. He skidded to a stop, then he and Lily ran toward the other vehicle and transferred the bags stashed in the cargo area. Seconds later, the journey to the airport resumed.

While Remy dodged traffic on side streets, Jake continued to check Veronica for injuries. "She hit her ribcage?"

"On the left side." He scowled. "Thin Man shoved her into the chair." Didn't hurt Adam's feelings that the two thugs were dead.

The medic handed Adam the flashlight, then lifted Veronica's shirt high enough to check for broken ribs. Finally, he looked up. "I don't feel any broken ribs. Bad bruising, though. Aggravated injuries from Silverman's work."

Jake dug into his mike bag for two chemically-activated ice packs. He shook them, then handed one to Adam. "Hold this against her ribs. I'll use the other on the goose egg."

Adam tugged Veronica's shirt down and pressed the ice pack to her side. The lights of the airport glowed a few blocks away when Veronica stirred. "Vonnie?"

"Cold," she muttered.

"Ice packs. You were injured."

"Lousy way to spend a honeymoon."

He chuckled, relieved she was alert enough to needle him. "I'll make it up to you. I promise."

"Everybody okay?"

"No other injuries on our team," Jake answered. "I think Curt might need stitches on his arm. I didn't hear of another injury from the teams."

"Hope we get hazard pay."

That brought laughter from everyone but Veronica. "Maddox takes good care of his people," Adam said. "Lily, let the PSI team know we're coming in hot."

Seconds later, she said, "Their medic is readying the back room for Jake to work on Vonnie."

Within minutes, Remy parked in the lot by the chartered jets and Adam climbed from the vehicle with Veronica in his arms. When Jake volunteered to carry her, Adam shook his head and hurried to the plane, flanked by his teammates.

Three of the PSI trainees positioned themselves between Adam's team and potential threats. He ran up the stairs, into the cabin, and straight to the back room where the PSI medic had spread a plastic sheet across the bed and laid out a basic medical kit kept on the plane.

"I need to wash my hands," Jake said as he set down his bag.

"Adam," Veronica murmured. "I'm okay."

He laid Veronica on her right side and brushed her hair away from her cheek. "You were knifed in the side, baby. That's not okay in my book."

"I've been knifed before. This one isn't bad."

"Jake's still looking at you." If Adam had anything to say about it, Sorensen would also check Veronica. He wouldn't breathe easy until the grumpy doctor gave Adam assurance that she would recover.

Jake returned to the room, glanced at King, the PSI medic. "Get my mike bag. I need antibiotics and a mild pain killer. We'll use the suture kit from my stash instead of the plane's med kit. We might need the supplies if we have more injuries to treat besides Vonnie and Curt."

"Yes, sir." A moment later, King brought in Jake's bag.

Jake yanked on a pair of gloves. "All right, Vonnie. Let's see what we have." He glanced at Adam. "You staying?"

A scowl. "What do you think?"

"I think you should hold your wife's hand while I check her side."

He could do that, relieved not to be forced from the room. Adam sat on the floor near Veronica's head and clasped her hand in a tight grip. He remained silent while the medic removed the pressure bandage, then poked and prodded Veronica's side.

Jake said, "You are a lucky woman, Vonnie. The knife didn't penetrate deep because the blade hit a rib and changed the trajectory of the cut. You'll need stitches and a round of antibiotics, but I think you'll recover fast. I want Sorensen to check you anyway and x-ray your ribcage. You squeamish about needles?"

Veronica frowned. "I'm not a fan of them, but do what you have to."

The medic numbed her side and stitched the entrance and exit wounds closed. Afterward, he administered an antibiotic and a mild pain killer. "The best thing for you now is rest."

"Thanks, Jake," Veronica said.

He closed his mike bag and walked to the door. "Same orders for you, Adam."

"When we're in the air."

"Jake, is it all right if I move to the cabin?"

"Sure. Might want to move before the numbness wears off."

"Get me up, Adam."

"Are you sure?" He wanted to insist she remain stretched out on the bed, couldn't.

She nodded. "Jake will have other injuries to treat." Veronica's gaze locked with his and her cheeks turned pink. "Besides, I want to feel your arms around me, Adam."

"Never a hardship, Vonnie. If you start hurting, we'll come back here and you can stretch out again." Maybe by the time they landed in Bayside, his blood pressure would be back to normal.

## CHAPTER THIRTY-EIGHT

Ted Sorensen yanked off his rubber gloves and tossed them in the trash. "Jake was right. The knife wound was shallow. I'll prescribe a strong antibiotic to prevent infection. I doubt the knife was sterilized before that clown used it on you. The x-rays showed hairline cracks in two more ribs. You'll be sore for a while, but you should be fine in a few weeks."

"Thank you, Dr. Sorensen." Veronica tugged down her shirt again. "How is your family?"

He beamed. "The kids are a joy, and my wife and I will celebrate our tenth anniversary next week. What about you and Walker? I hear through the grapevine you two are married. Fast work."

She rolled her eyes. "Maddox sent two people two Las Vegas to get married using our IDs. All the paperwork's been filed, according to Zane."

"Will you have Zane erase the trail?" He patted her shoulder. "Seems to me you two are emotionally involved already."

Involved was a mild way of stating how much she cared about Adam. "I'm in love with him."

"Mutual?"

She nodded. "I want to have the whole marriage experience with our friends."

"I don't blame you. Adam is a good man, Veronica."

Yes, he was. The question she had to answer now was did she let the marriage stand or have Zane erase the paper trail?

Dr. Sorensen flung open the door. Adam leaned against the wall, waiting for the doctor's report on Veronica's injuries.

He straightened. "Well?"

"Get her out of here. I might need the bed for a truly sick patient." The doctor glanced over his shoulder and winked at her. "Let me know what you decide to do."

She smiled and slid off the examination table. "You heard the man, Adam. Let's go home."

Adam walked into the room as the doctor disappeared down the hallway. "Maddox and the others are waiting at the airport. He said to hurry. Alexa's karate tournament is in a few hours."

In less than an hour, Veronica and the others were airborne, headed back to Nashville. Most of the operatives talked to each other while a few slept. Veronica glanced at Adam.

His eyebrow rose. "What is it?"

"What are we going to do?" she asked, her voice soft.

"About what?"

"The marriage."

His expression grew grave. "This isn't the way I wanted to win your hand. I'd planned to spend a few months courting you, then try to convince you to chance a lifetime with me. I want this marriage to be real, but I'm more interested in you being happy, Vonnie. If you want Zane to erase the trail and for us to start fresh, I'll have him do it as soon as we land."

She leaned close and kissed him. "Being married to you would be a dream come true."

"How soon?" He captured her lips in a deep kiss before easing back, his cheeks flushed. "Please tell me I won't have to wait long. I don't think I can take a long dating period."

Veronica smiled. "Four days from now sounds like a perfect date for a wedding."

"Are you serious?"

She nodded. "I want a church wedding although it doesn't have to be large. I want real wedding pictures to show our children one day."

"Do you want to invite your family?"

"They won't come, but I'll send an email to my mother."

He cupped her cheeks with his palms and they exchanged a series of long, deep kisses. "I love you, Veronica Walker."

A chorus of catcalls and whistles broke them apart.

"Hey," Eli Wolfe called. "Cut that out. You're making me miss my wife."

Adam stood up. "Veronica and I are getting married this Saturday. Details to follow as soon as we hash them out."

The operatives applauded and congratulated them. Maddox just smiled, satisfaction in his gaze.

Lily grinned. "This is one time I won't mind saying we need to go shopping, Vonnie."

The rest of the time in the air, Veronica and Lily brainstormed for ideas, and called Claire on the satellite phone to tell her the news and ask for advice. By the time the plane landed, most of the wedding details were in hand with Claire agreeing to take their wedding photos.

Once on the ground, Adam cornered Nate Armstrong and convinced him to prepare the food for the reception.

"Perfect." Veronica kissed Nate's cheek, which led to a red flush blooming on his face. "I can't thank you enough for doing this at short notice."

"Anything for you and Adam, sugar."

Veronica and her teammates climbed into Remy's SUV and returned to Fortress headquarters. Following a quick conversation with Zane about him changing the marriage date on the paperwork, she and Adam walked back to the garage. After they got into the SUV, Veronica turned to find Adam watching her. "Adam?"

"Are you sure, Vonnie?"

"That I want to be married to you? Positive."

He nodded. "Come on. Let's get you home."

"You don't want to take me home with you?" She held her breath, wanting him to say yes. They were technically married.

"Saturday." He slid an intense glance her way. "I love you enough to wait, baby."

Veronica's heart melted all over again. She wrapped her arms around his neck and kissed him.

Minutes later, he eased back. "We have to go now. My control is whisper-thin."

With her heart racing, Veronica realized the wisdom of Adam's words and released him.

The next few days passed in a whirlwind of activity, confirming wedding details and having her dress altered to fit. While the days were crazy busy, the evenings were fun and carefree. Adam insisted on continuing with his courtship plans, including dates every night and delivering flowers and small gifts to her doorstep each morning.

On Saturday morning, she woke to a phone call from Adam.

"I love you, Veronica Miles Walker," were his first words.

"I love you, Adam. This is going to be a fabulous day."

He chuckled. "Have you seen the weather forecast? Storms all day and into the night."

"I don't care about rain. All I care about is becoming your wife."

"A few more hours, baby. I'm sending a gift by way of Lily in a few minutes since I'm not supposed to see you until the ceremony."

Veronica sped through her shower and yanked on clothes when the doorbell rang. She dashed to the door. "Hi, Lily."

Her friend walked inside the house holding a small blue gift bag from an exclusive jewelry store in town. "Special delivery from Adam."

"What is it?" She followed Lily into the living room and dropped onto the couch beside her.

"Don't know. Adam made me promise not to peek." She handed over the bag. "Open it. I'm dying to see what he came up with this time."

Veronica reached into the bag and pulled out a small black box with a card attached. She read aloud, "You own my heart. Thank you for taking a chance on me. Adam." Tears stinging her eyes, she opened the box and gasped. Nestled on the black velvet was a diamond-encrusted heart on a gold chain.

"Oh, Vonnie," Lily murmured. "This will be perfect with your wedding dress."

She brushed the tears from her cheeks. "He has a heart of gold. I'm so blessed, Lily."

At seven o'clock that evening, Veronica walked halfway down the church aisle on Brent Maddox's arm where he stopped.

"One more gift from Adam," her new boss murmured and he inclined his head toward the tall man in dress blues who turned and stood.

Veronica's heart skipped a beat. "Charles."

"Congratulations, Veronica." He extended his arm. "May I walk you the rest of the way down the aisle?"

On the arm of her brother, Veronica continued her journey to the love of her life. "Thank you for coming."

"Thank Adam. He tracked me down and secured leave for me to be here for you." As they reached the end of the rows of pews, he said, "I have to return to the base so I can't stay for the reception, but Adam has my contact information. When you're back from your honeymoon, call me." Charles kissed her cheek and placed her hand in Adam's, then returned to his seat.

Veronica smiled at Adam, threw her arms around his neck, and kissed him. "Thank you," she whispered against his lips.

"All right now. You're getting ahead of the ceremony order," the minister said with a broad smile. Once the laughter subsided, Marcus Lang, the pastor of Cornerstone Church in Otter Creek, continued with the short, simple ceremony Veronica and Adam had chosen.

The small church outside Nashville was packed with Fortress operatives and their families as well as some of Veronica's friends from the DEA. In passing, she noted that Graham and Carol were sitting together in the pew. Cissy Carver sat beside Graham. Her mentor's wife mouthed a silent apology. Maybe something good would come from the horrible circumstances of the past two weeks.

After smiling at her three friends, Veronica shifted her attention to Adam. This, she thought, was what she'd been waiting for all her life. A man who looked at her as though she was his whole world, a man who would honor and cherish her for the rest of her life.

At the conclusion of the ceremony, Lang said, "Now you may kiss your bride, Adam."

Adam wrapped his arms around Veronica and kissed her. They walked down the aisle, hand-in-hand to greet their guests. Once Claire finished the pictures and they'd eaten enough to hold them off, Adam turned Veronica toward the room where she'd dressed for the wedding.

"Go change, Vonnie. We have a flight to catch."

"Where are we going?"

"Orange Beach."

Her eyes grew damp. He'd remembered her favorite place to vacation. "What about Gatlinburg, Adam?"

"Next week. Go on, Mrs. Walker. I'm ready to start our life together."

She pressed a hard kiss to his mouth, then hurried to change. She couldn't wait to see what was ahead for them.

# Resurgence

## ABOUT THE AUTHOR

Rebecca Deel is a preacher's kid with a black belt in karate. She teaches business classes at a private four-year college outside Nashville, Tennessee. She plays the piano at church, writes freelance articles, and runs interference for the family dogs. She's been married to her amazing husband for more than 25 years and is the proud mom of two grown sons. She delivers occasional devotions to the women's group at her church and conducts seminars in personal safety, money management, and writing. Her articles have been published in *ONE Magazine*, *Contact*, and *Co-Laborer*, and she was profiled in the June 2010 Williamson edition of *Nashville Christian Family* magazine. Rebecca completed the Doctor of Arts degree in Economics and wears her favorite Dallas Cowboys sweatshirt when life turns ugly.

    For more information on Rebecca . . .
Sign up for Rebecca's newsletter: http://eepurl.com/_B6w9
Visit Rebecca's website: www.rebeccadeelbooks.com